THE HOUSE AT BLACKWATER POND

The House at Blackwater Pond

Terri Gilbert

The House at Blackwater Pond
Copyright © 2024 by Terri Gilbert

All rights reserved. No part of this book may be reproduced in any form or by any electronic or mechanical means, including information storage and retrieval systems, without permission in writing from the publisher, except by a reviewer who may quote brief passages in a review.

Teagan House Books
Print ISBN 979-8-9914382-0-9
Ebook ISBN 979-8-9914382-1-6

Printed in the United States of America

For helpful librarians everywhere.

Chapter One

December 2018

Jillian Peters slammed her brakes when a dark car, horn blaring, careened past her and slid into the parking spot she'd been eyeing. Heart pounding, Jillian watched the driver, a tall man with a ponytail, jump out of the car and rush across the street into the funeral home. After carefully parking her red Fiat, Jillian headed that way as a cold wind blew her auburn hair across her face, blocking her view of the gathering snow clouds.

"Jillian, wait up!"

"Did you see that car, Elaine? It almost hit me!" Jillian asked her coworker, "Where's Larry?"

"Still fighting a cold, so I left him in charge of the remote." Smoothing her dark hair, Elaine asked, "How are you doing?"

"Okay, I guess. Ben always said I'd be late to my own funeral, but I never dreamed I'd be late for his." Jillian sighed. "I can't believe he's gone. To be honest, I've caught myself just staring into space this morning. I think I was half in love with the old geezer myself."

Elaine linked arms with Jillian and spoke with a gentleness uncharacteristic for her. "I know, darlin'. He wasn't just a boss. He was a good friend to us all, but he and Carol seemed to restore your confidence during your divorce. You've grown a lot."

Jillian's eyes filled with tears. "That's so sweet, Elaine." Jillian fumbled for a tissue. "I wouldn't have made it through that mess without my girlfriends, but Ben, Ben was special. He kind of filled a void in my life without asking anything in return." Jillian smiled a bit. "I'm going to miss flirting with the old guy."

"Ha, we all will, but it's time you started flirting with someone closer to your age. Fifty-four is far too young to give up on men. What about Clark Grebe over at Sweeney's? He's a looker!"

Jillian gave her friend an exasperated look, muttering, "Wrong place, wrong time," as they hurried up the steps. Located on a street of older homes converted to commercial use, Stone's Funeral Home had a rocking chair front porch and an enviable view of the Igohida River and the foothills surrounding Newton, Tennessee.

The women stopped to remove their coats before moving into the chapel, where they signed the guest book. The gravity, the finality, of the situation struck Jillian as she heard hushed voices and quiet notes from the piano. She could see the casket and almost smell the flowers surrounding it. "I need a minute," Jillian whispered, blinking back tears. She paused at the display of photographs and memorabilia. Pictures of Ben as a young man in his football uniform led to photographs of Ben in the Navy, with Carol at dances, their wedding, on picnics, with family, friends, and coworkers.

Elaine picked up a framed photo of the couple with their son. "Ooh, look at this cutie. I guess that's Andy from back in the day, huh?"

Jillian, thankful for the distraction, looked over Elaine's shoulder.

"I'd say so. I haven't seen him in years. He's much taller than Ben, with a lot more hair." Jillian smiled, remembering Ben's invitation to rub his bald head for luck before her first closing. In the photograph, a slender, sweaty teen with curly blond hair, wearing a smudged soccer jersey, stood with arms draped around his parents. *Hmm. He doesn't look much like Carol either.*

"He cleans up nice," Elaine commented softly, holding another photo of an older Andy standing beside two canoes, with three boys wearing orange life jackets. "His sons, I guess," she whispered before they began making their way down the aisle. "Was Andy at visitation last evening?"

"I don't think so, but his sons may have been," Jillian said quietly, remembering boys she'd noticed standing awkwardly with Ben's brother, Sam—boys she had assumed were Sam's grandchildren.

The opening bars of "Great is Thy Faithfulness" sounded as Jillian and Elaine joined coworkers in a pew behind the family. The preacher spoke about a life well lived, then one of Ben's former players began a moving eulogy. "He wasn't just a coach. He taught us life lessons. He had this saying from Confucius in his office: 'Study the past if you would define the future.' Once I tried to quit the team after screwing up. Coach asked me if I knew what it meant. I mumbled something about learning from mistakes. He said, 'Yes. Face the past. Recognize what went wrong in order to prepare for the future. Don't forget mistakes, but don't let them haunt you either. Focus on where you're going, not where you've been. Define your future, not your past.'"

Ben was right. It's more important to focus on the future. Jillian had married young and been married for twenty-seven years before realizing she didn't want to spend the rest of her life with someone whose idea of living was so different from her own. Paul had been a good provider, but theirs had often been a confining and contentious marriage, and after their children were grown, things worsened rapidly.

Was it any wonder she wasn't interested in dating? She'd grown used to doing things on her own and valued her independence. She had a successful career, a home, a good relationship with her adult children, friends she treasured, and the only companion she needed in Willie, the black and tan dachshund she'd adopted post-divorce. *Maybe Elaine has a point though. Is it time to get back out there?* Reining in her thoughts, Jillian silently promised herself to remember Ben's words, then listened as the speaker commented about Ben's propensity for practical jokes. Many in the congregation smiled through their tears when the middle-aged man's voice caught as he described Ben as a "wise man who was fond of wisecracking."

When the preacher called Andy Harrison to the podium, Jillian hissed, "He's the one who almost plowed into me." She looked closely at Andy. Dressed in a charcoal gray suit, white shirt, and blue tie, Ben's son was taller than the preacher, with dark blond hair pulled back in a neat ponytail.

"My father's favorite hymn," Andy said, then began to sing.

Jillian sat transfixed, all irritation about the near miss forgotten as Andy's tenor voice rang out, singing "Be Still, My Soul." She blinked away tears and smiled at the man, who appeared to be singing just to her. Then she blushed and looked down, wondering what kind of man winks at a woman during his father's funeral. *Did that even happen? Maybe I imagined it. No, it's the sort of thing Ben would've done.* Ben's compliments and winks had boosted Jillian's ego more than once. Initially embarrassed by the attention, Jillian knew Ben had Carol's permission to flirt with whomever he liked, so long as he saved the kisses for her. Their love had been obvious.

As the final chords faded away and the pastor offered the closing prayer, Jillian added her own prayer, thankful for Ben's friendship and hopeful that Carol might find solace in happy memories of their long and loving marriage.

"See you outside. I need a pit stop," Elaine whispered.

Jillian nodded and stood, thinking about how hard it must be to lose a beloved spouse.

A friend's voice intruded on her thoughts. "Jillian, I'm glad we caught you. We're not going to the cemetery," her neighbor Amy Taylor said. "The weather's looking bad. Be careful, and call me when you get home, okay? Don't worry about Willie. Stan and I will pop over and give your pooch a break."

"Thanks, guys. I'll call, but I'm sure we'll be fine. Elaine's used to driving in snow."

Jillian stopped to gather their coats, turning as she heard a voice behind her growling, "Not now." Jillian watched as Andy Harrison shouldered past Clark Grebe. *What has Clark done now?*

Her curiosity was forgotten as she stepped outside and looked with dismay at the low-hanging clouds and darkening sky.

Elaine appeared at her side, taking her coat from Jillian. "Ready to leave?"

"Yeah. I'm a bit concerned about the weather. Belford's on the other side of Bay's Mountain, and it looks like it's going to get dark early."

Elaine surveyed the sky. "Eh, it's only twenty miles. We'll be fine, but we should get going. Parking's liable to be tight, even though some people may just go home."

As they walked to the car, Elaine said, "Christmas is going to be rough for Carol. I'd had six months to get used to my first husband's passing, but that first holiday without him sure was lonely. Losing a loved one is always hard, but this time of year must make it worse."

"I'm sure it does, but at least her family's here, and I guess it's a relief to know Ben's no longer suffering." Jillian fastened her seatbelt. "Does thinking about Ben remind you of your own loss?"

"Yes, every funeral does," Elaine said, starting the car. "I was about your age when Ed passed. We'd built a good life together. After thirty years, it was hard to think about living without him." Elaine adjusted the heat. "My mother reminded me that life is for the living, and wallowing in self-pity and disappointment wasn't living. When Larry came along, I realized I still had room in my heart for love."

"Do you think I'm wallowing in self-pity, Elaine?"

Elaine reached over and took Jillian's hand. "No, honey. I think you're afraid of what *might* happen. So much so that you've cut yourself off from all the good that could come." At Jillian's silence, she added, "It's rough out there. There are a lot of frogs in the pond, and some of them are just looking for a nurse or a purse, as they say. But there are some princes too. Look at Larry."

"Maybe," Jillian said, reaching for a tissue, "but sorting one out seems too much trouble. I think I'm fine the way I am. Did you speak to Ben's son?"

"Andy? No, I had no idea who he was until he sang. What a set of pipes!"

"He has a great voice, but he was rude to Clark Grebe after the service."

"Well, Clark doesn't always have the best sense of timing," Elaine admitted. "He probably asked about the future of Harrison's." Elaine took her place in the processional driving to Belford. "Clark's heart is in the right place, but he can be tactless."

Jillian sighed. "I guess Tom will continue as acting manager."

"Maybe not. Rumor has it that Carol's ready to sell and Tom's ready to retire. No telling where that leaves us." Elaine sighed. "Personally, I'm not ready to retire or go gray despite my age. I'm sure we could find other employment, but Harrison's Realty has been home for twelve years."

"Nineteen for me," Jillian sighed again. "Ben stopped teaching and joined Carol at the agency right when I started. He saw things in me that I hadn't seen in myself. Ben's the one who encouraged me to stage homes and work on big projects, you know. Change is hard, but it can be good."

"I supposed that's true," Elaine admitted.

"Um, speaking of change, Elaine. What did you mean earlier? When you said that I'd grown in the years that we've known each other."

Elaine stopped at a traffic light and glanced fondly at Jillian. "Oh, my friend, you have come out of your shell. Do you remember when we first met?"

"Sure. At my very first closing. You were the buyer's agent."

"That's right. We'd talked on the phone, but that was our first face-to-face." Elaine laughed. "I've never seen anyone so nervous. I'm not sure the sellers saw your hands shaking, but I sure did. You were so prim and proper I was pretty sure you starched your underwear."

Jillian didn't laugh, she grimaced. "I never starched my underwear, but I did iron my pajamas. I tried so hard to be perfect and agreeable to please my mother and Paul and everyone else."

"Oh, honey, I know. I loved watching you grow more confident and competent. I did a little mental happy dance the first time I heard you disagree with someone. It was as if you'd finally realized you had a right to take up space and didn't have to hide in a corner."

"Was I really that bad?" Jillian sighed again. "Ugh, let's talk about something else."

"Well, let's talk about Andy. He's a looker, for sure, but I've never met him."

"Really? Paul and I met him a couple of times, years ago at one of those agency picnics. Carol introduced us, but I don't remember much more."

"Those picnics pre-date my involvement with the agency. How old is Andy anyway?"

"I don't know. Forty-five? Fifty? It's been a long time." Jillian thought about Andy's wink but decided not to mention it.

The conversation turned to office gossip and holiday plans. As they crossed the river outside Belford, Elaine said, "I know you're worried about snow, but the forecast is only one to three inches."

"Hmm, I guess it's odd to be so afraid of something and yet love it too. Sitting at home, watching the snow cover everything is one of my favorite things. It's so peaceful. Like God is giving us a chance to hit the pause button, a chance to start fresh."

Elaine turned from the main highway onto a sideroad, then slowly drove through a mix of newer commercial strip centers, the odd fast food restaurant, and older run-down structures housing paint stores and small businesses. As they passed the town limits sign on Main Street, the buildings took on a distinctly different look. Lampposts decorated with wreaths lined the street. A central courthouse of limestone topped by a brick clock tower dominated the town square. Brick buildings with decorated storefronts housed cute giftshops, boutiques, and professional offices.

"Wow," Jillian said. "Quite a change from when the kids played a soccer game or two here. The center of town is so cute now."

"Yeah, there's been a strong revitalization effort. I've heard some new company is moving in, bringing a lot of jobs." Elaine looked around as the processional slowed. "There's likely to be a lot of activity in Belford soon. Gorgeous views in the valley, and there's an old money section of town, believe it or not. A lot of rich folks used to live here: coal company owners and railroad moguls."

"I think the rich people must have left with the railroads. The downtown area appeared economically depressed when I was here last."

"Maybe so, but there are still some big beautiful houses, like that one." Elaine pointed to her left as they drove by an old two-story white house with columns and a balcony.

"Unfortunately, not all of them are in such good shape," Jillian said, noticing a row of Victorians with peeling paint. "It takes a lot of money to maintain old houses."

"Indeed, it does, which explains the good listing prices here. Things could be changing though. Possibly opportunities for historic restorations. I know you'd love to get in on that. What's the connection between Ben and Belford anyway?"

"Good question. I have no idea," Jillian said.

Elaine glanced at Jillian, hitting a pothole as she pulled into the city cemetery. "Sorry!" she muttered as she crept down the gravel drive and parked behind twenty or so other cars. They headed to the green canopy standing over the empty grave, joining other mourners shivering in the gusting wind. Andy and his sons sat with Carol, who smiled bravely and thanked everyone for coming.

The pastor said a few words, then led the singing of "Amazing Grace." When the casket was lowered, one member of an Honor Guard played "Taps." Another knelt before Carol, presenting her with a folded flag and thanking her on behalf of a grateful nation for Ben's service in the Navy. After a final prayer, Carol's son and grandsons escorted her to the waiting limo.

As the mourners dispersed, Jillian noticed the gently falling snow already covering the grass. She paused to speak briefly with a friend, then said to Elaine, "With this weather, we'd better head home."

Elaine hurried toward her car, anxious to get out of the wind. Rushing after her, Jillian tripped over a hidden footstone and tumbled to the ground as she heard Elaine say, "Damn, that tire is flat."

Jillian pulled herself up, brushed the snow from her dress, then dabbed at a little bloody place on her knee with a tissue from her pocket. *I should've worn my boots.* Standing on one foot, holding the dangling heel in her hand, she eyed the departing crowd. "I'll grab Tom. Maybe he can help with the tire." Jillian started toward Tom's car, but cried out in pain and sank toward the ground.

A strong hand gripped her elbow and helped her up. "I saw you fall. Are you all right?"

Jillian looked up to see Andy Harrison staring at her, concern etched in his face.

"Are you okay?" he repeated.

"I, I twisted my ankle, but it's fine. I'll be fine," Jillian stammered.

"Let me help you to your car," Andy insisted, looking around.

"I'm parked at the funeral home. I rode with a friend," Jillian said, pointing to the silver SUV, currently a beehive of activity as several men were assessing the situation, including Tom Smith, acting manager of Harrison's Realty, and Clark Grebe.

Elaine, all thoughts of the cold wind forgotten in the excitement, introduced herself to Andy. "As you can see, I've got a little problem, but nothing these handsome men can't fix."

Elaine put her arm around Jillian. "This poor thing though. Here she is, hurt and anxious to get home because of the snow, having to wait who knows how long to get this tire changed."

"It won't be that long, Elaine. Would've been quicker if you hadn't parked in the mud," Clark said, and the other men laughed. "I'll take you home, Jillian. Go get in the car."

"Jillian," Andy said slowly. "Huh. I can give you a ride if you like."

Jillian looked curiously at Andy, wondering why he'd said her name so slowly. Understandably tired, Andy's eyes, startling in their intensity, were puffy and bruised looking. "Oh, uh, thanks, but I'll wait on Elaine." She tried to balance without putting any weight on her ankle.

"I've got to stop back at the funeral home anyway to pack up the memory table, which apparently can't wait until tomorrow. That's where your car is, right?"

"Yes," Jillian said, wondering at his petulant tone.

He closed his eyes briefly, then spoke more calmly. "You should get off that ankle as soon as possible."

"Jillian, that makes sense," Elaine said. "It's out of Clark's way, and I'd have to double back if you rode with me. Ride with Andy, and take care of that ankle."

Jillian reluctantly agreed, despite Elaine's not so subtle plan. Leave it to Elaine to try to fix her up at a funeral. Elaine smiled as Jillian raised her eyebrows and mouthed, "Seriously?" as Andy left to get his car. Jillian muttered, "I cannot believe you."

"It's just a ride home, hon," Elaine said, "but he is awfully good looking."

"Really, Elaine, I'm not looking for a relationship, and this isn't the time."

"So you keep saying." Elaine laughed. "Riding with Andy will get you home sooner, and Clark's sure to notice. He'll be calling within the week," she added, walking off to supervise the men changing her tire.

Chapter Two

When Andy pulled up in a dark blue sports car, Jillian groaned. *Mid-life crisis, much?*

He frowned as he opened the passenger door. "Are you grimacing in pain or at my car?"

"Oh, I'm sure your car is very nice. I'd hoped to sit in back and rest my ankle, but . . ."

"But no backseat." Andy nodded. "Elevating your ankle is smart. I'll adjust the seat, and you can prop it on the dash. There you are, milady."

Jillian removed her coat and got in the low-slung car. "Oof," she giggled. "I hadn't expected the seat to be so low!" Jillian tugged at her dress, attempting to situate her ankle on the dash without flashing anyone.

Andy helped her buckle the seatbelt. "Thank you, kind sir," she said, blushing as she tucked her coat around her legs. Jillian typically liked meeting new people, figuring out what made them tick, but Andy's earlier wink, his harsh tone with Clark, and the idea of being alone with a virtual stranger made her a little anxious. She hoped the ride would pass quickly and the roads would stay clear.

Andy walked around to the driver's side. "I should've warned you about the seats. They take some getting used to."

"Oh, well, yes. Thanks for the ride. To be honest, I'm feeling a bit awkward. I should introduce myself. I'm Jillian Peters, an associate of your parents."

"I know who you are." Andy started the car. "I didn't recognize you at first but was pretty sure we'd met. When that pushy guy said your name, I put two and two together."

Hmm, Clark is pushy. Wonder what he said at the funeral home. Not my business.

"I think we met once at an office picnic," Jillian said, "but I'm surprised you remember."

"Oh, I've heard your name quite a bit through the years. A lot more so from Dad in recent weeks, to be honest." Andy glanced at her.

"Really?" Jillian asked. "Ben was talking about me? That's surprising. I hadn't seen him since before Thanksgiving. Carol said he wasn't up to having company."

Andy turned out of the cemetery. "It is curious. My folks often talked about people at the agency. Occasionally, they'd mention someone's family or more personal things to help me keep straight who was who. Dad said you helped him on that big Candler project, and Mom bragged about you staging homes. It's clear that my parents appreciate—" Andy sighed. "I mean, Mom appreciates and Dad appreciated your talent and work ethic."

Jillian bit her lip. "Oh, thank you, Andy. That's nice to hear. I'm grateful for the opportunities they provided."

Andy nodded. "If I'd known I'd be driving you home, I'd have paid more attention." He laughed, then sobered. "If I'd known about Dad, I'd have paid more attention to everything."

Wait. 'Everything?' What does that mean? Jillian remained quiet.

After a minute, he said, "Seven or eight months ago, Dad mentioned how you'd renovated your home after, uh, after your kids left home. He was impressed."

"After my divorce, you mean," Jillian said. It had taken awhile, but Jillian was no longer embarrassed or ashamed of her divorce. "It's surprising he was talking about that last spring. I renovated my home five years ago, long after the kids had flown the nest."

Andy didn't respond right away. "Yeah, well, I'm not sure why he mentioned it. Dad's mind wandered much of the last year, and his comments were often hard to follow. I couldn't be here as much as I wanted."

Jillian could hear the longing in Andy's voice. They rode in silence for awhile. "It's hard keeping up, staying current with family when we live in different cities and lead such different lives."

Andy nodded. "It is hard. I'm glad my folks were occupied with the agency. It gave them something to talk about all those years. Dad wouldn't have been happy sitting at home after retiring from coaching."

"No, he wouldn't," Jillian agreed. "Ben had the energy of many men only half his age. Up until last summer, he was in the office several hours a week, despite bad knees and chemo."

Andy nodded, but didn't respond.

"Your parents talked about you some too, but I can't recall any specific stories. I remember meeting you though. I think you were wrestling a screaming toddler while I was wrangling my three." Jillian smiled at the memory. "You live in Philadelphia, right? But you're not in real estate?"

"No, I'm a financial analyst in Philly," Andy said, slowing to a stop. "I've got three boys now: BJ, Will, and Seth. And yours are?"

"James, Sarah, and Elizabeth. James has finally found the one. About time; he's thirty."

Andy looked at Jillian before pulling out on the main highway. "You don't look like you have a thirty-year-old son. You must've been a child bride."

Jillian assumed Andy's remarks were meant as a compliment, but they needled a bit for reasons she didn't understand. "I married at twenty. James was born a couple of years later."

"Hmm, I was thirty when BJ was born. He's the screaming toddler you remember. Nineteen now, at Furman University." Andy paused. "I've never thought about it before, but my father was even older. Thirty-five when I was born. My folks married young though. At least a decade before my birth." Andy drove in silence for a few minutes.

Jillian noticed Andy's hesitation but let it pass. After another minute, she said, "I think I saw your boys last night at visitation. Would they have been with your uncle? He looks just like Ben."

"Yeah, probably. Seth and Will anyway. I can't imagine BJ abandoning Mom. He's always adored her."

"I was surprised not to see you." Jillian winced at his sharp look.

"I missed my plane after being unavoidably detained at the office. Otherwise, I would have been there, obviously. I didn't get in until after midnight," Andy explained a little testily.

"Flying is exasperating," Jillian said. "Since I'm being nosy, may I ask why you aren't riding in the limo with your family?"

"I could blame my Aunt Lois," Andy said as he slowed at a railroad crossing. "She's riding with Mom and the boys. I love her, but she hasn't stopped talking since Dad died. The truth is, with my late arrival, preparing for the service, and everything else, Mom knew I'd need some time to decompress between the service and burial. She understands that driving calms me and suggested I drive over separately, then pack up the photos and such." Andy yawned. "I've missed my Jaguar.

"Before you ask," Andy continued, "BJ's had it for a while because his truck's been in the shop. Since Thanksgiving actually. Ordinarily, we gather in Philadelphia, but with Dad being so ill, we spent the holiday in Newton. I drove down so BJ could use my car. I don't need it all that much in the city."

Andy paused. "BJ. Benjamin Andrew Harrison, Junior."

Jillian wondered about the non sequitur. "So you're named for Ben, but you're not the junior?"

"Right," Andy said shortly. "Dad's Benjamin Matthew. I'm Benjamin Andrew. I'm not sure why. I wish I had asked."

Andy changed the subject. "My sons are going skiing with their mother in a few days. I'll spend the holidays with Mom, then drive home."

That's interesting. His wife wasn't at the funeral. Jillian shifted, trying to get more comfortable.

"How's the ankle?" Andy asked.

"Throbbing a little. Talking keeps my mind off of it. It's hard watching kids grow up and go off to college. What's BJ studying at Furman?"

"Business," Andy answered without elaboration. He leaned forward and peered out the windshield. "The snow's really coming down. It's getting dark quickly too."

Does he regret offering me a ride? Better not mention the wife.

After a few minutes, Jillian said, "I enjoyed seeing the family pictures on the memory table. As often happens, some things surprised me. I knew Ben had coached before joining Carol in real estate, but I'd forgotten he'd been in the Navy. So much of a person's life is left untold. Photographs help fill in the blanks."

"True, but photos can lie. What looks like a happy family can be one with deep dark secrets. Obviously, people get to choose what they put out there, so the displays aren't necessarily reality."

Is he hinting at a big family secret? "You make it sound like social media, Andy. Funerals are different though. Surely there's nothing wrong with focusing on the good as we honor the departed. Don't we always want to present our best selves to friends and family on special occasions?"

"Of course," Andy sighed. "It's just . . . We're not allowed to speak ill of the dead, but sometimes people discover things that make them question how well they knew the departed." He paused. "My dad was a great guy, a great dad, well-loved coach, savvy businessman, a lot of fun, and obviously loved my mother, but there are things I'll never find out, questions I never thought to ask."

"Andy, I'm sorry. I talk a lot when I'm nervous, and driving in the snow makes me nervous. I didn't mean to pry. We don't have to talk about family. Or anything at all, for that matter."

"Yeah, we sort of do." Andy said, abruptly. "I'm actually glad you hurt your ankle because it gives us an opportunity to talk. I need to figure some things out, and you seem to hold the key."

Jillian suddenly felt chilled, almost guilty, though she didn't know why. She stared at Andy. "What are you talking about? Key to what?"

"My father was a flirt, as you well know. He flirted with everyone, but had a special place in his heart for beautiful women. Surely you realize he was quite fond of you."

Taken aback, Jillian spoke carefully. "And I was fond of him. Your father was a special man. A wonderful friend, who helped me a lot, both personally and professionally."

"Are you sure it wasn't more than that?" Andy asked.

Jillian froze, stunned into silence. Her mind reeled, then she spoke sharply. "We were friends. I was friends with both your parents. I'm not exactly sure what you're implying, but . . ."

"No, no," Andy protested. "I'm not saying there was anything inappropriate. It's just that Dad was insistent. He wasn't making much sense, you know. These past few weeks, he slept much of the time, but he'd talk. Often he was incoherent, but I distinctly heard him say, 'Talk to Jillian. She'll help,' and another time, 'Jillian will know what to do.' Can you explain that?"

Jillian shook her head. "No. I honestly have no idea, Andy. None whatsoever," she said, then reconsidered. "Unless, maybe he was reliving the Candler project, but that was years ago."

The intensity in Andy's voice made Jillian uneasy. She watched the snow falling in the headlights, wondering about Ben's cryptic comments.

Andy cleared his throat. "Dad's comments weren't the only reason I offered you a ride."

Jillian glanced at him sharply, but Andy stared straight ahead. "Seeing you during the service, when you were smiling at me, it's crazy, but I felt a connection, like I already knew you or had finally found you, like in the song. 'We shall meet at last.'" He paused and swore. "I'm not usually so hokey."

Curiosity overriding her embarrassment and discomfort, Jillian asked, "Did you wink at me?"

Andy rubbed his chin and avoided looking at her. "I did wink at you. I shouldn't have said anything about Dad's flirting. I guess I'm as bad as he is, but I'd noticed you earlier, and I'll admit I agree with his assessment of your voluptuous beauty."

Jillian blushed again. Suddenly aware of the darkening skies and being alone with a virtual stranger, Jillian felt uncomfortable and said so. "Oh my God, Andy, stop. Just stop right now. How dare you? You are a married man. We have literally just buried your father. A man who was a dear friend. Just a friend! And I'm still your mother's friend." Jillian tucked her coat more firmly around her legs. "Your comments are wildly inappropriate, and I don't appreciate being forced to listen to whatever sort of confession this is. Save your opinions and assessments, hokey or otherwise, for someone else!"

Andy rubbed his jaw. "I'm sorry I offended you. My comments were out of line."

Jillian looked out the window, grateful they were nearing Newton. *I am never letting Elaine talk me into anything like this again.* After a few minutes, she turned slightly and saw Andy's glowering expression in the light of passing cars as he navigated the twisting roads. Her breathing returned to normal with the passing miles.

I'm sure this has been a really difficult, emotional day for Andy. He's obviously shaken by Ben's death. As they passed her car, the only one parked on the city street, she said, "I appreciate the ride. I don't like driving in snow."

Andy nodded but didn't respond until he had pulled into the funeral home's lot.

He put the car in park and turned to her. "Just so you know, I am married, but in name only. The divorce will be final January third, as soon as these blasted holidays are over."

Oh, guess that explains why his wife wasn't at the funeral.

Andy pointed at the snow-covered lot. "Look, I don't want to scare you, but the roads are pretty bad. I'd rather see you to your door. It won't take long to load up all the photographs and junk. I'll leave the heat on for you."

As Andy opened the door, crisp, cold air blew in, and Jillian started apologizing.

"No, Jillian, don't apologize. This is on me. I'm sorry I made you uncomfortable. I don't know why I've bared my soul tonight. I'm usually a bit more reticent about flirting than my father, and I can assure you that I, at least, have never crossed the line."

Jillian sat in stunned silence as Andy walked into the funeral home. *What? Did he mean Ben had crossed a line? Surely not.* Jillian had barely realized she hadn't agreed to Andy's suggestion when he was back, putting the photographs in the trunk.

Jillian started gathering her things, dreading the drive home. "Listen, Andy, you've been very kind to give me a ride, but I don't want to cause you any more trouble. I can make it home, and I may need my car tomorrow anyway."

"It's no trouble, and with that ankle, you may need help."

Jillian motions slowed. "Oh, I hadn't thought of that," she said truthfully. "Are you sure? I don't want you going out of your way."

"I'm sure. I'm sorry about earlier. I'll happily be your silent chauffeur if you'll let me."

Jillian nodded and gave Andy directions, grateful for the ride but still a little miffed.

After a short drive in silence, Andy parked in front of Jillian's modest home and insisted on helping her up the snow-covered walk.

"I hear Willie barking. He'll be glad to see me." Jillian said as she unlocked the door but did not open it. "Thanks again for the lift and for your help," she said, gesturing at the sidewalk. "I'm sure Ben would've been proud of you for singing today. I imagine that was hard."

"Yeah." Andy reached out and touched the wreath of deep rose poinsettias on Jillian's door. "Christmas. Wow. I think I'd forgotten," he said slowly.

Jillian's reserve melted. "Oh, Andy, I am so sorry." She touched his arm. "I know this will be a rough holiday for you all. Please let your mom know I'm praying for her."

"Will do," Andy said. "I'll give you a call tomorrow to arrange getting your car back to you."

Andy squeezed her shoulder, then leaned in and kissed her cheek before calling out, "Get some ice on that ankle," and casually waving goodbye.

Staring after him, Jillian touched her cheek, then hobbled into her kitchen to get some ice.

Chapter Three

Jillian's throbbing ankle woke her before dawn. Grateful the agency was closed until the new year, she settled on the loveseat, iced her ankle, and flipped through television channels. Soon, unable to sit and be idle, Jillian showered, then moved to the kitchen.

Willie pranced as Jillian pulled ingredients from the cabinets and refrigerator. She sat at the counter measuring and mixing and beating. After rolling out the dough, she cut star-shaped cookies and placed them on the pan. "I know. It's not fair that you can't have any. Poor little dog." Jillian hobbled to the oven with the cookies. "Do you want a carrot?"

Willie turned in circles, eagerly awaiting his promised treat.

Jillian balanced on one foot as much as possible, washing up while the cookies baked. When the timer sounded, she opened the oven door, releasing a blast of hot air and a gingery aroma. As she transferred the cookies to a cooling rack, her phone rang.

"Jillian, Andy Harrison. I'm sorry to call so early. How's the ankle?" Andy asked.

"Oh, um, better but still swollen. I'm a little wobbly," Jillian said, wondering why he'd called.

"I'm on the way back from the airport. The boys had a slight change of plans in their skiing vacation. It's early, but if you think you can drive, I'll give you a lift to the funeral home."

Not wanting to be a burden on this man who had a way of unsettling her, Jillian replied, "Oh, that's not necessary. I can get a ride tomorrow. I don't have to go anywhere today after all."

"It's not a problem. If you could spare a cup of coffee and a few minutes, I'd like to talk to you anyway. I'm not ready to face my mother."

Andy's comment surprised Jillian and sparked her curiosity. *Not ready to face Carol? Wonder what that's about.* "Um, sure, okay. Coffee's ready." While she waited, Jillian prepared a tray with coffee and cookies.

"It's open!" she called, shushing Willie, who had started barking when the doorbell rang.

A gust of cold air ruffled Andy's hair as he stomped snow from his boots. After hanging his coat on a hook by the door, Andy bent down and patted the squirming dog. "Hello, little guy. You must be Willie." Andy straightened and said, "The roads are fine, but there's still snow on the shady parts of your sidewalk. It should melt pretty quickly though. I thought you might need this," he added, holding up an ACE bandage. "It'll help with the swelling."

"Oh, you didn't have to do that. I appreciate it though. I've tried to keep my ankle iced and elevated, but I haven't been a good patient. It's swelling again."

"Sit." Andy gestured to a seat near the fireplace. He knelt and said, "That's why you need the bandage: rest, ice, compression, elevation. Let me wrap it for you. I've had lots of experience with ankles. All my sons have had their share of sports injuries."

"Have you?" Jillian blushed as she pulled her pant leg up so Andy could wrap her ankle.

"Not really. I've always liked music more than sports. I played football as a child, but even Dad had to admit I wasn't cut out for it. Later, I played soccer and baseball and did okay." Andy patted her knee as he stood. "There, that should do it. How have you been a bad patient?"

"I made ginger cookies." Jillian pointed Andy toward the kitchen. "If you'll bring in the tray, you can have cookies and the coffee you asked for." His shifting moods intrigued and confused her.

Andy set the tray on an old trunk situated between two white loveseats flanking the fireplace. He sat down opposite Jillian, who poured the coffee. "What did you want to talk about? Is it Carol?"

"No. No, she's fine." Andy paused a moment. "What I've got to say is hard, but I'll go crazy if I don't talk to someone." Andy stood and paced as he talked. "Friends at home can't help. I need to know, and I can't ask Mom right now." Andy looked at Jillian. "I can't even look at her. You know my parents, and they trust you. I mean, Mom trusts you. Like I said last night, I've been trying to make sense of Dad's ramblings, but there's more."

Andy seemed to reach a decision. He sat down, took a sip of coffee, and continued. "I don't know you well, but honestly, it's sometimes easier to confide in strangers. You're not exactly a stranger, but . . ." Andy put his cup down. "Can I trust you?"

Jillian needed a minute to process Andy's confused plea. *What on earth?* "You can trust me to listen and not gossip. If I can help, I will."

"Okay." Andy breathed out heavily before beginning his story. "Over Thanksgiving, before Dad died, I was in his study sorting through papers, financial records and so forth. I found some letters and a copy of my birth certificate. My mother is listed as Ellen Grace Rafferty. No father noted."

Jillian's eyes widened. "You're adopted?"

"Adopted by the woman I call mother. But I think Dad is my father. Even though his name isn't on there, even though he didn't claim me, my full name is there. What other explanation can there be? My father had an affair, had an illegitimate child—me—and my birth mother disappeared from my life."

Jillian shook her head dismissively. "I think you're jumping to conclusions."

"So you've never heard a whisper of this?" Andy asked.

"No, never," Jillian said. "Maybe it was a surrogate kind of thing."

"The letters suggest otherwise. Anyway, test tube babies weren't a thing fifty years ago. Dad would've had to have been more, uh, directly involved. Regardless, they should have told me!"

"People used to keep quiet about adoption and fertility issues," Jillian said gently. "Maybe they were embarrassed. What did the letters say? Maybe you're misinterpreting them."

Andy pulled an assortment of envelopes out of his shirt pocket and handed them to her. "Read them. See what you think. It's all there in black and white—or rather blue and yellow."

Jillian opened a yellow envelope. "August 12, 1965. Dear Ben, it was great to meet you Saturday. I've never felt such an instant connection with anyone. I look forward to getting to know you much better. Let's keep in touch, Ellen." She glanced at Andy who nodded at the other envelopes.

The second envelope also held a thank-you note. "April 14, 1966. Dearest Ben, thank you so much for the lovely tulips. No one has ever sent me flowers before! They brighten up my dorm room. All the girls are teasing me about a secret boyfriend. Can't wait to see you again. Fondly, Ellie."

"Still think I'm jumping to conclusions?" Andy asked. "Go on, it gets worse."

Jillian unfolded the flowery yellow stationary. "January 11, 1967. Dearest Ben, it's been a long time between phone calls and dinners out. Our schedules have been pretty crazy lately. Knowing you love me enough to drive to Cookeville in the snow for such a short visit warms my heart. This college girl feels very lucky to have such a loving man in her life." Jillian scanned the rest of the letter that contained news of Ellen's new classes and a little story about her roommate.

"The last letter is postmarked July 1968. I think Ellen had come to regret being involved with my father, but she obviously didn't end things since I was born a year later." Andy took the envelope from Jillian and read aloud. "Ben, I'm sorry I got so angry at dinner the other night. I love you, but no one tells me how to run my life. Maybe your wife and the boys you coach let you boss them around, but I won't live like that. I've been on my own for a long time and make my own decisions. You can call, but I don't need your help moving. I need to do this on my own. Ellie."

"Without any context, the letters do appear pretty damning

evidence of some sort of close relationship," Jillian admitted. "But there's got to be an explanation other than adultery. Your father would not cheat. I'm sure of it. Can I see the birth certificate?"

Jillian looked but could find nothing to refute Andy's explanation. The mother's name was there—Ellen Grace Rafferty—but the father's name was conspicuously blank. She handed it back. "How have you made it to fifty without ever seeing your birth certificate?"

"Forty-nine. I won't be fifty until July," Andy said, glancing at the document before returning it to his pocket. "I remember needing one for my driver's license, but Dad held on to it. I've had a passport since I was ten and didn't need the certificate to renew. I got married in Vegas, so didn't need one there either. I guess my folks took care of any other paperwork that would've required it. How often does one need a birth certificate anyway?" Andy shrugged. "I searched for Ellen's name, but no joy. Another oddity: I was born in Belford."

"What?" Jillian said, getting caught up in the mystery. "I totally overlooked that. I didn't know Belford had a hospital."

"It may not. Place of birth is city, county, and state. No hospital name. No street address. The mother's address is in Gentry, so that's another mystery as to how she met Dad and why she was in Belford." Andy shook his head as he looked at Jillian. "I never expected this of my dad. I'm furious that he never told me anything, and now it's too late to know the truth.

"I'm telling you, Jillian, it's the weirdest feeling. Surreal, somehow. I'd never knowingly been to Belford before yesterday. Never even heard of it. I've never doubted my parents or their relationship. But now . . ." Andy rubbed his jaw. "I don't know. When I questioned Mom about the burial plot, she said Dad thought the grass was greener in Belford, and if he had to be below ground, he wanted something pretty to think about. Typical Dad eccentricity, right?"

Jillian laughed. "I don't know how many times he told me that any day above the grass was a good day. It's odd though. I wonder about the connection to Belford."

"I do too, and I intend to find out. I can't seem to let it go. The ghosts of the past are constantly whispering in my ear. I can't sleep for wondering about it." Andy's phone buzzed. He pulled it from his pocket and glanced at the screen. "Mom. I need to pick up some eggs."

Andy stood and stretched. "I've intruded long enough. I'll take this to the kitchen," he said, picking up the tray. "Thanks for your input. It helps to have someone listen. Ready to get your car?"

"Yeah," Jillian said, following Andy into the kitchen. She bagged up some cookies. "I think Willie wants to ride along." Jillian put a little coat on her little dog. "Wanna go for a ride?"

They made the short drive to the funeral home in near silence, each lost in thought. Andy took Jillian's hand and thanked her again. "And you too, boy," he said, rubbing the small dog's ears.

"Oh, Andy. Thank you for all your help. I hope—well, you know. I hope your Christmas is as good as it can be, given the circumstances. I'll be thinking of you." Jillian handed him the small bag of home-baked cookies and carefully made her way home.

"I'm sure I *will* be thinking of him and this whole mystery," Jillian admitted to herself. "What do you think, Willie? He's pretty intense, but he can be nice too."

She'd liked his thoughtfulness in wrapping her ankle and appreciated his trust in confiding in her. It was nice to have a man listen to her. "Unlike Paul," she said aloud. "Paul stopped caring what I had to say decades ago, and he definitely didn't trust my opinion on anything. If Andy lived closer, I think we could be friends."

Chapter Four

The days before Christmas passed quickly. Jillian's friend Amy, familiar with ankle injuries from her dance career, delivered lunch and books early in the week. Elaine finished Jillian's holiday shopping, wrapped the gifts, and insisted on buying her groceries. Clark Grebe called asking about her ankle twice and suggesting they meet for coffee. Jillian finally agreed to meet him after the holidays.

When the phone rang Wednesday morning, Jillian was in her living room, ankle elevated, waiting on Elaine. *Please don't be Clark again.*

"Hi Jillian, it's Andy Harrison. Thought I'd call and check on you. How's the ankle?"

"Getting better every day, Andy. I'm not as talented at wrapping as you are, but I'm managing." Jillian closed her eyes and smacked her forehead. *Argh, please don't think I'm hinting that you should wrap it.* "How are you?"

"Oh, okay. I'm keeping Mom company, sorting through paperwork. That kind of thing." Andy paused. "Uh, thanks for the cookies. Care to share the recipe?"

Jillian's eyes widened. *Andy? Baking?* "Be honest now. Do you bake?"

Andy gave a short laugh. "Truthfully, no. To be completely honest," Andy breathed out audibly, "I wanted to hear your voice again and be reminded of what contentment sounds like."

"Oh," Jillian said in a small voice, knowing that while she was content, getting there had been a struggle. *Poor guy. I'm sure he's reeling with the divorce, Ben, and now all this uncertainty.* "Things will get better, Andy. Give yourself some grace as you deal with everything.

"Yeah. Mom's actually doing better than I am. Lois has helped."

"Lois is your aunt? Will she be there for Christmas?"

"Yes, she went home yesterday but is coming back. She's been through this and knows what to say or not say." Andy laughed a little. "Mostly say. Lois talks a lot. She's trying to talk Mom into taking a cruise in the spring. If nothing else, she's a distraction and a better cook than I am."

The doorbell announced Elaine's arrival, so Jillian rang off, promising to send the recipe.

"Good golly, Elaine, did you buy out the store?"

"I stuck to your list," Elaine said, dumping bags on the counter. "Well, with a few extra things, but it's Christmas. I didn't know how much baking you'd be able to do." Elaine unpacked a coconut cake.

Jillian reimbursed her and said, "I appreciate your help, Elaine. Especially since you and Larry are leaving tonight."

"Friends help friends. Our plane doesn't leave until six, and I'm already packed. Now, is there anything else I can help with?" Elaine looked around. "Maybe decorations?"

"It's a little bare," Jillian admitted. "I hung the wreath weeks ago, but that's as far as I got. If you'll bring in a box from the garage, maybe I'll finish before the kids arrive."

Elaine brought in the box and accepted the cup of tea Jillian handed her. "Are you going to tell me about your ride home with that good-looking man, or am I going to have to drag it out of you?"

"Oh, Elaine," Jillian said, sipping her tea. "It was just a ride home." Knowing that Andy's story wasn't hers to share, Jillian said nothing about his concerns with Ben. "Andy was understandably quiet but talked about his kids some. He was nice enough to bring me home and help me get my car after the roads had cleared."

"Okay, Willie. I think we're ready," Jillian said, surveying her living room on Friday morning. She'd added Christmas towels in the kitchen and tucked some brightly dressed elves among the dishes displayed on open shelves. She'd placed greenery and candles on the fireplace mantle, holiday throws and pillows on the loveseats, and a stuffed Santa in Willie's toy basket. The tree would wait until her children arrived.

Jillian's 1940s ranch sat inside a loop road atop the ridge surrounding Newton. The home was full of character, the bedrooms light and airy, and Amy's lot was just behind her own. Jillian had found the house during an agent preview and made a fair offer before it ever hit the market.

Jillian felt content with her quiet little life. Renovating her home had helped her feel that way. With every stroke of paint, Jillian had covered her pain and shed her resentment. As walls came down, so did the expectations that had confined her. Making all the decisions herself had empowered and enabled her to change roles from a dutiful daughter, wife, and mother to an independent homeowner and career woman. Stronger for having made the journey, Jillian wasn't sure a relationship was worth giving up her freedom, despite her friend's encouragement to get back out there.

Willie's barking interrupted her musings. Jillian rushed to open the door and was quickly engulfed in a hug. "James! It's so good to see you." Jillian welcomed her only son. She reached up and ruffled his auburn hair. "I like your new haircut!"

James let her go and greeted Willie. "It's good to see you too, Mom. Sarah and Elizabeth not here yet? Move, boy, and let me in." James lugged in a large suitcase.

"They should be here soon. Elizabeth texted when they got off the interstate. How was the drive from Acworth?"

"Not bad once I got out of metro Atlanta, which these days stretches all the way to Cartersville." James patted his mother's shoulder. "I need to call Meg and let her know I've arrived. We'll catch up when the girls get here," he said, pulling the suitcase to the office and craft room, where he would sleep on a daybed.

Jillian returned to the kitchen to refill the teapot. James had been a strangely quiet and serious little boy. By earlier standards, he'd been almost verbose today. Meg had definitely been good for him. Jillian pulled out a veggie tray and cheeseball she'd prepared earlier, then replenished the cookie and candy tray. Fudge was hard to resist, after all.

"Mom, we're here!" Sarah called, and Jillian's small home was suddenly full of life and laughter and suitcases. Sarah and Elizabeth had both attended the University of Tennessee's Chattanooga campus. Now they shared an apartment in the small city. Only eighteen months apart, slender with dark curls like their father, the girls were often mistaken for twins.

"We brought food," Elizabeth said, carrying a covered dish. "A chicken casserole and veggies to fix later." She put the casserole in the refrigerator and began unpacking a canvas bag. Fruit, crackers, olives, and pickles soon competed for space on the countertop.

Sarah carried their suitcases to the guestroom, then returned to the living room. "Let me see your ankle, Mom." Massaging the ankle, Sarah said, "It's healing nicely. This will help the lymphatic fluid drain."

"Nice to have a home visit by my personal physical therapist," Jillian said with a smile.

"Glad to help." Sarah looked around. "Where's your tree? It's Christmas Eve!"

"In the garage. I didn't think I should climb a ladder," Jillian said.

"True. We'll decorate it together. I'll get the tree. James, start a fire. Sis, you're in charge of music."

"On it," James said, flipping the starter switch for the gas fireplace, then hurrying after Sarah.

Elizabeth found the Christmas playlist on her mom's iPod, and familiar tunes soon filled the air. Sarah lugged in a box of ornaments as James carried the box containing the small, flocked tree Jillian had chosen for her home.

Soon, Jillian was sitting on a loveseat, adding hooks to ornaments, listening to her adult children reminisce about Christmases past, remembering favorite toys, waiting for Santa, and hiding gifts from each other.

"Remember those Christmas programs we used to do at church?" Sarah called from the kitchen where she refilled her plate with veggies, fruit, and cookies before returning to the living room.

"I remember the one where we all dressed in Christmas pajamas," Elizabeth said.

"Except James," they added, laughing and toasting each other with a cookie.

"Hey, I was already the biggest kid in the choir," James said. "Give me one of those," he added, taking a cookie. "No way was I wearing red-and-white-striped footie pajamas. I'd have looked like an overstuffed sausage or something."

Jillian delighted in having her three children together again. For a moment, she felt bad Paul was missing this. During *his* holidays, the kids usually met him at a restaurant to share a meal.

"Y'all are falling behind," she said, gesturing to ornaments remaining on the trunk top.

Jillian watched her children interact. *I'm so glad they're friends. I guess we did something right.* Her brow furrowed. *But maybe our problems scared them away from marriage. Many of their high school friends are married. By the time I was their age, I had three kids.* Jillian pinched her leg to stop her spiraling thoughts. Her children were doing well, finding their owns paths. As she wondered whether she'd been a terrible role model, too passive in hiding her feelings around Paul, Elizabeth interrupted her thoughts.

"The tree's done, Mom. I'll put the casserole in the oven, then we'll fix the veggies and rolls. After we eat, we can do the tree lighting." Elizabeth patted her mother's shoulder. "You okay?"

Jillian smiled. "Of course. That sounds wonderful. Do you need any help?"

"Nope. We've got this," Elizabeth said, pulling Sarah toward the kitchen.

At least I finally found the backbone to stand up and reclaim my life.

"Actually, hang on, you two," James said. "I want to talk to everyone."

"Wait. That sounds serious," Sarah said, hands on her hips. "You didn't forget our presents again, did you?"

James blushed. He had, indeed, forgotten their presents one year. "Ten years, Sarah. It's been ten years. Let it go."

"I'm kidding, bro. What's up?" Sarah said, joining Elizabeth on a loveseat. Jillian looked curiously at her son. James was nervous but also confident.

"Well, Meg and I've been dating awhile now. Even though she's younger, just twenty-four, I know she's the woman I want to spend the rest of my life with, and I know she feels the same way about me. Nothing's official yet, but . . ." James reached in his pocket and pulled out a ring box. "I'm going to ask her to marry me."

Now that he'd made his announcement to the delight of his family, James was more talkative than usual. "I'm ready to ask her, but I want it to be special. A lot of people get engaged at Christmas, so I'll pick a random day in January."

"Better go put that ring back in your suitcase before you forget it." Sarah laughed after everyone had congratulated James. When he left the room, she whispered to Jillian, "We already knew. We helped him pick out the ring!"

"After Meg told us what she wanted, of course," Elizabeth added, leading Sarah back to the kitchen to finish the dinner preparations.

James joined Jillian on the loveseat. "I talked to Dad last night and told Meg's parents when we went to Savannah last month. Sorry you're the last to know, but I wanted to tell you in person."

"No worries, James," Jillian said, hugging her son. "Your feelings for Meg and hers for you have been evident every time I've seen you two together. When's the wedding?"

"The sooner the better, as far as I'm concerned, but Meg says weddings take a lot of planning. She doesn't want a huge wedding, but it won't be a Justice of the Peace either.

They moved into the kitchen and sat around the table, listening to the girls describe wilder and wilder proposal scenarios their friends had experienced. James appeared to consider the merits of riverboats and rooftops, messages spelled out in rose petals or candles, rings hidden in hollow books or fortune cookies. Finally, he put up his hand. "Stop. I don't think Meg cares about any of that, and I know I don't. I'll figure it out. So, enough about my love life. Still seeing Brandon, Sarah?

Sarah nodded and said Brandon was now tending bar at O'Shea's, a new rooftop bar in Chattanooga. Elizabeth said the bar was nice, but Jillian noticed she didn't offer any opinion of Brandon. Sarah didn't have the best record with men.

Elizabeth had found her soulmate at seventeen, but she and Liam were intent on establishing their careers before marrying. Elizabeth was already working in interior design, but her boyfriend had two remaining years in his doctoral program of psychiatry.

When her children asked if she was seeing anyone, Jillian blushed, thinking about the date she'd made with Clark. "Oh, for goodness sake. No news. You'll be the first to know,"

As they cleared the table and moved back into the living room, Jillian thought about their question. Her daughters had fully supported the divorce and encouraged her to see people. James had been a little slower to come around to the idea but had given his blessing when Paul found someone. Jillian wasn't sure she wanted to rock the boat. *They don't need to know about every coffee date. I don't expect anything to come of it anyway.*

"All right, are we ready for the great tree lighting?" James asked, turning off a lamp.

"Story first," Sarah said, pulling Jillian onto the loveseat between her and Elizabeth.

The tree lighting ceremony had been Paul's idea, Paul's tradition, but Jillian loved it. Now James took his father's place, sitting in the dark at the base of the tree, petting Willie and waiting.

Each year Jillian shared the story of annual childhood visits to the Rich's Department Store in Atlanta with her grandmother, aunt, and cousins. They'd ride the Pink Pig, a monorail that ran through the toy department and around the base of a giant tree perched on a pedestrian bridge. One special Thanksgiving, they'd returned to see the lighting of the Great Tree. "It was cold and late. I had pajamas on under my coat. We waited in the middle of a huge crowd, listening to a choir in the bridge."

Jillian fell silent as James played a recording of "O Holy Night." When the high note sounded, James turned on the tree lights and Sarah said, "Aw, it's so pretty."

After hugs all around, Sarah ran to get hot chocolate while Elizabeth laid out puzzle pieces on a card table by the tree. While her kids worked the familiar Santa puzzle, Jillian snuggled with Willie, reminiscing.

Her marriage hadn't been all bad. She could admit that now. Those early years, creating a home filled with second-hand furniture, him sanding, her painting, her culinary failures, and his mishaps with home maintenance—somehow they'd laughed their way through all that. Even then, Paul had shown a propensity for staying at home. She'd wanted to go places, do things, enjoy his time away from work. "We have a house now, let's enjoy it," he'd said. So Jillian had learned to occupy herself with books and crafts and children. When her youngest started school though, Jillian took advantage of her new-found freedom and earned her real estate license. Had that been the beginning of the end?

"Mom, come join us," Sarah called.

And Jillian did.

They finished the puzzle before midnight. Everyone stood and stretched and wished each other a goodnight. Jillian prepared for bed, then tiptoed into the living room, adding three stockings to the pile of presents that had mysteriously appeared since they'd said good-night.

ON CHRISTMAS MORNING, she followed the voices and laughter into the kitchen, where her three children were hard at work preparing their traditional Christmas breakfast of biscuits, bacon, scrambled eggs, grits casserole, and a fruit bowl.

"Sit down, Mom. Rest your ankle," Sarah said as Elizabeth brought her a cup of coffee.

"Everything smells wonderful," Jillian said.

"The eggs are almost ready," James said as the girls began pulling things from the oven and refrigerator and bringing them to the table.

When they'd been younger, they'd opened gifts and dressed before breakfast. Traditions had flipped as they'd reached their twenties. Now they leisurely breakfasted in pajamas, then showered and dressed before opening presents.

"Oh my goodness! What a beautiful coat," Jillian said, opening the box from Sarah and Elizabeth. James and Meg's gift was a coordinating cashmere scarf.

They enjoyed the day watching holiday movies, snacking on Christmas cookies and candies, and playing board games. As the afternoon waned, Jillian asked if anyone wanted to walk by the river. The weather had turned warm again after the early snow the previous week.

"Are you sure? What about your ankle?" Elizabeth asked.

"I think it'll be fine. If not, I'll find a bench. I've been housebound for almost a week."

Jillian's phone rang as everyone gathered their jackets.

"Jillian, it's Andy. Just wanted to say Merry Christmas. I won't keep you," he added as voices and laughter and barking sounded from the hall.

"Is Willie coming?" Sarah called.

"No, we're stopping for Chinese after," James said to a chorus of groans.

"The kids are here, obviously," Jillian said to Andy. "Just a second." She waved at her family. "James? Take Willie out for a potty break. I'll meet you outside," Jillian said before returning to the call. "Sorry about that, Andy."

"It sounds wonderful. It's been awfully quiet around here today."

With his mother in mourning, his dad gone, and his boys skiing with his soon-to-be ex-wife, Andy was having a very different sort of Christmas. "You're right, Andy. It is wonderful. Paul and I trade off holidays now, so I understand that unnatural quiet too well. How are you?"

"I'm okay. I made a big show of dinner prep. I don't bake, but I can grill steaks and bake potatoes. We ate early and will snack for supper."

"That sounds nice. I'm sure Carol appreciates your efforts.

"She does, and I'm grateful for Aunt Lois. She's kept Mom company. Enjoy your kids. I'll talk to you later," Andy said and hung up.

Jillian wasn't crazy about Chinese food, but James and Paul loved it and had their own tradition of Chinese takeout in front of *A Christmas Story*. The girls pretended to hate the movie and the food, but it was part of their Christmas tradition as well. This year, they'd already watched the movie, so they'd eat at the restaurant.

Traditions were important in keeping a family close, but Jillian knew it was smart to be flexible. She was happy but recognized things were changing. James might be with Meg's family next year. The girls could decide to get married or to spend holidays with their boyfriends' families. If divorce had taught her anything, it was to appreciate what she had while she had it.

NEW YEAR'S EVE FOUND JILLIAN sitting at home alone, appreciating the coziness of her little nest. Her tree lights twinkled, and Christmas music played softly. After an early dinner, she'd poured a glass of wine and curled up in the living room with a book and her little dog. When her phone rang, she at first resented the intrusion but smiled seeing Andy's name on the screen. "Happy New Year, Andy! Back in Philadelphia?"

"Nope, still here in Newton. I know it's last minute, but I thought we might go out for a drink or a bite to eat and celebrate the New Year."

Is he kidding? "No," Jillian said, a little abruptly. "Andy, I appreciate the offer, but . . ." Jillian paused. "You know what? I actually don't appreciate the offer. You're still married, and even if you weren't, it's much too soon for you to start dating." Silence. *Did he hang up?*

Finally, Andy spoke. "Oh, um, I meant casually getting together as friends. Not a date."

Jillian blushed. "Well, that's a relief."

Andy gave a short laugh. "Ha. Am I that bad? Don't answer that. I've pretty much oscillated between seething anger and frustration to inappropriate comments. Forget I asked."

"If you'll forget I offered an unsolicited opinion on your social life, we have a deal," Jillian said. "To be honest, Andy, I'm not one for New Year's celebrations. Besides, Carol might appreciate your company this year."

"I asked, but she declined. New Year's Eve has never been a big deal around here either. Hey, is that the Lennon Sisters?" Andy asked as "Winter Wonderland" was playing.

"Yes," Jillian said. "I'm surprised you recognize them."

"My parents had their Christmas album. It definitely brings back memories. I gotta say, Jillian, you have eclectic taste. First, Boyz II Men, then the Lennon Sisters, and now Kenny Rogers."

"Well, my ex-husband gets credit for that," Jillian said. "Despite our differences, he loaded my iPod with tons of music. Christmas seems to be the only time I slow down enough to enjoy it."

By the time they hung up some twenty minutes later, Jillian and Andy had shared a lot about their favorite songs and genres and Jillian had forgotten her irritation at the disruption of her evening.

Having fully enjoyed the blessings of another family Christmas, Jillian began cleaning up and preparing to return to work. As she packed away the last of the boxes, Elaine called.

"Hey, girl! I wanted to check on you. We got home last night. How's your ankle? Did Clark call? How are the kids? Decorations put away?"

Jillian laughed at the barrage of questions. "Happy New Year, Elaine. My ankle is much better, thanks. The kids stepped up and took care of all the meals. I spent most of the holiday with my foot propped and Willie on my lap."

"You've got good children, girl. Mine would've still expected food on the table three times a day," Elaine groused.

"I know better than that. Your boys love their Mama. They'd have ordered pizza at least. I wish you'd come help me eat all these cookies and fudge though."

"Womanly figure still expanding?" Elaine laughed.

Long ago, Jillian had told Elaine about the first time she'd ever heard that term. At nineteen, she'd been shopping for bridesmaid dresses with friends who'd looked fabulous in gowns that Jillian couldn't zip closed, regardless of size. A kind saleswoman had firmly escorted her across the store saying, "Sugar, you'll find dresses more suited to your womanly figure over here." Jillian had felt beautiful in the saleswoman's selections and resolved to appreciate her curves.

"Yes, indeedy. Either I start walking at lunch or invest in a new wardrobe. How was your trip?" Jillian asked, taking a bite of fudge before resolutely tossing the Christmas goodies in the trash.

Elaine and Larry had flown to New York to visit her sons and their families. Elaine complained about the weather. "I'd forgotten how much I hate slogging through slush. Enough about me. Did James get the ring? Did he pop the question?"

"He did buy the ring. It's a lovely, rose gold tapered band with an oval diamond surrounded by some smaller stones. The girls helped him choose, after asking Meg for input, of course."

"Was she thrilled?"

"Well, he hasn't given it to her yet. You know James. 'Christmas is so cliché.' He plans to pick a random day in January."

"He's a strange one, that boy," Elaine said fondly. "Elizabeth still dating Liam?"

"Of course. Liam's family went skiing in Colorado for the holidays. Elizabeth will probably join them next year."

"And Sarah?" Elaine prompted.

"We're wondering if she'll ever find the one. No, I'm teasing. It's fine if she never marries. That girl never lacks for company. Apparently, she's now dating a bartender."

"Hmm, I don't imagine he'll get many weekend evenings off," Elaine said. "Sarah may get tired of that. I would. What about you, Jillian? Did Clark call? Have you been out with him?"

"He did, and I haven't." At Elaine's silence, Jillian protested. "The kids were here. I've told you I'm not looking for anyone."

"Promise me you'll have coffee with the man, Jillian. Your little nest may be comfortable, but your birdies are fleeing. Besides, there's nothing wrong with a little competition."

"Competition! Elaine! I'm not some prize to be won by Clark or Andy or anyone else."

"Andy? You know I never mentioned him, don't you?" Elaine laughed.

Jillian huffed before filling Elaine in on Clark's phone calls, carefully avoiding any mention of Andy's visit or calls.

After hanging up, Jillian returned to her chores. She hadn't thought about Clark much. But sometimes, even in the holiday bustle, she'd remember Andy's arms supporting her as he'd helped her to the door, the woodsy scent of his aftershave as he'd kissed her cheek, and their shared conversations. It had been so long since she'd let anyone close to her that it was natural she'd feel a little . . . interested, right? It didn't mean anything.

Jillian sighed. Andy seemed to like her, but they probably should just be friends. After all, he lived in a different state, could be moody, and definitely needed time to get over his divorce. Maybe Elaine had a point. "Guess I'll see how things go with Clark," Jillian told Willie before continuing her cleaning.

Chapter Five

As Harrison's employees returned to work in the new year, Tom warned them of challenges they'd face in a slowing market. Nearing retirement in his late sixties, Tom also assured everyone that he would continue as acting manager a bit longer.

Jillian planned to check for new listings and set some goals for the month. But first, knowing Andy's divorce would be final today, she sent a quick 'thinking of you' text.

His response was immediate. "It's over."

A second text followed. "Feels weird. Leila a no-show. 20 yrs. The end."

Jillian replied, "Know it's hard. Give yourself time, it's normal to grieve," followed by a 'hang in there' emoji.

She put away her phone and began figuring out how to best represent her clients in what promised to be a tight market of increasing interest rates and lower inventory.

TRUE TO HER WORD, JILLIAN MET CLARK for coffee a few days later. She'd scheduled a home showing at noon so there was a definite end to her date in case things didn't go well. She'd known Clark for years but couldn't recall a single conversation with him that didn't involve real estate. An agent for a competing firm, Clark was in his mid-fifties, with a shaved head and a fit physique.

"Jillian! Over here," Clark called, standing beside a corner table holding two cups. "I took the liberty of ordering plain coffee for two. I figure we can all use a little restraint this time of year," he added as she joined him, patting his flat stomach.

"Thanks, Clark," she said, though she'd have preferred ordering a latte and maybe a cookie too. *Isn't the whole point of Starbucks to treat oneself without counting the calories?*

"How's the ankle?"

"Completely healed, thanks. My children were home for Christmas and wouldn't let me do a thing." Jillian laughed. "I was ready to get back to work! Did you have a nice holiday?"

After Clark's comments about visiting relatives, conversation dragged a bit until they touched on office gossip. Clark was very curious about the future of Harrison's Realty.

"I'm not sure, Clark. Carol hasn't been in the office in months. Tom Smith is running things as usual, and if he knows, he's not telling."

"Well, if you hear anything, I'd appreciate you letting me know. Ben Harrison was a smart investor. I'd be interested in some of his rental properties if Carol sells out."

Jillian tried to turn conversation from work to other topics, but her patience ran out before Clark's interest in real estate. "I'm sorry to cut this short, Clark," she said, "but I have a showing soon."

Clark looked surprised but stood and said he hoped they could get together again. He shook her hand, and Jillian left with the distinct impression that their meeting had not been a date after all.

After the showing, Jillian returned to the office where she helped a young agent get ready for a closing, then headed home. She'd just let Willie back inside when the phone rang.

"Jillian, it's Clark. Look, I talked too much about work this morning. I'd like to get to know you better. How about dinner at Applebee's this weekend, say Saturday, about seven?"

"Oh, well, um, thank you, Clark, but I have plans," Jillian said, glad she'd made plans to visit Carol. "Perhaps another time," she added, then wished she hadn't. *Why is it so hard to just say no?*

―♾―

AS PREDICTED, THE MARKET WAS SLOWING, so Jillian stayed busy at work, encouraging new sellers to counteract longer stays on the market by allowing her to stage their homes. Many buyers had difficulty seeing beyond personal furniture and décor choices. Staging shifted the focus from family photos and crayon drawings to the house. Faster sales at higher prices usually allowed sellers to recoup the additional fee.

When Clark phoned again mid-week to invite her to dinner, Jillian was in the middle of her call list and agreed just to get him off the phone. Since she'd already lost momentum, she called Amy.

"Please explain to me why I agreed to go out with Clark Grebe again. We have nothing in common other than real estate. He's very into nutrition and exercise. He'll probably insist on ordering for me again. Something low fat, I'm sure. He doesn't read or care for music. I know we're not a good match, yet I agreed to go out with him. Again."

"Well, Jillian, maybe you're reluctant to hurt his feelings."

"Maybe. Although to hear him talk, I'm the only person he's ever had to ask twice. He seems a bit stuck on himself. Why would he tell me that?"

"Good Lord, Jillian, I haven't dated in decades, and I'm not a relationship coach. Stan, on the other hand," Amy said of her husband, a retired mental health counselor, "Stan would say your job is to figure out you, not him. You've been restless since Christmas. What's going on?

"Oh, Amy, it's too quiet around here. My normal activities seem kind of boring. I miss the kids. I miss conversation. Last Saturday, I had lunch at Bruno's with a total stranger. Willie ran up to this guy's dog at the lake. We started talking, and Steve—that's his name—asked if I'd like to get a sandwich, so we did."

"Nothing wrong with that."

"I know, but it was his first date in forty-four years. Forty-four years! He's sixty-five, and his wife died about six months ago."

"Did you like him?"

"More than Clark," Jillian admitted. *But not as much as Andy.* Jillian sighed. "Doesn't matter anyway. He's not ready to date. We talked about his poor wife's struggles with cancer a lot."

"Maybe meeting Steve is a little nudge from the universe about dating again."

"I don't know about the universe nudging me, but Elaine sure is. I have a good life. I like my life. I'm not sure I want to be married again, but for the first time since I left Paul, I'm a bit lonely."

"Well, you're fine the way you are, Jillian, but if you're feeling lonely, then there's nothing wrong with dating. Go with the flow, honey. Don't force anything, but don't get out of the river either. You'll figure it out."

ONE DAY IN LATE JANUARY, after her first appointment, Jillian parked next to a dark blue Jaguar in the agency's lot. She listened to her voicemail and grimaced at hearing Clark's voice. Their dinner date had not gone well. From Jillian's perspective, at least. Clark had monopolized the conversation by discussing his new fitness routine and repeatedly inviting her to join him for early morning runs. Having survived a second date with him, she was determined there would not be a third. Gathering her things, she made her way into the office.

"Jillian, Adam Brown needs you to call him immediately," the office receptionist said, handing her a stack of messages. "I think he's already called six times, and Clark Grebe called twice."

"Thanks, Barb. I'll call Mr. Brown right away. Could you bring me some coffee?"

Exasperated at Clark's persistence, Jillian crumpled his messages and tossed them in the trash. She hung her coat on its hook, turned on her computer, and reached for her phone, entering Mr. Brown's number. As she was leaving a message, a steaming cup of coffee appeared on her desk. "Oh, thank you, hon," Jillian said, ending the call.

"You're quite welcome, dear," a deep voice replied.

Jillian spun around and saw Andy smiling down at her.

She stood and started to hug him but stopped and kind of awkwardly touched his arm. Despite their growing friendship, Jillian hadn't seen him in weeks. "Andy! What are you doing here?"

"I've got a meeting with Dad's lawyer this afternoon. I hope you'll have lunch with me before that." Andy lowered his voice. "I wanted to ask your opinion on some personal matters. I don't want to burden Mom right now. I could use a friend, Jillian. Can we talk outside the office?"

Jillian looked at her calendar. "Yeah, I can do that. I don't have any other appointments for today. I don't know that I can help, but I'm willing to listen." Jillian wondered if Andy had discovered more about his family history.

"Sounds good. I know you'll be honest," Andy teased. "That's all I'm asking. Where do you recommend?"

"Dimitri's. If we plan for eleven, we'll beat the rush. Does that work?"

"Sure. I need to be back at one thirty-ish. I'll pop by in about forty-five minutes."

Picking up her coffee, Jillian smiled, looking forward to lunch. Andy's phone calls since his divorce had been sporadic but welcome. They'd talked about life after divorce, family, books, and music. She wasn't sure why, but she'd kept their conversations private, not mentioning them to Elaine or Amy, with whom she usually shared everything.

JILLIAN DIRECTED ANDY toward an older section of town with brick storefronts. Dimitri's, a fixture in Newton, served a huge variety of plentiful, reasonably priced Greek, Italian, and American food.

As they made their way toward the back of the restaurant, Jillian spotted Clark Grebe dining with a slender blonde woman. She waved casually, but Clark walked over, so Jillian introduced them. "Andy, this is Clark Grebe, a colleague from Sweeney Realty. Clark, Andy Harrison."

"Oh, now, Jillian, we're a bit more than colleagues," Clark said, frowning slightly. Shaking Andy's hand, he continued, "Sorry for your loss. I imagine things are a bit shaky at Harrison's."

Andy's eyes narrowed. "Not really. If you'll excuse us, we have business to discuss. Jillian, shall we?" Andy took her by the elbow and led her away. "A bit more than colleagues?"

Jillian glanced over her shoulder at Clark, who appeared frozen in surprise. Clark glared at Andy's back, then turned and stomped back to his table.

"Nope, definitely not." Jillian blushed. "We've been out a few times recently, but no."

"I see." Andy leaned close to Jillian. "That guy, Clark, has a lot of nerve," he hissed. "He tried to corner me after Dad's funeral to ask about his inventory of rental houses. I don't even know the man, and he's got the gall to ask something like that at a funeral! You should steer clear of him."

Jillian eyes widened. *Whoa. Not your business who I see.*

Shaking his head, Andy picked up the menu. "What do you recommend?"

After they ordered, Andy said, "Thanks for agreeing to this. I need a second opinion. My ex-wife is taking the boys out of school for a trip to the Gulf Coast. They'll only miss a couple days, but I think she's bringing a 'friend.'"

Jillian's eyes widened in surprise as Andy reached for her hand.

"Speaking of friends, old Clark is staring daggers at us. No, don't turn around." He leaned back.

"A male friend?" Jillian asked as she tried to forget about Clark and his foolishness. *For goodness sake, we've been on two dates, counting the coffee, and he's with another woman. Why is Clark being weird?* Focusing on Andy, Jillian asked, "What makes you think that?"

"This 'friend' is the reason for our divorce. I can't imagine Leila going without him."

"Your wife had an affair?" Jillian asked in surprise.

"Yeah. Affairs, plural. Third time's the charm." Andy shrugged and studied the table.

"You're joking."

"I'm not." Andy sighed and sipped his water. "The miserable truth is that Leila has a long history of infidelity. I should have listened to my gut, but I was blinded by her beauty and sophistication. She was seeing someone when we met. By the time I found out about him, she was pregnant and I was asking her to marry me.

"Two kids later, I was working a lot of hours. Leila felt hemmed in by the mommy lifestyle and had a short-lived tawdry fling with her tennis instructor. She admitted it. We went to counseling. I forgave her, and she went back to work. She works in the fashion industry. PR stuff. I thought it was a one-time thing. Turns out, it wasn't."

Jillian's eyes never left Andy's face. She shook her head, unable to imagine the pain of a spouse's repeated affairs.

"With three kids and two careers, life got busy, you know? Music lessons, school, team sports, appointments, and so on."

"Those are hectic years with everyone going in different directions."

Andy nodded. "Yeah, anyway, a few years ago, Leila started with the business trips, late meetings, and mysterious phone calls. The kids were catching rides from neighbors when it was Leila's turn to shuttle them around. Then Will's coach called me at the office. Leila hadn't picked him up. I confronted her, and she admitted she'd been seeing an accountant she'd met at work for six months. I moved into the guest room. She ended things, we tried counseling again. I blamed myself for not giving her enough attention. I thought she was insecure, worried about aging, about the boys growing up."

Andy paused. He fiddled with packets of sugar and rearranged the salt and pepper shakers.

Sensing he had more to say, more he needed to say, Jillian waited patiently.

Finally, Andy blew out a breath and looked at Jillian. "I tried. I tried to understand, to do what I could. I sent flowers, bought gifts, tried to make her feel special. Things seemed to be getting back to normal, so I thought I'd surprise her by moving back to our bedroom. Instead, I found her in our bed with the drummer from my band. I left, called my lawyer, and filed for divorce the next day."

Whoa. No wonder he's so angry and hurt. It's one thing to suspect, but to see?

Andy leaned his chair back and glanced around the restaurant. Letting it drop to the floor, he confided, "Leila claimed she ended things. I don't believe her. She was more discreet, but the home front was more stressful than ever. When BJ left for college, Will and Seth felt it was unfair that they had to live in the midst of our fighting, so I found a boarding school for them."

"I assumed it would be temporary, but we're well into year two, and they want to continue. I hated sending them off to school so young, but at least they didn't have to witness the marital downfall." Andy rubbed his eyes. "The divorce was a contentious, stressful process. We had a lot of assets, and Leila fought me every step of the way. She wanted full custody of the boys, which was never going to happen. January third was the light at the end of a very long, lonely tunnel."

Jillian's eyes filled with tears listening to Andy's listless recital of his wife's infidelities. Her heart stirred seeing his vulnerability. *Poor guy, no wonder he's so grouchy.*

The arrival of their food preempted any expressions of condolences, so Jillian thanked Andy for trusting her with his story. "Are you planning to warn your sons that their mom may bring a boyfriend on the trip?"

"I think I have to. Don't you?" Andy asked, picking up his steak sandwich.

Jillian thought as she added dressing to her salad. "No. It's natural you'd want protect them, but they're going to be hurt either way. I obviously don't know your sons, but I think they'd resent any warning you give them, whether you're right or wrong." Jillian buttered a roll, then said, "Your ex-wife should be the one who has to deal with their feelings and ensuing behaviors, whatever they may be. She can choose her actions, but none of us gets to choose our consequences.

"I'd just remind them that the divorce is between you and Leila, not them, and while the family dynamic has changed and may change again, the way their parents feel toward them hasn't changed. Maybe let BJ know that you'd appreciate him keeping an eye on his younger brothers. Make sure they all know how to contact you if they run in to any problems."

Andy picked up a French fry. "That makes sense. Leila's insensitivity makes me furious. It's got to be awkward for teenage boys to think about their mother sharing a room with a new man six weeks after divorcing their father."

"Yes, but kids are resilient. As long as one parent behaves like a responsible adult, they should be okay."

"Forgive me for asking, but was infidelity something you dealt with?" Andy asked.

"No, thankfully," Jillian said, sipping her water. "Although that might've been easier. Paul and I grew apart. He sort of, I don't know, gave up on life around forty. He stopped taking care of himself, stopped doing chores around the house, stopped doing anything, really."

Andy reached out his hand again. "How would infidelity have been easier?"

Jillian frowned and ignored Andy's hand. "Choosing divorce was hard. It felt shameful. We'd been married so long, I thought I should stick it out, despite my unhappiness. Then I learned in counseling that there are all sorts of ways to leave a marriage. Infidelity is one." Jillian shrugged. "People understand that. Paul's way was quieter, less visible to our families and friends, some of whom were a little judgy. He didn't seem to care how I felt. I could hire people to do chores, but marriage is about companionship and love and respect, and I wasn't getting any of that. Anyway, when I finally accepted things weren't going to change, I decided to leave.

"You sound like you've made peace with divorce. How long does that take?"

"Gosh. A long time. It took forever to decide to leave, then a year's separation before the final proclamation. Then I had to grieve, all those hopes and dreams and expectations. It took two, maybe three years before I stopped thinking of myself as less than married." Seeing Andy's crestfallen expression, she added quickly, "Most people move a lot faster."

As they finished their lunch, Andy said, "Thanks for suggesting this place, Jillian. The food was good and advice even better, but we'd better get back to the office now that the coast is clear."

At Jillian's confused look, Andy added, "Now that Clark has left the building."

"Oh, good grief. I had forgotten all about him," Jillian said truthfully.

※

THEY WALKED INTO THE REALTY OFFICE TOGETHER but separated as Andy went toward Carol's office. In minutes, Andy was back in Jillian's office, waving an envelope in front of her face. "You've been summoned, Jillian. It's the reading of the will. I understand why I'm needed, but I don't understand why you are. Would you care to enlighten me?"

"I don't know," Jillian said, "but your tone is a bit hostile. I'd like you to leave."

"Conference room in twenty minutes. Don't be late." Andy tossed the envelope in her lap.

Jillian was sitting, holding the envelope, and staring after Andy when Elaine walked in. "Was that Ben's good-looking son who just left? What's going on?"

Jillian opened the envelope and quickly scanned its contents. "I've been invited to a reading of Ben's will. I don't know why. Andy's not being very nice about it though. 'Don't be late!' He's not my boss! That man's moods are enough to drive me insane." Jillian stood, shaking with anger, and threw the envelope on her desk. Andy's behavior had obviously touched a nerve.

"Oh, now, I hear he took you to lunch today. Did he behave badly? Do I need to talk to him?"

"It's fine. I'm overreacting. Lunch was fine, but now, well, his coldness reminded me of Paul, and I didn't appreciate it."

Elaine patted Jillian's shoulder. "Fill me in after the meeting, okay?"

Chapter Six

Twenty minutes later, Jillian sat at the conference table beside Tom, the agency's acting manager. An older gentleman sat at the head of the table with several files in front of him. Tom greeted Carol warmly. Carol, looking rested and lovely in a blue pantsuit and her trademark silver jewelry, shook his hand, then hugged Jillian.

Scowling, Andy strode into the room and sat beside Carol.

The lawyer cleared his throat. "Good morning. I'm Patrick Sullivan, Mr. Harrison's attorney. Thank you all for coming. Mr. and Mrs. Harrison filed updated Last Wills and Testaments with our firm last year. The bulk of Mr. Harrison's estate passes to Carol Harrison. Rather traditional bequests to his son and grandchildren have already been discussed with the family. Today, we'll discuss some special dispensations Mr. Harrison dictated. Mrs. Harrison is in agreement with these arrangements."

Jillian glanced at Andy, who looked as confused as she felt, while Carol beamed broadly.

Mr. Sullivan continued. "The second bequest depends entirely upon the first, so we'll begin with Mr. Smith.

"Mr. Smith, Mr. and Mrs. Harrison placed their trust in you when

Ben's health began to fail. It is their wish that you continue to head the firm as its new owner if you so choose. The firm, its building, furnishings, and holdings, in their entirety, are available for you to purchase at, to use Ben's words, 'a heck of a steal.'" At this, Mr. Sullivan passed along a folded paper to Tom.

Tom opened it, and his eyes widened. He grinned but shook his head slowly. "If I were a younger man, I'd jump at this. It is a 'heck of a steal.' But the missus and I want a slower pace of life. We've been talking it over and think a little cabin in the mountains is calling our name. So, I thank you, Carol, and thank you, my absent friend," Tom said, glancing upward, "but I'll help transition the new owner, then wet a hook or two in between naps and long strolls with my family."

Carol smiled and nodded. "We expected you to say something along those lines. We appreciate your help and Mae's patience more than we can say. Pat?"

Mr. Sullivan slid an envelope along the table toward Tom. "Mr. and Mrs. Harrison respect your decision and thank you for your years of service. Please accept this check as down payment on that mountain cabin."

Tom opened the envelope. "Carol, this is most generous. I'm not sure I—"

"Tom," Carol interrupted, "we want you to enjoy your retirement."

After Tom left, the attorney looked at Jillian and Andy. "The next bequest involves the two of you and is contingent upon certain conditions. Mr. Harrison purchased a property in need of restoration to its former glory several years ago, intending to complete the renovations himself. It's a large home built in 1873, situated on twenty acres outside the town limits of Belford."

Jillian and Andy's eyes met across the table.

Mr. Sullivan continued, "To my son, Benjamin Andrew Harrison, I leave fifty percent ownership, contingent upon agreement to terms of this offer, of the real property located at 473 Blockhouse Road, Belford, Tennessee, in the hopes that it will help him reclaim his roots, find his heart, and unburden his soul. To my friend and coworker, Jillian Renee Peters, I leave fifty percent ownership, contingent upon agreement to terms of this offer, of the real property located at 473 Blockhouse Road, Belford, Tennessee, in hopes it will help her find the joy she so richly deserves."

"Are you kidding me?" Andy said slowly and quietly, looking first at his mother and then Jillian. "What the hell?"

"Carol?" Jillian asked. "What was Ben thinking? What do you think about all this?"

"I know what I think. The old man was up to something," Andy fumed. "Unburden my soul!" Andy rubbed his face and muttered, "Maybe it's not my soul that needs unburdening."

Carol patted Andy's shoulder and smiled at Jillian, saying, "Ben was impressed with your work on the Candler Estate. He appreciated the integration of modern conveniences with period elements to make the original house the development's centerpiece. He also admired your personal home renovations. Had things turned out differently, he would have enjoyed working with you on this project. Ben trusted your judgment and your aesthetic sense, just as he trusted Andy's financial sense. Ben and I believe you two are perfectly suited to bring the property in Belford back to life."

"But why Belford, Mom? What's the story there? What did he mean by reclaiming my roots? Why did Dad buy a house in such a random place? Why was he buried there?"

"Ben moved from Belford when he was very young, but it held a special place in his heart. The valley's quite beautiful, so when he said he wanted to be buried there, I agreed, even though we never lived there.

"He found the house online. I've actually only been in it once," Carol said quietly. "If his health hadn't failed, I'm sure we would've visited more often. It's not that far to Belford, but life seems to run at a different pace there, like stepping back in time."

"Well, that's great," Andy said. "But unless Jillian's got a half-mil in her back pocket, she'd be a fool to start renovations on a house that old. Those things are always money pits. We'd be better off selling it and splitting the proceeds."

"As to that," Mr. Sullivan continued, "should either Mr. Harrison or Ms. Peters, or both, decide not to pursue this arrangement, the property will be sold, with proceeds going to the Parker High School football program."

Andy fumed. "Dad seems to have forgotten that I have a life in Philly. A job, boys in school." He stood and paced behind the table. "Is all this a ploy to get me involved in agency business? Am I supposed to tell Jillian to have at it and send me the bill?" Andy, looking furious, returned to his seat. "That ain't happening."

"Well, no. That's not what your father had in mind," Mr. Sullivan said. "There's a second part of this bequest that doesn't involve Ms.

Peters. If she's willing to accept half-ownership of the Belford property, we can get to that. Ms. Peters?"

Jillian looked at Andy and Carol before looking at Mr. Sullivan in confusion. She took a deep breath and shook her head. "I'm not equipped to make a decision today. I'm honored to be considered, of course, intrigued and enticed by the possibilities, but I don't know. I mean, honestly, I'm just stunned. Can I see the property and think on it awhile?"

"Of course. Perhaps follow up with your financial advisor, but be aware there's a three-month window of opportunity, so to speak. Shall we say mid-May? Please speak with Mrs. Harrison to gain access to the property at your convenience. My office will be in touch regarding your decision in the coming weeks."

JILLIAN CLOSED HER OFFICE DOOR, sank into her chair, and closed her eyes. What had Ben been thinking? Why on earth would he leave her a share in a property? Could she work with Andy for months of renovation? His moods were aggravating. Was he even interested?

She was intrigued. Renovating a period home was a dream come true but also a lot of work. Could she continue working at the agency and oversee such a project? Could she afford a leave of absence to complete the job? Was she even going to have a job since Tom had turned down the offer to purchase Harrison's? Her head was swimming with questions.

First step: research the property. Jillian typed in the address and found an old listing with a few blurry photos of a brick exterior. The windows, five across each floor in the front and three on the end, were covered with boards. A sagging front porch and side addition were obviously not original.

A lot of potential, but a lot of work, and a ton of money.

Jillian studied the photographs, trying to get a feel for the property. She couldn't imagine living in such a big house. It had to be five or six thousand square feet. *Hmm. Federalist design, built in 1873, but the Federalist period ended before that, didn't it? Four chimneys, probably two main floors with an attic. Dormer windows. Maybe a basement too. Argh. Why are there no interior views?*

Hearing a knock, Jillian quickly minimized the website and motioned for Elaine to come in her office. "Close the door," she said softly. "I barely know where to start. Tom was offered an opportunity to buy the company at a good price, but he declined. No one said what happens next as far as that goes. Then, this is crazy. Don't tell anyone, but Ben left me half-ownership of a property in Belford."

"What?! What do you mean half-ownership? Who gets the other half?" Elaine looked at Jillian's raised eyebrow. "You don't mean it! Andy? What? How? Why?"

"I barely believe it myself. And there are conditions. If Andy doesn't want in, the property will be sold and neither of us gets a dime. It's a huge old house in Belford." Jillian turned and pulled up the listing. "Here, look. It'll take months of work to renovate. Ben had hoped to do the rehab himself but decided Andy and I together had the necessary skills to make his dream come true."

"Wow. It could be lovely. I don't remember seeing it. Where's it located?" Elaine asked.

"Blockhouse Road, outside the city limit. Not much point in thinking about it until Andy decides if he wants in or not. He didn't seem interested in the meeting." Jillian voice filled with regret and disgust as she remembered Andy's attitude.

"Somebody was still being grouchy, huh?"

"And then some. He can be downright rude sometimes."

"And at other times . . ." Elaine said, smiling. "Why did Ben buy the property?"

"Who knows? Carol said Ben's family had lived in Belford when he was young. Maybe he was feeling sentimental or thought it would be a good investment. Enough speculating," Jillian said, picking up a file folder. "That meeting disrupted my routine. I've got to get back to work and think about something else for a while."

"Good luck with that, hon." Elaine laughed and closed the door behind her.

Somehow Jillian did manage to get some work done. She worked right through the afternoon and jumped when the door opened.

"Hey, Jillian. You've been awfully quiet back here. I thought I'd better deliver your messages before I head home," Barb said.

"Home? Is it that time already?" Jillian asked. "Is Carol still here?"

"No, that meeting broke up almost two hours ago. Everyone involved pretty much skedaddled after that. Carol looked great, didn't she? That son of hers though. He was not too happy leaving the meeting. I'd love to know what that was all about."

Jillian didn't say anything. After all, she didn't know what had happened in the meeting after she left, and she saw no reason to fuel the fire of office gossip. Unlike Elaine, Barb really couldn't keep a secret.

Chapter Seven

Ten days later, Jillian was home, checking listings and planning stagings for the spring season, although the house in Belford was never far from her mind. She knew the house could be a good investment but needed to see the inside and have the house inspected before making any decisions.

Jillian glanced out her kitchen window as she answered her phone. *Still raining.* "Jillian Peters speaking. How may I help you?"

"You can talk me out of renovating a house in Belford."

"Andy! I was just thinking about you. I mean, the house. And you," Jillian said.

"It's hard not to think about it. It's—what was it you said?—enticing, intriguing, something along those lines. I'll admit to similar feelings. What are your thoughts now?"

"Still the same. I haven't had much success with internet searches or much time to call prior listing agents. The man who sold the property to Ben has moved or passed away. No one seems to know for sure. I want to see it. Do you?" Jillian asked.

"Yep. That's why I'm calling. I'll be in town in the next couple of weeks. Pick a day. We'll go look at it."

They set a date, then Andy asked, "Will I need my heavy coat?"

Jillian laughed. "I doubt it. It's been unusually warm and rainy, but weather around here is crazy. Wait five minutes and it might snow again."

"Guess I'll be a good scout and come prepared for everything."

Throughout the afternoon, Jillian's thoughts turned to Belford and Andy more than she'd like to admit. *Thirty minutes before my Zoom call. Guess I'll see what I can find out about the town.*

Belford was incorporated in the late 1700s. The valley's rich soil attracted surveyors, who bought land from early settlers to create the town. The railroad arrived in the mid-1850s, boosting the growth of coal mines, and a nearby limestone quarry provided the material for the historic courthouse in the town square.

The kids are going to be so surprised about all this.

∞

AFTER ATTENDING TRAINING on video-conferencing years ago, Jillian's son James had convinced his mother and sisters that the Zoom platform would help them stay in touch, since they lived in three different cities. At first, Jillian had found the video calls disconcerting. It was hard to see her kids and not be able to hug them. Over time though, they'd all come to enjoy their twice-monthly virtual visits.

Once everyone was online and the kids had shared their updates, Jillian said, "I have some news. It's pretty crazy, but I've inherited a half-interest in a house."

After the surprised squeals and questions, Jillian explained about the inheritance.

"There's not much to add right now. I'm riding back to Belford with Andy Harrison next week to view the property. We'll check it out and see if it's feasible to rehab."

"That's so weird. Remember Skylar Wilson, from middle school?" Sarah asked. "Brandon and I ran into her at the River Market. She's working part-time at the library in Belford."

Jillian's face betrayed her befuddlement.

"You don't remember her, do you, Mom?" Elizabeth asked. "I'm not surprised, honestly. Skylar's super smart but kind of fades into the background. By choice, I think. Her family moved to Chattanooga a long time ago."

"No, I don't remember her, sorry," Jillian said. "So is she a librarian now?"

"No," Sarah said. "She double majored in history and folklore, then got a Master's in archival studies. She just finished an internship at the Smithsonian. Great experience, but her stipend barely covered living expenses. She's had a hard time finding a permanent job, so she's commuting to Belford from her parents' basement. Aren't you glad we're gainfully employed?"

"Considering I don't have a basement, yes," Jillian teased. "I'm not getting my hopes up about the house until we look at it. Rehab may not be feasible since it's been sitting empty for years."

"Wait, how are you going to rehab a house and do your regular work?" Sarah asked.

"Valid question," Jillian said. "We haven't made any decisions yet.

We may sell it as-is." Jillian didn't mention that Andy's shifting moods might hasten such a decision.

ON A BEAUTIFUL, SUNNY TUESDAY that promised an early spring, Jillian dressed simply in jeans and a floral tee, then packed some snacks and drinks. Surprised at being ready early, she grabbed a jacket, notebook and pens, and waited on the front porch swing. Hidden behind a budding forsythia, Jillian admired Andy as he approached the porch. Dressed casually in gray jeans and a long-sleeved green T-shirt, his curly hair was loose and his face unshaven. *Ooh, he looks so good.*

"Oh, hey. Good morning. You ready to go?" Andy asked.

"Yes!" Jillian blushed as she stood and picked up the cooler. "I'm ready. Where's your car?"

"In Philly. I flew down last night, so I've borrowed Mom's. I picked up a couple lattes on the way. What's in the cooler?" Andy asked, taking it from her.

"Snacks and water bottles. Thanks for getting coffee," Jillian said a little stiffly, remembering Andy's rudeness during the meeting with the lawyers.

As Andy opened the car door, he said, "I owe you an apology. Dealing with Dad's estate on top of my divorce is a bit overwhelming, and it's making me grumpy."

The mood lightened as they crossed the river out of town. Jillian began feeling like a child on school holiday. "I did a little research on the origin of Belford's name."

"Oh? Do I have to guess or will you enlighten me?"

"Every chance I get," Jillian said, blowing on her coffee. "Belford is from Bell's Ford. Get it? Back in the day there wasn't a bridge across the river—"

"This river?" Andy interrupted, sipping his latte.

"No. Well, yeah, actually. It's all the Igohida River. It snakes around through the county, but I mean where we cross going into Belford."

"Wasn't it Heraclitus who said you never step in the same river twice?" Andy asked.

"I don't know, but it's true. Rivers flow one way. Anyway," Jillian said, drawing out the word, "Mr. Bell owned the property near the river's ford, so they named the settlement after him. That and he had a bell for people to ring if the water was high."

At Andy's glance, Jillian laughed. "It has a nice ring to it. Bell's bell."

Andy snorted. "You've got a cute sense of humor."

"I almost forgot the punchline to my own joke with all the interruptions." Jillian laughed again.

"What's the name of the river again?" Andy asked.

"Igohida. It's Cherokee for 'eternity.' Didn't you grow up in Newton?"

"No, Springdale. I've never lived in Newton. Before Dad got sick, I'd only visited the town a handful of times. It was easier for my folks to fly to Philly than for us to travel with the kids. I guess everyone just said 'the river,' or maybe I wasn't paying attention." Andy shrugged and was quiet a moment, seemingly lost in thought. "I haven't actually lived in Tennessee since I was twelve. I went to boarding school from seventh grade up."

"Ooh, why? Were you a troublemaker?" Jillian teased. "Inquiring minds want to know."

"Inquiring minds, huh?" Andy said with a laugh. "No, I was just good at math. I took Algebra I at the high school in sixth grade. When I aced the state test, my parents found a more challenging program. Dad told me later they felt it was too soon, but when I started winning our stock game, he knew it was time."

"Stock game?"

"Yeah, virtual stock trading. We'd scour the *New York Times*, investigating stocks to pretend to buy and sell. It was a fun bonding experience, even after I started boarding school. We talked on the phone every Wednesday and Sunday."

"That's pretty precocious. I guess you really are a math whiz."

"Yeah, pretty much. Did you grow up in Newton?"

"Me? No, I'm a Georgia girl. I grew up in Aiden, north of Athens. I sort of moved to Tennessee by accident." Jillian laughed.

"How so?" Andy slowed at a railroad crossing.

"Well, after I graduated from high school, my Aunt Rose invited me to fill in for a secretary on maternity leave from her realty office. I loved it. Knoxville was such a change from Aiden. A whole different vibe. Rose lived in a condo community with a pool and lots of college boys. That's where I met Paul actually."

"Are you a UT graduate?"

"No, I'd planned to go to UGA like every other senior in Athens, but after that summer with Aunt Rose, I didn't go home. It was too late to apply at UT, so I attended a community college, but quit when I got married."

"We're getting close," Andy said as they crossed the Igohida River again.

Heading through town to the lower valley, they passed by several stately older homes. Andy whistled. "Dang, that's unexpected for this area. Somebody had some money back then."

Jillian nodded. "Coal companies and railroads. That's how this town made its money."

The road cut through a beautiful valley of fallow farmland bordered by the Cumberland Plateau. At the crossroads mentioned in their directions, Andy squeezed Jillian's hand. "Here's to the beginning of a grand adventure."

Blockhouse Road was paved but barely wide enough for two cars. Occasionally spotting a barn or farmhouse in between pastures and fields, Andy drove slowly until arriving at the red brick house they'd come to see. "Dang!" He said again. "It's huge."

The four-story house included an attic and basement, whose windows hadn't been obvious in the online pictures. A grove of pecan trees bordered the sparsely grassed, mostly level lot. A large pond stood between the road and the house, and a ridge rose up some distance behind it.

"The porch and door aren't original," Jillian commented. "The front entry would've been a lot grander with two curved brick staircases meeting in the middle. The door would've been larger, probably with transom windows to the side and a fan window built into the brick above it. I'm almost afraid to see what other renovations have been made."

"Well, we won't know until we head in," Andy said, unlocking the front door.

"Brr. It's chilly." Jillian pulled on her jacket. "And dark. With the windows boarded up, we're not going to be able to see much. Do you have a flashlight?"

"Yeah, here you go. I'll try to pull down some boards outside."

"Can you do that? Is it legal?" Jillian asked.

"We're the de facto owners. It'll be fine," Andy called as he walked back out the door.

He returned after a few minutes. "Well, that's a bust. I can't do anything without a ladder. The windows are ten feet off the ground. You'll have to share the flashlight."

As they walked through the lower level, Jillian noted a marble fireplace, wainscoting, and embedded columns and archways separating rooms. Two large rooms of similar dimensions stood on either side of a wide hall that ran from the front door to a porch. A curving staircase dominated the hall.

"This might've been a library," Jillian said. "I'd guess the other rooms were a dining room, maybe a drawing room, and a formal reception area."

Opening a door that led into the addition, a miasma of mold and mildew floated out. "Ugh. It stinks!" Jillian put her hand across her nose. "Nothing in here looks salvageable. The ceiling is sagging, and the floor looks rotten. Tearing it down and moving the kitchen into the original structure makes more sense than trying to save this monstrosity."

"I agree. Why'd they put it out here anyway?" Andy asked.

"Kitchens were often separate from the main house because of the risk of fire. Some homes had basement kitchens though. We might find evidence of that, but I'm not exploring a dark basement with just a flashlight! That's the stuff of horror movies."

"You are surprisingly knowledgeable about historic homes, Jillian, but you're also a big chicken." Andy laughed, taking the flashlight and racing upstairs.

"Don't you dare leave me in the dark," Jillian squealed. Upstairs, they found two large bedrooms separated by a narrow bathroom, and across the hall, two more bedrooms, each divided into four separate quarters by thin sheets of plywood.

"Weird," Andy said. "Servants quarters?"

"Servant quarters were probably in the attic. Maybe the owners were trying to house a lot of people here. Maybe they had a lot of kids. It's curious," Jillian said. "Let's check upstairs."

A closeted off servants' staircase led to a narrow hallway with eight rooms that, though smaller than the ones downstairs, could easily accommodate at least two beds. Andy's flashlight beam darted around the rooms. "I don't see any leaks."

As they walked back downstairs, Jillian noticed a bathroom. "Also not original."

"Huh. Want to grab some water and walk around outside?"

"Sure. It looks good, right?" Jillian said. "I didn't notice any huge red flags."

"Yeah, but I want a home inspection." Andy locked the door.

"Agreed. And we need to find the biggest gossip in town to find out everything we can about this place. If it's haunted, I want to know before I sign on the dotted line," Jillian joked.

"How do you propose to do that?"

"Barbara," Jillian said. "I'll give her a mission of chatting up the local realtors. She'll love it, and someone is bound to know something!"

"Great. Let's get out of here and enjoy my favorite season." Andy started singing the Indigo Girls' song "Southland in the Spring Time."

Jillian joined in, laughing at Andy's surprise. As they drove through the valley, Andy sang the first verse of "Down in the Valley," before saying, "Oh, Miss Jillian, you do intrigue me."

Chapter Eight

As Andy drove up Bay's Mountain, Jillian made notes and sketched the floorplan. "I'll arrange for an inspection to identify potential problems."

"Absolutely," Andy agreed. "You know, I have to give Dad credit for knowing there's no way I'd do this alone. He always hoped I'd take a larger role in the company, but we'll rely on your expertise in real estate and renovation." Andy rubbed his jaw. "I'll continue working through Dad's financial records. You make a list of possible contractors, particularly those that have experience with older homes. See which ones are willing to work in Belford."

"Will do, boss," Jillian said, hoping Andy understood that she didn't expect to be ordered around. She made another note and dedicated several pages to listing renovations required to make the home livable again.

Andy looked at her but didn't speak.

"I hope the wiring is in good condition. It'll take thousands to rewire the house. Oh, Andy. It's fun to think about restoring such a beautiful home, but where's the money going to come from? And to what end? What will we do with the house when it's finished?"

"I don't know the end result, but the lawyer told me about some, shall we say, arrangements Dad made. Your job is aesthetics. Mine is finances.

"If we move forward, that is. I'm still thinking on that one." Andy flipped the visor down to block the sun. "Dad had a lot of nerve foisting this off on us. He should have been more upfront about his intentions."

With that, Andy turned quiet again and met all Jillian's conversational forays with surliness, so she occupied her mind, imagining color choices and wondering which of Andy's rapidly changing moods was normal for him. She enjoyed being with him when he was in a good mood, but she'd had enough of grouchy men to last her a lifetime.

About ten minutes later, Andy impulsively turned into a pullout and looked at Jillian. "I always seem to be apologizing to you. Today's been great. I enjoyed exploring the house, being with you, getting to know you better. I like your company, and I hope I haven't offended you too badly with all my questions and moods." He paused. "Or my bossiness. My dad's secretiveness about Belford is bugging the hell out of me."

Andy turned off the car and pounded the steering wheel. "I don't like being manipulated, and that's what this feels like. Part of me is tempted to forget it. At least you could get a sale's commission. Maybe we should move on with our lives and forget Belford ever existed."

Andy stepped out of the car, slamming the door behind him. He walked to the railing, gazing at the valley below.

Jillian inhaled, opened her door, exhaled, and joined him. "I won't try to talk you into anything, Andy. Something like this requires total commitment. I understand the temptation to walk away. I truly do. I have doubts of my own." *Like whether I can put up with your moods.* "Walking away would be easiest." Jillian shielded her eyes and looked out over the valley, waiting.

When Andy didn't comment, she continued. "It's scary, but every decision has risks and consequences. Sometimes not deciding is the worst decision one can make. A long time ago, I chose not to live in fear of what might happen or what might go wrong." Jillian turned to look at Andy. "I'm not always successful, but I'm always mindful of my choice. Decisions are hard. I don't make them hastily, but I rarely second-guess myself. Once I decide something, I'm all in. If I make a mistake, well, at least I've learned from the experience."

Andy turned toward her. Jillian continued. "I've also learned I'm not in control. I spent the first five decades of my life doing exactly what was expected of me with the expectation life would work out the way society told me it was supposed to."

Jillian turned and looked back over the valley, then spoke more quietly. "I felt betrayed when my marriage failed. I believed it was my responsibility to fix it. I thought I had all the answers, but I didn't. I tried to control Paul and failed miserably. I learned several lessons there." Turning back to Andy, she said firmly, "I won't try to influence your decisions, but I'll tell you this: God, the fates, Ben—someone or something is throwing us together and leading us to Belford, and I'm really curious to know why."

Andy stared at her, then nodded. "Call the inspector. We'll make a more informed decision afterward. Meanwhile, do you feel like a short hike?" Andy pointed to a sign for Bridal Veil Falls.

The sun was warm, the sky blue, and a brisk breeze stirred the branches above them. Jillian was surprised but grabbed her jacket, and they headed up the trail.

"I noticed the sign on the way over," Andy said. "It'll be nice to think of something other than old houses for awhile."

Jillian agreed. "It's been rainy though. I hope the trail's in decent shape."

"If it's not, we'll turn back. No need to ruin your shoes."

Jillian laughed. "Oh, please, I'm not worried about that. They'll wash. I just don't want to lose one in the mud."

The trail was a bit muddy in places, but Andy gallantly helped Jillian skirt around puddles and climb over branches blocking the path. They startled a deer as they made their way uphill and nearly stepped on a box turtle when the trail turned down after a few hundred feet.

"This is an odd change in elevation, Andy. Do you think we're going the right way?" Jillian skidded on some loose gravel.

"Yep, shouldn't be far now. I think I hear it." Andy held out his hand, which Jillian gladly took. They rounded a bend and soon found the falls. Water cascaded gently over multiple layers of mossy rock on the side of the mountain, falling about thirty feet. "Well," Andy said, "I'm not all that sure the reward was worth the journey. If there hadn't been rain recently, there wouldn't have been much of a waterfall."

"Sometimes the journey is the reward," Jillian said, leaning against a large rock. "The falls are probably prettier in spring when all these dogwoods are blooming, but every bride is beautiful." They sat in silence a few minutes, watching the waterfall. "Are you ready to go back? You may have to drag me up the hill. Hiking out is always twice as steep."

"I'm happy to help in exchange for some food." Andy took her hand and pulled her up. He didn't have to drag Jillian, but he continued to hold her hand all the way back to the car, where they enjoyed the chicken salad sandwiches and fruit she'd packed.

"If I hadn't been so ill-tempered earlier, I might've noticed the beauty," Andy said, gesturing to the tapestry of farmland below.

"Good to know the clouds have lifted." Jillian laughed. "It's a beautiful valley. I don't know why we never explored this area. Too caught up in 'getting and spending,' I guess."

Andy look at her quizzically. "Wordsworth?"

"Yeah. I've always enjoyed poetry," Jillian said, furrowing her brow.

"I like poetry too. I was just surprised. Ready to head home?"

Jillian's feathers were still a little ruffled by Andy's assumptions. That was twice today he'd been surprised by her knowledge. Her lack of a college degree did not mean she was ignorant. Why wouldn't she know the same songs he did or have knowledge of books and poetry? Why would her knowledge of old homes surprise him? Why did she care what he thought anyway?

Looking at her curiously, Andy said, "Thanks for indulging my whim."

Jillian realized she'd been scowling, feeling oversensitive about her limited formal education. She smiled falteringly. "I enjoyed seeing the falls. I'm glad you suggested it. I was thinking about my ex-husband and my mother," she fibbed.

"That seems random." Andy started the car and pulled out. "What's the connection?"

"Oh, well, neither would've ever spontaneously gone on a roadside hike. They'd have been appalled at picnicking on the hood of a car in muddy clothes." Jillian smiled. "But it was fun.

Jillian fiddled with the vents. "My mother demands perfection and has impossible expectations. Unfortunately, she and my ex share a lot of the same qualities. I went from my mother telling me what to do to Paul telling me what to think. For a long while, I let him." Jillian glanced at Andy. "Honestly, I didn't get out much. I went shopping, ran errands, went to the library and church, and had dinner on the table when he got home from work."

"Sounds familiar. I know Leila got bored being at home. Is that when you started working in real estate?" Andy asked.

"Not until after all three kids were in school. Once I got my license and started working, I realized I disagreed with Paul's outlook on life. A lot. I began to do things on my own. Paul didn't like that. He was never physically abusive, but he could be hateful, and he never seemed to care about my opinions on anything. It's hard to be held in contempt all the time."

Andy reached for her hand and gave it a squeeze. "I'm sorry, Jillian. I've shared about my marriage. Do you want to talk more about Paul?"

"No, not now anyway. Over and done with. I want to hear more about boarding school. Did you like it?" Jillian asked, changing the subject.

For the rest of the ride, Andy shared tales of his youth, the initial strangeness of dorms, uniforms, and all-male classes, leading to stories of sports teams and mixers with girls schools.

"I bet you were popular with the girls."

"Ha. I was the classic ninety-pound weakling. Tall, super skinny, big feet, total math geek. Yeah, I was real popular."

"Oh, come on. Everyone has an awkward stage. I bet the girls loved you."

"I wouldn't say that," Andy protested. "I'm serious about being super skinny. I was premature and took a good while to fill out, as Mom used to say. Once I'd added a little muscle and formed a band, I managed to get a girlfriend sophomore year. Marie Whitworth. She liked me being in the band but decided she liked the lead singer better."

"Ouch, first heartbreak."

"Yeah, but not the last." Andy sighed and went quiet.

First Marie, then Leila. Wonder why they cheated on him?

As they neared her street, Andy reached over and took her hand. "I'm grateful for you, Jillian. Call me when the inspection comes back, okay?"

"Okay. Take care." Jillian felt a little bereft that Andy hadn't walked her to the door but decided a business arrangement was probably better than a relationship, despite the fun they'd had.

JILLIAN NEEDED TO CLEAR HER HEAD and attempt to reconcile her feelings. Deciding a little girl talk was in order, she invited Amy and Elaine for dinner, pulled a lasagna from the freezer, put a leash on Willie, and drove to the river that bordered Newton.

Jillian's side of the Igohida had walking trails, restaurants, and parks. The other side, the outskirts of Knoxville, had a golf course and expensive homes with great views. Although she'd never listed one of them, she'd once helped Elaine with an open house. At the time, Jillian had wondered why anyone would need such a large home, and now, here she was, almost half-owner of one even larger.

Jillian sat on her favorite bench about halfway between Bruno's and the main parking lot overlooking a little crook in the river, watching the ducks and turtles sun themselves on logs, thinking. *Do I want to work on the house? Yep.* Renovating a historic property was a personal goal. Jillian felt capable of handling the challenges involved. She could coordinate the appropriate workers, keep meticulous records, and be frugal with money. *But where would the money come from? And then what?*

Jillian sighed. She didn't want to live in Belford. Restoring the house would be a huge undertaking, and she had a full-time job in Newton. What she'd told Andy was true. It would be easiest to walk away.

JILLIAN PULLED THE LASAGNA FROM THE OVEN and saw Willie whining and wagging his tail at the back door. "Come on in, Amy. The door's unlocked," Jillian shouted as she sliced a loaf of French bread.

"Hey there, little buddy. Are you glad to see me? Yes, you are," Amy cooed as she carried the wiggly dog into the kitchen. "Something smells yummy. I brought wine."

In her early sixties, Amy was still lean and graceful and always styled her long gray hair in a braid wrapped around her head. Jillian admired her grace and beauty, but she was most impressed by Amy's zest for life. Amy's husband, Stan, was pretty much a homebody, cheerful and unperturbed by Amy's myriad involvements in community activities. The two women had been neighbors for five years and friends for twenty, ever since Jillian's girls had taken dance at Amy's studio.

Elaine knew Amy through her friendship with Jillian. She arrived a few minutes later, having picked up a cheesecake from the bakery.

Amy made herself at home, pulling out wine glasses and a corkscrew while Jillian served up lasagna and salad. "So, start talking. How was the house?"

Jillian talked and talked as they ate dinner and enjoyed the wine, describing the house and imagined renovations, her curiosity about its history, and Andy's reluctance to move forward.

Elaine listened carefully. "You obviously want to do this. Do you know how you'll market it?"

"No, it's hard to imagine it as a single family home, but I can't envision a commercial use for it either, since it's quite a distance from town. Maybe a B&B or small inn if the rooms were reconfigured and bathrooms added."

"I've heard rumors of increased jobs in Belford, and we saw evidence of revitalization downtown," Elaine interrupted.

"That's true. It's a big decision, fun to think of the possibilities," Jillian admitted.

"I'm sure it'll be gratifying to bring such a beautiful house back to life. It might work as a private school or an artist colony," Amy said.

"I hadn't thought of that. The area is gorgeous, so I can see painters loving the environment. And writers might appreciate the solitude."

"Or a wedding venue. Old buildings are in vogue right now," Elaine suggested.

"Oh my goodness. I can totally see that. Lovely pictures. The grounds need work, but there's potential," Jillian said enthusiastically. "My marketing campaign will have to suggest different uses." She sighed. "Oh, listen to me. Old grouchy face probably won't agree to move forward anyway."

Amy laughed. "Elaborate on that one, please."

So Jillian did. She told her friends about Andy's moodiness but also how good he had looked that morning and how much fun they'd had creeping around the dark house with only a flashlight, how they'd held hands during their impromptu hike to the falls. When she shared about them singing together, Jillian had blushed and sighed, "I sound like a teenager."

"No, you sound like a woman who's falling in love," Amy said.

"I'm not falling in love with that man! How could you think that? He is so moody, so bossy. Yes, he's reminding me of feelings I thought I'd buried so deep they'd never see the light of day, but he's also grouchy and cynical and wounded and doesn't even live in the state," Jillian protested.

Elaine hooted and attempted to quote Shakespeare, "Methinks thou doth protest too much."

"Oh, stop laughing! I am not falling in love with him!"

Amy smiled and began clearing the table.

"Maybe you should give Andy a chance, Jillian. He's been pretty nice around the office," Elaine said. "And you have to admit he's easy on the eyes," she added as she loaded the dishwasher.

"Elaine," Amy said firmly. "It's Jillian's decision."

"I'm not falling in love with him," Jillian insisted to herself after her friends left. "I can't be. I don't want to be. It's too early for him. I'm not looking for a relationship. I like being single. Being a rebound would kill me. Oh my god, I have got to be careful. I don't want to get hurt."

Above her protestations, Jillian could hear her own voice telling Andy how she refused to live in fear. Was she afraid to love again?

Chapter Nine

Jillian awoke resolved to put matters of love aside and focus on what needed to be done. She'd call Mike Chapin and order an inspection when she got to the office. Jillian knew the boards would need to be removed from the windows and the electricity reconnected. *I assume the HVAC will need replacing to be up to code. What else? What else? Water? Sewer? No, probably septic tank. Hopefully Mike will have some contacts in the area.*

Jillian was surprised to learn Mike had previously inspected the property for Ben. At that time, the first floor addition had been occupied by some sort of caretaker. "Well, the old guy said he'd been there pretty much all his life. Doing what, he didn't say. Good news is, structurally, the main house was in pretty good shape. But," Mike added, "it gave me the creeps. All that empty space, them little cubical rooms upstairs, wallpaper hanging, mousetraps in the corners. Probably bats in the attic, although I didn't see any. I couldn't see why Mr. Harrison wanted it.

"Anyway, I can't get to it next week, but in a week, maybe two, I can fit you in," Mike said.

"And I don't turn the water on, right?" Jillian asked, doodling on a legal pad.

"Not unless you want to mop up a flood," Mike said. "Washers and plumbing rings dry out and leak without water. Probably best to plan on a big ol' plumbing bill. I 'spect you'll want new bathrooms anyway. It's better to plumb while you're renovating."

Jillian's sketch of bats and a mop went unfinished as she took notes and Mike rattled off details.

"Have the well and septic tank inspected separate. I'll check for termites and window cracks, so get them window boards off. I got a guy in Belford does handyman work. You want his number?"

"Yes! That would be very helpful. I'll call the utility board about the electricity. I appreciate your help, Mike. I'll be in touch."

Jillian hung up and laid her head on her desk, feeling panicky as the reality of undertaking such a massive project sank in. *I need you, Ben. I can't do this by myself. There's too much that I don't know.* Having Andy in Philadelphia wasn't going to work. She'd call him tonight.

As the day progressed and Jillian dealt with clients and solved problems and answered questions from less experienced agents, she regained her equilibrium. She didn't know everything, but working on the Candler Project had given her valuable experience and contacts. *I'll wait for the inspection. There's no point in quitting before I start.*

While driving home, Jillian thought about her daughter Sarah, who used to shut down when faced with big projects. Through the years, Jillian had taught her to break big assignments down into more manageable steps. *That's what I need to do. One step at a time.*

I can't do anything else without the inspection, but I can begin a property history investigation. Maybe we'll figure out why Ben bought it. I need a cover story to convince Barb to help. No need for her to know Andy's involved.

The next morning, Jillian stopped by Barbara's desk with a fairly plausible story. "Good morning, Barb. I'm hoping you'll help me with something. It's an odd request from Wendy Seivers," Jillian said, making up a name, "with the Knoxville Paranormal Society. Are you familiar with them?"

"No." Barbara frowned. "Are they associated with the Newton Ghost Hunters?"

"Possibly. Ms. Seivers is searching for properties with paranormal activity, particularly abandoned buildings, with a history—at least a hundred years old, with boarded-up windows, that sort of thing. They want to hunt ghosts, not buy the buildings, so we can't spend a lot of time investigating, but we might build some goodwill with a large number of potential clients by helping her out, right?"

"Absolutely. Did you tell her about the old hotel and the warehouse out near the railroad?"

"Yes, I gave her a couple leads around here, but when we were in Belford for Ben's funeral, Elaine mentioned a number of old houses there. Would you be interested in talking to some agencies over there? Kind of ask around?"

"Oh my gosh, yes. That sounds like fun. I'll get right to it."

"Wonderful. Harrison's work first. But if you have time, I'd appreciate it, Barb," Jillian said. "Oh, if you hear of anything, get the addresses, of course, but also ask about the property history. Ms. Seivers is interested in places with lots of activity, big buildings, somewhere with more chances for ghosts, I suppose."

"You mean like a prison or hospital or something?"

"Or even a large private home that's changed hands frequently or been empty a while."

"Got it," Barb said, rubbing her hands together. "I'll let you know."

Jillian smiled and headed to her office. Her instincts had been right. If anyone could find information on the mystery property, Barbara could. Reassured, Jillian called the utilities board and the handyman so that the inspection could proceed as soon as possible.

OVER THE NEXT SEVERAL DAYS, Barb smiled and winked every time Jillian saw her. "I'm on it," she'd say with a grin.

On Tuesday, Barbara stopped Jillian. "Success, kiddo! I left a report in your office."

"What? You found one? Already?"

"I found seven! Belford seems to be a hotbed of paranormal activity—or rumors at least. I don't believe in that stuff, personally," she said before answering the phone. "Harrison's Realty. How may I help you today?"

Jillian hurried to her office and opened the folder Barb had left on her desk. She flipped through the pages eagerly. A stone motel on the outskirts of Belford, the upper floor of a furniture store with an apartment that wouldn't stay rented, a school building with odd occurrences during renovation, the block house they'd passed, and the red brick house by the pond. Jillian glanced at the last couple pages to calm her nerves. A fancy Victorian built by a railroad employee who'd lost everything in the Great Depression, and finally, a vacant theater from the 1940s that had fallen into disrepair. *I'll have to buy Barbara coffee and doughnuts tomorrow.*

Returning to the notes about the house on Blockhouse Road, Jillian found the same listing she'd seen earlier, but Barb had made notes: "Blackwater Manor, among oldest houses still standing in valley. Talk to Nola at hist. soc. re: orphans. Home of Dr. Wm. Clement for years. Son inherited, he lives out west. Bobby Hixon caretaker. On market 3 yrs before sold. Bobby w/dau near Elwood."

"Blackwater Manor! Time to do some sleuthing of my own!" Jillian began searching.

Having a name made a difference. She found documents posted by the Richardson County Historical and Genealogical Society with directions to the house and clues she tracked down to gain more information. By lunch time, she'd reached a dead end but felt good about what she'd learned.

Blackwater Manor was built in 1873 by Samuel Bunch, who moved his large family south from Lancaster, Pennsylvania. An 1880 census listed Samuel and Margaret Bunch, ten children, and eleven servants. Ownership passed to Walter Hixon in 1919. Jillian noticed that Hixon's wife was Malinda Bunch, one of Samuel and Margaret's daughters. The property passed to Daniel Clement in 1977. Although it had been listed numerous times, the next sale had been to Ben in 2010.

Jillian was confused. She reread Barbara's notes and double-checked census and genealogy sites but couldn't find a Bobby or

Robert Hixon anywhere. *Where did this caretaker come from? How could he share a last name with the property owners and not be related?* Jillian wondered how Dr. Clement fit into the picture and why his son inherited the property. She'd ask Barb about that, the orphans, and Nola.

After speaking with Barb, Jillian knew she needed to call Andy. She wanted to share everything she'd learned but felt uneasy. Should she disturb him at work? What if he was in a bad mood? Jillian decided to text him: "Still no word from inspection, but some news. Call when convenient."

Almost immediately, he called. "Hey, Jillian. What's up?"

Good mood, then. "I thought I'd share the results of Barbara's investigation."

"Wow. Quicker than an inspector, the intrepid investigator dishes the dirt," Andy joked. "How did you arrange this?"

Jillian shared the story of the paranormal investigators to a disbelieving Andy.

"Remind me to not believe half of what you say," Andy teased. "That's some pretty fancy creative talent."

"Do you want to hear what she found?"

"Of course. What did our master sleuth discover?

"The house is called Blackwater Manor." Jillian shared the remaining details before adding, "There's a contact at the historical society, a Nola Robbins. Should I call her?"

"Yes, set up an appointment, maybe Wednesday or Thursday of next week. I'll be in town awhile. My days will be pretty full with different aspects of Dad's estate, but I can spare a day, or an afternoon, at least. Hopefully the inspector's report will be back before I leave, and we can make some decisions. Let's find out all we can. I'm still confused about that rabbit warren upstairs."

"I was hoping you'd be able to come," Jillian said. "I'll call her today."

"Are you going to chase me up the stairs again?" Andy teased.

Jillian knew she was attracted to Andy. He could be a lot of fun, and from the first time she'd looked into his emerald eyes, she'd wanted to get to know him, to be close to him. Seeing him dressed casually, with his hair hanging loose the way it had been the last time they went to Belford, she'd had to physically restrain herself from reaching out and brushing the curls from his forehead.

Maybe her friends were right. Maybe she was falling in love.

But those moods. Being afraid to call him, feeling like she had to walk on eggshells around him. Those weren't healthy feelings. Jillian didn't want to get back into a relationship where she lost herself trying to keep a grumpy man happy. She wasn't responsible for Andy's moods, but they did affect her. She wouldn't sit quietly and pretend they didn't. *I can walk away, let him know he needs to act right if we're going to work together.*

Jillian's feelings were confused. Andy was nice most of the time. She felt younger and more attractive and more desirable around him than she'd felt in a long time. She felt better about herself. The attraction seemed mutual. He'd winked at her, been very kind about her ankle and kissed her cheek that first night she'd ridden with him. He'd taken her hand in Belford and always seemed to be touching her arm or waist as he stepped around her or guided her into a room.

She yearned for his touch, that much was true. But was it Andy, or would she feel that way about any man? Well, any man but Clark. It had been a long time since she'd let anyone get close to her. Andy was moody, but given the circumstances, given everything he had gone through in the last few months, that too was understandable. After all, she'd been angry for months after her divorce.

Maybe I'm being too judgmental. Divorce is hard. Then again, maybe I'm running scared. Maybe I should listen to Amy and stay in the river.

Even though Andy's marriage had been over long before its official end, his mood swings suggested a lot of unresolved feelings. Jillian knew the chances of having a meaningful relationship down the road depended on building a friendship first. Jillian wasn't sure she wanted a relationship that led to marriage, but she did know she wasn't interested in a casual fling. Working together on the house at Blackwater Pond would give them a chance to build a friendship or maybe more.

Chapter Ten

Having planned a return visit to the house she and Andy had inherited, Jillian was determined to find Ben's connection to it. Since Barb's notes had included a contact name, Jillian called the Richardson County Historical and Genealogical Society, which she learned was a big name for a small group of volunteers who'd gathered an impressive collection of books and papers currently housed in the county library. The librarian, Martha Small, listened as Jillian explained her interest in Blackwater Manor.

"There's information to be gleaned from the collection, but it would take a month of Sundays to prise it out from these family histories. I'd suggest talking to Miss Nola," Martha said.

"Do you have a number for her?" Jillian asked, twirling her pencil.

"I do, but you'll be missing a treat if you don't visit with her in person. If you like, I can call her great niece, Faith Boyd, and set up a meeting. Nola lives with Faith and her husband just off Main Street here in town."

"That sounds wonderful," Jillian said. "What can you tell me about Miss Nola?"

"Oh, land, she's about ninety pounds soaking wet and near ninety years old but sharp as a tack. She's pretty much a walking history book of Richardson County and, as I'm sure she'll tell you, a descendant of some of the first families in the valley. She made it a mission in life to write a family history book for each of the original twelve families. Then she wrote a history of the railroad and coal companies and their activities in Belford. Now I think she's working her way through the alphabet of all the newcomers." Martha laughed. "She's a real pistol."

"She sounds delightful. I look forward to meeting her." Jillian gave Martha her contact information and promised to stop by the library after their visit.

⁂

ON THE FOLLOWING THURSDAY, Jillian and Andy drove to Belford again. Nola lived, as Martha had promised, a block off of Main Street on Catawba Avenue, diagonal from the public library.

"Ha," Jillian laughed. "We really do have to update Martha. She's sure to notice a strange car!"

"Can't hide this little red torture machine," Andy groaned, unfolding his long legs from Jillian's Fiat. "I thought realtors all drove SUVs or big sedans."

"I used to, but most of my clients prefer to meet at the property. Besides, this car is more energy efficient," Jillian said as they walked down the sidewalk through the corner lot filled with flowering hydrangeas.

Faith Boyd met them at the door of a single-story red brick house with a wide front porch. "Oh, do come in. Aunt Nola's excited to have visitors to talk to about the valley. I'll get you settled in the front room and let her know you're here."

Faith led them into a living room redolent of lemon furniture polish, where she moved a wooden dining chair from the corner closer to the couch. "Aunt Nola prefers this chair. She says it makes her feel queenly, but really, it's easier for her to get up and down. I'll be right back."

Jillian and Andy stood when Miss Nola appeared in the doorway. The tiny woman was barely four feet tall. Neatly dressed in a long-sleeved dark blue dress with pleats and tiny buttons up the front, Nola walked unassisted to her chair, tucking a strand of her white hair back into a bun.

"Thank ye for coming to sit with me. I'm always glad of visitors. Martha said you were inquiring after the house at Blackwater Pond."

"Yes, ma'am," Jillian began. "Andy's father Ben Harrison bought the property several years ago but passed away before he could restore it. We're curious about its history."

Nola looked at Andy closely, peering into his green eyes. "I'm sorry for your loss, young man. Death and loss sometimes bring life and gains we don't expect. How much do you know about the history of Richardson County?"

"Not much, I'm afraid," Andy said. "I only went through seventh grade in Tennessee, so I missed the local history. Could you tell us a bit?"

"She sure can," Faith interrupted. "I brought you all some coffee." She placed the tray on the table in front of them before leaving the room.

Miss Nola said, "Cream and sugar, please. I'm partial to sweets. Well, let's see. Richardson County was settled in 1797 by twelve families. Their names were Abram, Bell, Boyd, Bunch, Gamble, Hale, Hixon, Jeffries, Robbins, Shannon, and White," she recited, ticking them off on her fingers. "Who did I miss? Oh, yes, the McTeers. Where do you suppose these families were from?"

"Scotland and Ireland, I'd guess," Jillian ventured, grinning at Andy as she poured the coffee. "Isn't that the typical ancestry for Appalachia?"

"Yes, typically, but nine of those families were English. What might have brought the English families to the wilds of Richardson County in 1797?"

"Religious freedom?" Andy guessed.

"No, the last big religious migration was the Quakers in the early 1700s. By 1797, it was famine. Up along the Scottish–English border, massive crop failures led to a burgeoning of immigration from Scotland, Ireland, and England. This county, with its lush valley, clean water, and rolling hills, reminded the folks of home. Early homesteaders included my four-times great grandpa Adam Bell, for whom the town is named, and my husband's ancestor William Robbins, a farmer and a self-styled Methodist preacher. He was one of three learned men who came here. The others were Abram, who studied law, and Hale, who studied medicine. Still do, come to think of it."

"Miss Nola, were you, by any chance, a teacher?" Jillian asked.

Miss Nola took a sip of her coffee and set it down carefully before responding. "Yes, I was. I taught for forty years at Belford Academy before the County took over. Eighth grade history mostly. History is my passion. I want the young people of this valley to learn where they came from and of the sacrifices and good works of their ancestors.

"As I was saying, the house at Blackwater Pond," she continued, "was built by Samuel Bunch in 1873. He mined an iron deposit on the property and sold it to the railroads at quite a profit. He built the manor to house his family. Had ten children, you know. The property passed to his daughter, Malinda, and son-in-law, Walter Hixon. Walter was a godly man. He and Malinda had three children, Isaiah, Matthew, and Francine. Believing that Bible verse about rich folks and the eye of a needle, Walter felt led to help folks out. When the valley fell on hard times in the 1920s and 1930s, Malinda and Walter did what they could to ease the suffering."

"They sound like wonderful people," Jillian said, picking up her coffee cup.

"Oh, they were," Miss Nola said. "Many here in the valley suffered. Folks lost money, land, homes. Some hired themselves out, others moved on. One or two killed themselves over the shame of loss and debt. And some did the unthinkable and abandoned their children because they couldn't feed them." Nola pursed her lips. "Walter Hixon let it be known that anyone could have a place to live and work to do at Blackwater. In the fall, they'd pick pecans and harvest crops. In the spring and summer, they'd work the fields, dig iron, or saw lumber. Women cooked and cleaned and learned a little nursing. He set up a school and taught the young ones of the valley in exchange for a chicken, ginseng root, squirrels and doves—whatever the families could give. He didn't need money. He knew folks needed to pay their own way to retain their dignity.

"After the depression ended, most folks moved on with their lives. The Hixons never stopped helping. They took in orphans, the elderly with no one to look after them, and young girls in trouble. All those little rooms upstairs were filled with people needing care. Everyone was treated with kindness and dignity. Not a one was made to feel ashamed or denied care because they had sinned. That wasn't the Christian way nor the Hixon way." Miss Nola paused for more coffee.

"Where did the house get its name?" Jillian asked.

"From that pond or the creek that feeds it. Blackwater is slower moving and brackish with decaying leaves and such. Some say that's where the polio started. Belford had not had a single case until the church picnic out there in 1952, when some children waded in the creek and took sick.

"Two children died. Lots more sick near to death, weakened badly. Two cases at the manor. Bobby Bunch and that pretty little girl with the blond ringlets. Francine Hixon was a particular friend of mine. We were born the same week and were friends all our lives. She saved those children, nursing them around the clock."

"Bobby's still living, isn't he, Aunt Nola?" Faith asked as she came bustling back in the room. "I wanted to make sure you're not too tired. Do you want to lie down?"

"No, I do not. I want to talk about Francine. Thank you though, dear. It's so good to talk about old friends with new ones, and this young man needs to hear my story."

"Well, now my curiosity's piqued, for sure," Andy said. "I'd love to stay and listen, but we can come back another time if that's better."

"I'll continue. The little girl I mentioned, the one who caught the polio, came to Blackwater in 1948. She had big green eyes, a little blond fuzz on her head, and a solemn little face. Everyone was quite taken with this baby girl, not yet two. We knew she'd be adopted before long. Malinda worked to place the babies born here, you see. Sure enough, a wealthy family from Kentucky came calling. The woman wanted a baby and hadn't been blessed with one. They decided on our green-eyed beauty. Called her Susan and took her home with them.

"Six months later, she was back. The woman, now in the family way, no longer wanted the child. Devastated and overjoyed at the same time, Malinda vowed to be more particular about who adopted her little ones. Francine was seventeen when the child returned. She never married, you know. She loved all those children at the Manor like they were her own. Baby Girl, that's what she called the child, became quite the pet. Had Malinda tried to adopt her out again, Francine would've stopped it.

"By then, I was spending less time at the Manor because I was courting. I'm a Robbins by marriage. My maiden name was Bell. I may have already said that. Then 1952 brought the polio. The child would've died without Francine's constant ministrations. Bobby Bunch's father left him on the front porch, and him as sick as could be. Francine moved from one sickbed to the next, a ministering angel." Nola's voice rose in frustration. "Wore herself half to death caring for others. When it was all over, she adopted Bobby. His father had left town the same day he left Bobby to die."

Bobby Hixon. The caretaker. That's where he came from. Francine adopted Bobby Bunch.

"By that time, Dr. Clements and his son had moved to the manor. Francine convinced him to doctor the other residents in exchange for room and board. He was widowed, so it worked out well."

"Did she adopt the little girl too?" Jillian asked.

"No. Baby Girl had a family, and Francine was determined to find them."

"A family? I thought she was orphaned," Jillian said.

"Well, now, she was, but after she'd been taken by the Kentucky family, her uncle came looking for her and her older brother. The uncle had a letter from his brother, the children's father, begging for help. Their father was in the Army, still overseas despite the war finally being over, and had been told his wife was poorly and not expected to live. The father wanted his children to stay with family, but the uncle didn't receive that letter for some time."

Miss Nola was watching Andy closely. "By the time this man heard about the children, his brother, the children's father, had been killed in service, and little Ellen was gone."

When Andy heard the name Ellen, he raised his eyes and asked, "Ellen who?"

"Ellen Harrison, son. I do believe she was your mother."

"My mother's name was Ellen Rafferty," Andy said.

"Yes, that is what the birth certificate said. I know because I registered all the babies born at the house on Blackwater Pond, and that is where you were born. You do look remarkably like Ellen. Your eyes are just as hers were."

Andy stood. "I, I need a minute. Will you excuse me, please?"

As he walked to the front door, Jillian said, "Andy? Are you okay?"

"Let him go, dear. There's more, when he's ready to hear it."

Faith rushed into the room as she heard the front door open. "Is everything all right?"

"It's fine, dear. Set a couple extra plates, won't you? We'll finish after we eat a bite," Nola said as she stood.

"We don't want to impose," Jillian protested.

"Nonsense. We would enjoy the company."

When Andy returned, Jillian went to him. He smiled thinly. "It's what we came for, right? Answers to our questions. I'm okay. Just a bit of a shock. Where is everyone?"

"In the kitchen, putting dinner on the table. We can leave if you'd rather. It's a lot to take in."

"I'd like to stay," Andy said.

They walked into the kitchen. "Wow! This is quite a spread," Andy said eyeing the ham, kale, deviled eggs, beets, sliced tomatoes, field peas, and cornbread.

Faith introduced her husband, Rex, who was able to walk home from his job for lunch.

"What are those trees lining the street?" Andy asked, gesturing toward the front. "The ones with the big heart-shaped leaves."

"That's a catalpa tree. You may have noticed the street's Catawba

Avenue. There's some discussion about the spelling and the origin. Some say it's from the Indians, but others say the tree," Rex explained. "Please, have a seat."

"It's an unusual looking tree. My dad used to talk about Catalpa worms," Andy said.

"Oh, yes, some folks feel the worms are pests because they attack the trees. Others say it's God's way of providing the best catfishing bait around."

"Every cloud has a silver lining," Miss Nola said.

"Were there many Native Americans in this area?" Jillian asked, passing the bowl of peas.

"Yes, primarily Cherokee and Chickasaw, I think," Rex said, reaching for the ham.

"The Chickasaw were mostly in West Tennessee," Nola corrected. "There were likely others: Catawba, Muscogee, and Shawnee. Of course, the Indian Removal Act of 1830 forced Indians in great numbers from their homes. Blockhouse Road is named for one of the stockades of that era."

"Andy, I understand you live in Philadelphia. What is it you do there?" Rex asked.

Andy talked about his work and family and asked questions of the Boyds. Miss Nola shared more about the town's history and her years as a school teacher. Before long, Rex returned to work, and Faith urged them back into the living room to finish the story. She hinted that Miss Nola might like to lie down soon, so Jillian and Andy didn't offer to help clean up the kitchen.

"I do not know the end of the story," Miss Nola said, returning to her chair. "But there's a bit more if you would like to hear it."

Andy and Jillian sat side by side on a low couch. Andy's long legs bumped against the coffee table as he sat down. "I'm ready to hear whatever you can tell me."

"Well, we left off with the polio," Nola said. "Ellie recovered but used crutches for some time. She was weak in her legs and had accepted that she'd never be adopted. Malinda and Francine kept looking for her family but did not have any luck. As Malinda and Walter got older, Francine decided to host a big party, a sort of reunion for anyone associated with Blackwater Manor. She advertised in newspapers in several states and prepared for a big to-do.

"This would have been about 1965. I was not at the party. I was quite ill, ended up losing the only child Mr. Robbins and I ever conceived."

Jillian looked up from her notes. It's easy to think of older people as having always been old, but Nola had been a bride once. She'd had a full life as a teacher and historian, but her voice conveyed her sorrow at her personal loss from so long ago.

"Francine told me later about Ellie meeting her brother. I suspect her brother noted a family resemblance to one of their parents. He was a good size boy when they passed.

"Ellie, by that time, was a freshman at Tennessee Tech, studying education. She came home for the reunion. She graduated later. Francine went to the ceremony. The next thing I knew, Ellen was back at Blackwater Manor, helping in the kitchen and staying in one of the little rooms upstairs. She was about six months gone.

"Pregnant," Miss Nola said, answering Andy's unspoken question.

"I didn't see her again until she had fallen and was in labor. I was told her man was in Vietnam. A letter arrived that upset her. She ran out the door and fell down all those steps. She concussed and went into labor. I was there for part of it, poor thing. Crying for her man. Begging Francine to call her brother. When the child was born, she said his name was Benjamin Andrew Harrison. Francine told me to leave the father's name blank and write Ellen Grace Rafferty as the mother.

"Francine never said, but I suspect Ellie wasn't married. In those days, unmarried mothers were shamed." Nola shook her head. "That was the last time I saw your mother. Francine said Ellie's brothers came to get her. We never found out anymore." Miss Nola finished her tale.

Brothers? Jillian looked at Andy to see if he had noticed, but his expression hadn't changed.

Nola stood. "I am right proud to have met you, Andy. God works in mysterious ways. His ways are not our ways, nor his timing our timing." She paused. "When I start talking in clichés, it is time for me to rest. I do believe I'll go lie down now."

Faith had been listening from the doorway. She helped the old woman to her bedroom, then came back and said her goodbyes to Jillian and Andy.

Andy paused by the car. "I'd rather not talk to the librarian today. Make my excuses, will you? I'll walk around a bit. Don't be long."

"I'll let her know we learned a lot of property history and see what resources the library has. I shouldn't be more than ten minutes."

Chapter Eleven

Leaving Belford in relative silence, Jillian waited until they were chugging up Bays Mountain to speak. "I can't imagine what's going through your mind, Andy. Do you want to talk about it?"

"Not really." After few minutes, he said, "I don't have any clear thoughts. I keep hearing Nola repeating her story. I'm numb." Andy huffed. "And mad. I've been kept in the dark too long."

Jillian gripped the wheel tightly and glanced at him. She didn't want to anger him but hoped to defuse some of the tension. "Do you believe her, Andy? Nola believes the story, but it's possible she has her facts confused, right?"

"She could, but she didn't hesitate with names or dates. It obviously made an impression." A full minute passed. "I want answers, dammit! What happened to my birth mother? Who was my father? Why haven't I ever been told any of this? I'm calling my mother. She's going to have to talk to me today!" Andy punched numbers in his phone. "No answer. Typical."

Jillian's heart raced as Andy's voice rose. She wouldn't pretend his anger didn't affect her. The days of not speaking up were over.

"Andy, please calm down. You're understandably frustrated, but go easy on your mother. Ben shares the blame for their silence. Do you really want to hound your mom before her trip? Carol's had a couple of rough years. She's a grieving widow." Jillian continued quickly, stifling Andy's protest. "She is grieving. Yes, she's leaving for a vacation, but she's putting on a brave face, trying to move forward."

"If wandering around graveyards is a vacation. That's another thing I don't understand—this sudden interest in family history. Aunt Lois has always been into genealogy, but Mom never cared."

Jillian breathed out softly. "Maybe it's a way of dealing with her own mortality, thinking about those who came before. Maybe she would've felt guilty researching a family, knowing your dad was orphaned. Maybe it's just a way of staying busy, keeping her mind off things."

"She and Lois bought tickets for an Alaskan cruise in May. That's a bit more than staying busy."

Jillian tried to be sympathetic regarding Andy's mood. He was grieving, but so was Carol. Her way of coping was different. Surely Andy could understand that. "Oh, Andy. I'm sure it's hard to see going on a cruise as grieving, but Carol and Ben talked about that trip for years. I'm glad she's going. Ben would've wanted her to, and I'm sure she'll be thinking of him every day." Jillian glanced at Andy, who was still seething. "Is there anyone else you can talk to about Belford?"

Andy consulted his phone. "Turn on Highway 127 toward Lakewood. It's coming up on the left. We'll talk to my uncle, Sam. Nola didn't mention him, only Dad and Ellie. Sam would've been at Belford too, right? He's seven years younger than Dad. Maybe he remembers something. If I don't get answers from him, I'm talking to Mom before she disappears. I'm not waiting three weeks."

"That's true, Andy. Miss Nola didn't mention Sam by name. She said, 'Ellie's brothers came to get her.' I wondered then if you'd noticed." Jillian glanced at Andy, who remained silent. "I met Sam, very briefly, at the funeral home. It's puzzling Miss Nola didn't mention him."

Andy called Sam and told him to expect them. Sam lived in an older one-story home on a small farm. When they arrived, he came out of his workshop to meet them, wiping his hands on a large blue handkerchief.

"Sam. Thanks for agreeing to see us on such short notice," Andy greeted his uncle.

"Anytime, son, anytime." Sam shook hands with Andy. He nodded to Jillian as they walked toward the door. "I believe we met at Ben's visitation. It's nice to see you again. Come on in."

Andy and Jillian followed Sam into his living room to a well-worn sofa. Sam sat in a nearby recliner and asked, "What can I do for you, son? You seemed pretty serious when you called."

Andy said, "Well, I've got some questions, Sam. Mom's gallivanting all over town getting ready to leave on a trip, so you're pretty much the only one who can answer them. You see, the thing is, Dad left us," Andy pointed at himself and Jillian, "a property in Belford called Blackwater Manor."

Sam's eyebrows rose.

"We've been doing some digging, talking with folks over there, and are coming up with a lot of questions. We've gotten some answers, but they've led to more questions."

Sam nodded slowly. "I expect that's so. Your daddy didn't talk much about Belford, but I know a little bit. Go on and ask your questions. I'll answer what I can."

"Am I adopted?"

"You'll want to talk to your mother about that," Sam hedged, leaning back in the chair.

"I'll save that one for later then." Andy looked at Jillian before continuing. "Were you at Belford? Were you and Dad orphans?"

"Well, son, I never did know too much about it." Sam rubbed his forehead. "I was about eight years old the first time I met Ben. I remember it clear as anything. My dad drove over to Belford, been gone all day, which was unusual. Since he'd come back from the war, he'd worked at home all the time, you see. He was a small farmer and mechanic. Well, he come back in his big ol' truck with Ben, fifteen or so, quietest kid I'd ever seen. My ma came out on the porch and said, 'Where's the girl?' Dad said, 'Gone,' and Ma took to crying and carrying on—scared me bad. I'd never seen that before.

"Dad told me to show Ben the barn. Said, 'This here's your cousin Ben. He's your brother now.' And he was. He was a good big brother. A good fella. Biggest heart ever. And not a bit quiet after that first day."

"And you didn't ask about it later? Never wondered where he'd come from?" Andy asked.

"No, things were different in those times. Lots of blended families, to use a more modern term. Parents didn't confide in children like they do now. Even if I'd asked later, I expect I'd have been told to leave it alone. We accepted things as they happened. I had a new brother, Ben had a new family, and we just got on with it." Sam moved the chair into an upright position.

"The girl, was her name Ellie, or maybe Ellen?" Andy asked.

"Might have been. Ask your mother, boy." Sam stood up. "She'll know more than me."

"Thanks for your help, Sam. I think we'll be going now," Andy growled.

"It's not my story to tell, Andy, but it's kept for nigh on fifty years. You can wait a bit longer." Sam embraced Andy and shook Jillian's hand before walking them to the door. "You all drive safely. Come back anytime."

⌘

JILLIAN BACKED HER CAR OUT OF THE DRIVE and turned down the highway without saying anything. Anger seemed to be rolling off of Andy in waves.

"What if I don't want to wait?" Andy said petulantly. "Why should I have to? I've waited almost fifty years. It's time somebody told me the truth."

Jillian bit her lip, fearful that anything she said would make his anger worse.

"Andy," Jillian said a few minutes later as she eased to a stop sign, "I don't know why things are working out as they are, but maybe ease up a bit. Go with the flow and see where it takes you."

Jillian turned onto the highway back to Belford and heard Andy take a deep breath and blow it out slowly. When he didn't speak, Jillian added, "To continue with the metaphor, rivers flow one way. Stop trying to swim upstream. Forcing things doesn't work. When things aren't working out the way I expect, it's usually because I'm trying to control more than I should. Maybe we should focus our energy elsewhere."

Andy's ringing phone interrupted Jillian's philosophical thoughts. She was relieved to hear him answer his mother's call in a tone somewhere between relaxed and strident.

"No, Mom, nothing major. I hope you and Lois have a great trip. I love you. We'll have lots to talk about when you get home."

Andy hung up and looked at Jillian. "The fates are conspiring against me. I'll wait, even though it's eating me up inside. Where should we look next?"

"Let's search for more about Ellen Rafferty and her boyfriend," Jillian suggested.

"Or husband. Despite what Nola said, they could've been married. Rafferty could be her married name."

"It could," Jillian said. "It's odd he wasn't named on the birth certificate if that's the case. I wonder . . ."

"What?"

"Well, there's no way of knowing, but maybe Francine, who told Miss Nola to put Rafferty as the last name, was sort of giving Ellie the benefit of the doubt. Maybe she knew about Ellie's boyfriend and their plans to marry when he returned home."

"Except he didn't," Andy said. "At least, it seems that way. Nola said Ellie received a letter, and Ellie's man was in Vietnam. It sounds like he died, right?"

Andy looked at Jillian. "I'm not ready to let this go. I want to keep searching. What say we grab a pizza? Lois is picking up Mom around four, so she won't be home." Andy explained, "They're wanting to get an early start tomorrow. We can eat and look for Ellen Rafferty without you worrying about me hassling Mom. You know you'd be making the same searches if you went home."

"You're probably right," Jillian admitted. "I'll call Amy and ask her to take care of Willie."

∞

SEARCHING FOR "ELLIE RAFFERTY" and "Ellen Rafferty Tennessee" and even "Ellen Harrison Rafferty Tennessee" didn't produce any relevant results. Andy finally remembered that his birth certificate included the middle name Grace. While "Ellen Grace Rafferty" was unsuccessful, "Ellen Grace Harrison" yielded results. The first hit from the *Gentry Observer* pictured Ellen along with several other new teachers in Gates County, Tennessee.

"Can you make the picture larger?" Andy asked. "I'd like to see her." Although a little blurry, the picture showed a tall, slender young woman with long blonde hair held back with a wide hairband. Andy stared intently at the woman wearing a short plaid skirt and thin sweater.

"Can I print from here?" Jillian asked.

"Yes. Good idea. Let's print off everything we find."

"Do you think she's your mother, Andy?"

"Yeah, most likely. There's some resemblance, and with what Nola said, I think so." Andy breathed out heavily. "Yeah. Weird."

They noted the school's name and the town before continuing their search. After finding several more articles with school news and one featuring Ellen as a bridesmaid in a wedding, Andy said quietly, "I think this is an obituary."

"Oh no. I'm so sorry, Andy," Jillian whispered, rubbing his shoulder.

"Yeah." Andy breathed deeply. "I've been expecting it. Maybe even hoping it. It'd be worse to find out she was living and didn't want me." He clicked on the link.

Together they read the short notice. "Ellen Grace Harrison, 26, passed from this life suddenly September 18, 1972. A teacher at A. J. Dills Elementary School in Gentry, Miss Harrison loved singing and playing guitar, reading, and spending time with her students. Preceded in death by parents John and Mary Ellen (Andrews) Harrison, Ellen leaves behind to mourn her passing: Family Ben Harrison (Carol) of Springdale, Sam Harrison (Mildred) of Lakewood, and special friends Miss Francine Hixon of Belford, Randy Keith and Beth Ann Rafferty of Gentry, members of the New Hope Methodist Church, coworkers, and many students."

Andy pushed back from the table and stared blindly at the screen before putting his hands over his face. "One sentence. One sentence about her, about my mother as a person." Andy reached out and caressed the screen, then shook his head. "No cause of death listed."

Jillian saw that Andy's eyes were red with unshed tears. "I'm so sorry, Andy. It seems very unfair that Ellen died so young." Jillian took Andy's hand and sat with him in his sorrow.

"I was, what, three when she died? Yet I have no memory of her. Where was she? Where was I during all that time?" Andy shook his head. "Mom's going to have to come clean. I deserve to know what happened. I need to know about her." Andy gestured toward the computer.

Jillian looked back at the screen. Noting Ellen's parents' names, she asked, "Do you think the Andrew in your name comes from Ellen's mother's maiden name of Andrews?"

"Maybe. I was kind of hoping it came from her boyfriend, my father, assuming the dead Vietnam boyfriend was my father. Do you think it's odd he's not mentioned in the obituary? Those 'special friends' listed, what were their names?"

Jillian read from the screen. "Miss Francine Hixon of Belford, Randy Keith and Beth Ann Rafferty of Gentry." Jillian looked up. "Boyfriend's parents? Is that what you're thinking?"

"Well, maybe. I mean, if Rafferty wasn't Ellen's birth name, it's likely to be either her adoptive name or a married name, right?"

Jillian made a face. "I doubt she would've kept an adoptive name since the family returned her. It's possible that Randy Keith is a friend entirely separate from Beth Ann Rafferty. Keith could be a last name, right? Maybe they both lived in Gentry. To me, it makes more sense that Randy Keith and Beth Ann Rafferty are husband and wife." Jillian looked at Andy, who was shaking his head. "Well, if you disagree with my theory, what's yours?"

"I don't know," Andy admitted. "Two unrelated people, maybe coworkers. Maybe Beth Ann Rafferty is my birth father's sister. Could be his mother, I suppose. Randy Keith could be a friend." Andy pulled the laptop in front of him. "Argh. I don't know. We're just going in circles. I think we should search some service records."

Andy was obviously growing frustrated again. Jillian patted his arm. "That's a good idea, but maybe this is enough for today. Let the discoveries about your birth mother sink in a bit before digging deeper." Jillian stood and stretched. "I'm going home. It's been a long, eventful day. You're not leaving until Monday. We don't have to find everything tonight."

Andy followed her to the door. "About that, I'm not leaving Monday. I'm thinking about relocating to Newton, at least temporarily. If we move forward with Blackwater Manor, living nearby will make things easier. The boys are happy at their boarding school, so I don't have to worry about uprooting them, and I've been renting a condo since before my divorce. I can terminate the lease or sublet. What do you think?"

"I'd feel better about Blackwater Manor if you were local." *Being local would give us a chance to get to know each other better too. A chance to see if the moodiness clears up.* "It'll be a big job, and I was concerned about how it would work with you out of state. So yeah, I'm relieved. What about your job?" Jillian asked. *I like having you around.*

"I'm still trying to decide about that. On one hand, it's crazy considering giving up the salary with three kids to put through college, but Mom and Dad envisioned me taking over Harrison's Realty if Tom didn't want it. There's a lot of opportunity there. I'm tempted, truly. It'd be a learning curve, but I'm confident about the financial aspect, and Tom can bring me up to speed pretty quickly on other aspects." He rubbed his eyes. "Maybe it's too many changes though. Maybe I'm running away from Philadelphia because of the divorce."

"Or maybe you're running toward something," Jillian offered. "Could you extend your visit and see how you like living in Newton? Your mom's trip is three weeks, right? Stay in Newton, spend some time at the office, and get a feel for things. We can continue searching for Ellen. The inspector's report should be back soon, and we can see what Blackwater Manor looks like with the lights on."

Andy nodded and drew Jillian into a bear hug. "All good ideas. I'll call my boss," Andy said. "I can do some work remotely and arrange coverage for what I can't do from here. I hope you know how much I appreciate your calm, rational approach to all this craziness. I'm glad you were with me," Andy murmured softly as he pulled her close and kissed her hair. "I'll walk you to your car."

Oh my, his hugs feel so nice. Staying in town is a good idea.

As she drove home, Jillian thought about Andy and his reaction to finding his mother's obituary. *What did he say? Something about it being better to find out Ellen was dead? Hmm. I wonder if he feels abandoned and that contributed somehow to his wife cheating on him. Is that crazy? Probably. He didn't even know he was adopted then. Better leave the psychoanalysis to professionals.*

Chapter Twelve

Jillian awoke Saturday morning dreaming of Andy's arms around her. *Would it be so bad to have a little fling? Do I want a real relationship?* Jillian stretched and crawled out of bed, thinking it was time she took her own advice. *I'm going to get a feel for things and see how things go with Andy.*

Although they'd just met a few months ago, they'd had many serious talks. And even though Andy's divorce had been final only a few months, Jillian knew the marriage had truly ended a year or more before it was official. Andy seemed interested, and Jillian did not want to live in fear. *Only one way to find out.*

Jillian took a deep breath and called Andy. "It's a beautiful day, Andy. Care to join me for a picnic at Igohida Park?"

"A picnic? Yeah, that sounds great. I'll pick you up. Around eleven?"

"See you soon." Jillian wished she could bring Willie, both because she knew he'd enjoy the outing and because she felt like she might need a chaperone. Dogs weren't allowed at the park, however, so she played with Willie in the backyard before getting ready.

Jillian felt anxious. How should she approach this? Talk first and share what she was feeling? Kiss him and see what happened? What if he backed away? What if he wasn't ready? What if he got mad? "Willie, I hate feeling like a teenager again. This is ridiculous. I'm a grown woman," Jillian chided herself. *Just be there. Things will happen as they're meant to. Stop pushing.*

It was sunny, but a little cool, so Jillian dressed in jean capris and a scoop neck green tee topped with a cardigan. As she finished packing sandwiches, chips, fruit, and drinks, the doorbell rang.

"Good morning, Jillian. Thanks for suggesting this. I'm looking forward to a day off, spending a beautiful day with a beautiful woman."

"I'm glad it worked out." Andy appeared relaxed, casually dressed in jeans and a denim shirt with the sleeves rolled to his elbows. His hair was loose and his chin unshaven. *Very sexy.* "It'll be nice to get outside and show you the sights," Jillian said. "If you'll carry the cooler out, I'll meet you out front after I get Willie settled."

"You be a good boy, Mr. Willie." He rubbed the little dog's head and took the cooler to the car.

After Jillian joined him, she directed him toward the river park, pointing out various sites along the way—the schools, churches, bookstores, and theaters. Before long, they arrived at a service road marking the park entrance.

"This place is kind of hidden away, isn't it?" Andy said.

"Yes, it's mostly used for boating and fishing, but there's a small beach and a picnic area out on a peninsula. We'd lived in Newton for ten years before I knew it existed," Jillian said. "I still forget about it. It's beautiful but a bit too isolated for me to feel comfortable by myself, and they don't allow dogs, so I usually stick with the river walk."

"It's sad women have to think about safety all the time," Andy said. "Are you ever afraid at home?"

"No, but I bought an alarm system to appease my children. Plus, Willie's really good about letting me know about every intruder: squirrels, cats, leaves. He doesn't discriminate. Plus, I try to not live in fear." Jillian paused. "That's part of what today is all about."

Andy gave her a quick look. "Is this the way to the peninsula?"

"Yes, turn left by the sign to the beach and left again to get to the peninsula. There are eight or ten tables if I remember correctly."

Only a handful were occupied, so Andy carried the cooler down to a sunlit table near the river. Jillian spread a tablecloth and unpacked the food. Andy walked down to the shore and skipped a rock or two before wandering back.

"It's beautiful here. I'm glad you remembered this place."

Jillian smiled and patted the seat beside her. "Sit here, and we can both enjoy the view."

"Oh, I can enjoy the view from here," Andy said, leering and wagging his eyebrows before coming to sit beside her. Jillian pushed him playfully, then handed him a plate. They ate in companionable silence for a while, enjoying the sunshine, the blue sky, and the sound of the water lapping on the shore.

After they finished eating, Andy started cleaning up. "Tell me more about not living in fear."

Jillian blushed. "I enjoy your company. I like talking to you and spending time with you." Jillian paused, then plowed ahead. "I have feelings for you, Andy, and wonder if you feel the same. I don't want to rush things, and I suspect you'll want to move slowly too—if you're interested at all—but I don't want to shut down my feelings in fear of what may go wrong either."

Andy stood motionless, holding the bag of chips and staring at Jillian.

"It's okay if you don't feel the same way," Jillian started.

"I do." Andy quickly put down the chips and moved beside her. "Jillian, you're on my mind constantly. I hear a song and want to share it with you. If someone makes a comment at work, I wonder what you'd say about it. You must know I've wanted to kiss you for weeks now," he said, stroking her hair. "Let's clean up and take a walk."

Jillian smiled slowly, a bit flustered, but pleased that her feelings were reciprocated. *All that worry for nothing.* She helped Andy clear the picnic items, then took his hand as he led her to the shore.

They walked out to a point of the peninsula railed to keep visitors off the rocks. Andy leaned back on the railing and pulled Jillian close. His green eyes focused intently on her hazel ones. "I'm going to kiss you now, okay?" he asked softly.

Jillian gulped and nodded. Andy's lips met hers. Andy gave a little guttural moan and pulled her against him, deepening the kiss. Jillian moved her hands down his broad shoulders and felt his muscular arms. Suddenly, Andy moved his hands from her back to her upper arms and pushed her away gently. "Someone's coming," he said quietly.

Jillian heard the voices then. Some children laughing and parents calling. She looked at Andy and smiled. They nodded hello to the intruders and walked toward the picnic tables, hand in hand.

"It's gotten warm." Jillian took off her cardigan.

"Yep, things have certainly heated up," Andy agreed, unbuttoning his denim shirt.

Jillian laughed, then admired Andy's physique, shown off by the tight black T-shirt he wore beneath the denim one. "I didn't know you had tattoos. Isn't that kind of unusual for a financial analyst?"

"Not when he's in a band. You're looking at the lead guitarist for the Wall Street Boys."

Jillian laughed again. "Seriously? What kind of music do you play?"

"Mostly 80s tunes. We cover everything from The Clash's 'Should I Stay or Should I Go' to U2's 'With or Without You.' Occasionally, we'll try something original, but our audiences want to dance and sing along."

"My kids and I used to have our own dance parties with songs like that," Jillian said, thinking that the titles he'd named aptly reflected her indecisiveness. "Who else is in the band?"

"Well, it kind of fell apart awhile back, but we had a couple brokers, an accountant, me, and Chad." Andy frowned. "I've only got two tats—the armband and this guy." Andy pulled up his left sleeve, displaying Kokopelli playing a guitar. Andy shrugged. "Remnants of a different life. You don't hate them, do you?" he asked, taking her in his arms.

"No." Jillian embraced him around the waist before leaning back and running her hands up his arms. "I was surprised, but they're kind of sexy. I like the Kokopelli. I hadn't seem him depicted with a turtle shell before."

"Yeah, I liked the way it looked, blending the spirits of music and inner peace." Andy leaned down and kissed her. "Why don't we drive over to the beach area? I saw some benches overlooking the water as we passed it." In the car Andy said, "Since it's too cool to swim, maybe we'll have a bit more privacy."

As Andy drove, Jillian asked, "Is Chad . . ."

Andy stopped, turned toward her and shook his head, tracing her lips with his finger. "No talking about family drama, kids, parents, or work. No house or exes, okay? Today is about you and me. Just us, just now, just right here." He kissed her softly but intently. "Agreed?"

Jillian readily agreed. She could barely think straight after that kiss. Today, she was going to enjoy falling in love. Tomorrow, she'd worry about what that meant.

Soon, Andy parked at the small beach and pulled a guitar from the trunk of his car. "I thought I'd serenade you," he said, holding the guitar by its neck with one hand and taking her hand in his other. They walked to a bench beside the swimming area. Jillian sat down, but Andy propped his foot on the bench, winked at her, and strummed a few bars of Dylan's "Lay, Lady, Lay" before laughing and switching to Stevie Wonder's "Overjoyed."

Jillian listened to Andy sing and remembered his first wink, how she'd been transported by his voice at Ben's funeral, and how she'd felt he was singing just to her. And now he was.

When the song ended, Andy leaned the guitar against the bench, then sat beside Jillian and cupped her face in his hand. "I am overjoyed to be here with you. I plan to kiss you, a lot, but I don't want to mess up this relationship by moving too fast. I want to be with you more than I can say, but I think we should wait until all that stuff we're not talking about today is a bit more settled. Do you believe me?"

Jillian nodded and reached for Andy's face, drawing it close. "I do, Andy, and I believe we're worth waiting for." She kissed him softly, sweetly, and sighed, resting her head on his. "But don't make me wait too long."

Andy laughed. "I love a passionate woman!" Then he grabbed his guitar and started playing "Green Eyed Lady" by Sugarloaf.

They sang and kissed and sang and kissed some more. When the sun dipped behind the clouds, Jillian shivered. "I may have a new favorite bench."

"You have a favorite bench?"

"Yep. Along the river, between the parking lot and Bruno's. It's my thinking spot." Jillian kissed Andy again. "Right now, I think it's time we head back to town."

"Yeah, probably so," Andy agreed, pulling her close for one more deeply passionate kiss. "You are one sexy lady, Jillian Peters. Let's get out of here before I lose my mind."

Chapter Thirteen

Andy called early the next morning. "Want to skip church and have breakfast with me?"

"I can do that," Jillian said. "Where do you want to go?"

"I want you to come here. I make a mean omelet, but I was thinking French toast. Which would you prefer?"

"French toast sounds yummy. Can I bring anything?"

"Just your luscious self."

Is he expecting more than just breakfast?

Jillian could hear Andy rustling in cabinets. "And syrup. Mom doesn't seem to have any."

Probably not. We said we'd wait. Best not to rush things.

Andy met Jillian at the door wearing a navy T-shirt covered with flour and a frilly white apron tied around his waist. Holding a spatula awkwardly away from their bodies, he leaned in for a kiss. "Right on time. I need to turn the toast."

Jillian followed Andy to the large eat-in kitchen. The table was set with napkins, silverware, and glasses of orange juice. A vase of freshly cut tulips stood on the kitchen counter.

"Have a seat, milady." Andy moved the flowers to the table.

"Coffee?"

"You've gone to a lot of trouble, Andy," Jillian said, pouring two cups.

Andy dusted the French toast with powdered sugar, added sliced strawberries, and carried the plates to the table. "I'm glad you're here," he said, squeezing her hand. "Yesterday was great, taking a break from all the craziness of the past months . . ."

"But . . ." Jillian said as he paused.

"But time is passing quickly. I want to continue investigating my parental mystery and go back to the house on Blackwater Pond."

Jillian sampled the French toast. "Yum. So good." She nodded. "Continuing the investigation makes sense. Any ideas?"

"Drive to Gentry. Maybe someone there knows something, remembers something. I need to know more than the one line from the obituary." Andy took a swig of juice. "I want to locate Randy Keith and Beth Ann Rafferty if they're still living, find out what they know. Find out why they never tried to be a part of my life. Ask them about my father too. I think they were probably his parents, don't you?" Andy asked, adding more syrup to his toast.

"Maybe, but I worry that you're making too big a leap, Andy. It's possible the Raffertys were Ellie's boyfriend's parents. Probable even, but not certain. They may have been her friends. Maybe she was scared, felt alone, so she just used their name." Jillian took some more strawberries. "If their son was your father, it's also possible they didn't know about you. I worry about a fifty-year-old grandson turning up on their front porch."

"Forty-nine," Andy reminded her with a mock growl, holding his hand up in a scout's pledge. "I promise to break the news gently, but I need to follow this lead."

Jillian nodded. "I'll call the school where Ellie taught on Monday, see what I can find out."

They cleared the table and made room for Andy's laptop. "I've had a thought. It's possible the Andrew in my name comes from my bio-mom's side of the family, but it might be from the Rafferty side, from Ellen's boyfriend."

Jillian's eyebrows rose as she considered this. "It's worth a shot," she said slowly, "but why not look for Randy Keith first?"

"I've already looked," Andy said glumly. "After you went home last night. I didn't think about looking for an Andrew until late. I thought I'd run it by you first. Am I completely crazy?"

Jillian rubbed Andy's shoulder. "No, since you struck out with Randy, we may as well try to find an Andrew."

They tried searching the paper wherein they'd found Ellie's obituary but had no luck. Then they tried searching for Andrew Rafferty in Gates County, in Gentry, and in Tennessee, but still found nothing. Andy was getting frustrated. "Maybe this is a wild goose chase. Maybe Andrew Rafferty doesn't exist."

"Why don't you look for a list of deaths of soldiers from Tennessee during the Vietnam era?"

Andy's search led to a Virtual Wall Memorial. Names of deceased soldiers were listed by county. Scrolling down to Gates County, he saw it.

"It's here, Jillian. He's here. Andrew Keith Rafferty."

Andy searched again, adding Vietnam to the complete name.

Several sites listing the casualties of Tennessee popped up. Andy clicked on one, entered his birth father's name, looked at the photograph, and pushed the computer away.

"Oh, Jesus. He was so impossibly young." Andy reared back in his chair. "Damn!"

Jillian jumped and reached for Andy, but he let his chair fall back to the floor, stood, and paced behind it. "Will you read it?"

She pulled the computer toward her and read, "Andrew Keith Rafferty, born May 22, 1949; expired in a traumatic event resulting in a loss of life on July 17, 1969. Circumstances of death attributed to hostile actions; died from wounds received in helicopter crash, South Vietnam, Quang Nam province."

"He died a week before I was born. He never even knew he had a son."

"I'm sorry," Jillian said softly, standing and wrapping her arms around him.

Andy bent his head and wept silently. Jillian held him as he grieved the loss of a man he'd never known.

After some minutes, Andy wiped his face. "I want to know more about him. I want to know who he was, what he was like, more than that he died in the war. I need to know."

They searched, finding only a graduation photograph from Davis High School's class of 1967.

"Maybe we can get some information from the school or city library. Do you want me to make some calls tomorrow?" Jillian asked.

"Yes. That's a start. Someone should remember the family at

least. Someone's got to."

Jillian picked up their empty cups and carried them to the sink. As she was rinsing them, Andy came up behind her and wrapped his arms around her waist, nuzzling his face in her hair. Jillian was surprised but pleased. She dried her hands and turned in his arms.

"Thanks for not thinking I'm crazy to cry about a man I never met."

"Oh, Andy," Jillian said, brushing his hair from his face. "Finding your father only to find he died so young, right after learning about your mother, has got to be intense. It's perfectly natural to cry." She reached up and gently kissed him.

Andy increased the pressure of the kiss and moved his hands down her back until he was cupping her bottom, pulling her close. Jillian's desire built, matching his. Andy led her into the living room. They lay intertwined on the couch, kissing one another deeply. When Andy's hand moved under her shirt, Jillian's breath quickened as she tried to rein in her own desire.

"Andy," she gasped. "Stop, please."

Andy's hands immediately stilled. "You don't want this?" he asked.

"I'm so sorry, Andy. This isn't right; the time's not right. I do want you, but not like this."

Jillian felt very torn. Her body certainly wanted Andy's touch, craved more, but her mind knew that what was happening between them was a reaction to his earlier discoveries.

They sat up and straightened their clothes, avoiding looking at one another. Andy rose and walked down the hall without a word.

Jillian sighed, then returned to the kitchen. Soon, Andy came in and wrapped his arms around her, again resting his chin on her head.

"I'm sorry. I'm embarrassed and don't know what to say. I guess I got carried away."

"What happened was pretty normal, Andy. You experienced a loss and wanted a connection. I did too, but since we'd just talked yesterday about waiting, I felt we needed to stop."

She turned, still enclosed in his embrace. "I want to make love with you, Andy Harrison. It is going to happen, and it will be worth waiting for, but we agreed to settle some things first. Right?"

Andy pulled her close. "We did." He stepped back and looked at her. "Jillian, I've screwed up every relationship I've had by moving too fast." He pulled her into his arms again and kissed her hair. "I don't want to do that with you. We've got a real chance for something special." He hugged her tightly. "I can't believe I'm saying this, but I think you should go home now."

"I think so too." Jillian gathered her things and left after a chaste goodbye kiss.

Chapter Fourteen

When Jillian got home, she called Amy. "I need some emergency girlfriend time."

"Be right there. Have you eaten?"

Jillian was grateful to have such a good friend living nearby. Amy was at her backdoor within ten minutes, carrying salad, French bread, and a bottle of wine. "What's going on, girlfriend?"

After a quick hug, Jillian sat at the kitchen counter while Amy bustled around getting out napkins, plates, forks, and glasses. Jillian talked about her weekend as Amy poured the wine.

"I'm so confused, Amy. You were right, I'm falling in love. I know I am, but what if I'm not?"

"Sugar, you're not making sense. Everything you've said points to falling in love. What makes you think you might not be?"

"What if I'm in love with the idea of being in love? Just loving the attention? How can I be sure of that?" Jillian demanded.

"Oh, honey, you've received plenty of attention from men through the years but didn't give them the time of day because you weren't interested. What are you afraid of?"

Jillian didn't answer for several minutes. "I'm afraid of making a mistake, of making a fool of myself." Jillian paused. "Maybe I fear

Andy will turn out like Paul, or that I'll revert back to how I was with Paul. I like who I am now. I don't want to lose myself again."

"Jillian." Amy reached for her hand. "I've known you for over twenty years. I've watched you crawl into your shell, and I've watched you crawl out. You're stronger now than you've ever been." She released Jillian's hand and sat back. "Living on your own has helped you realize who you are and what you want. You're finally seeing yourself as others see you—kind, smart, loving, capable, and deserving of good things in life." Amy sipped her wine. "We love Andy's parents, and Elaine seems to like him. Maybe—"

Jillian interrupted. "But what if it's just physical, Amy? Maybe Andy looks at me as being convenient, needy, or desperate. He doesn't know me that well. I don't want to be used."

"What does your gut tell you?"

"To take a chance?" Jillian covered her face. "But I'm afraid of being wrong."

"Then you continue to set the pace, Jillian, and stop all this worrying about Andy's feelings. You're not responsible for them. Trust yourself. Do what is right for you."

"That's the problem. I don't trust myself. I was so wrong about Paul." Jillian ate her last bite of bread. "I also worry about Andy's ups and downs. His moods, especially the anger."

"Well, Lord knows the man has a lot on his plate. Listen, Jillian, don't cheat yourself because you're afraid. Enjoy each day as it comes. You deserve happiness and love, and if it grows and lasts, wonderful. If it doesn't, well, life goes on. Andy isn't Paul any more than Stan was Jimmy," Amy said, referring to a long past boyfriend.

"Life gives us second chances if we're willing to take them."

Jillian began clearing the dishes. "I'd feel better with a second opinion of that second chance."

"Easy enough. Tell Andy he's invited for dinner Wednesday night. We'll grill some burgers, have a little social gathering. Should we invite Elaine and Larry? Maybe Carol too?"

"Oh, Amy, that sounds perfect. Carol's out of town, but inviting Elaine and Larry is a wonderful idea. I'll bring deviled eggs and potato salad, and we'll all get to know Andy better."

Without going into detail, Jillian told Amy about finding some connections to Andy's family and their plans to go to Gentry. Naturally, the conversation turned to the house at Blackwater Pond.

"We're still waiting on the inspector's report. It's odd though, how many ghosts we're already uncovering with all our research. It's quite the journey."

"Jimmy used to talk about ghosts of the past lighting the paths of the future. At the time, I thought he was really deep. Now I think he was probably stoned." Amy laughed.

"What a character. Where did you meet him anyway?"

"Oh my. I thought I'd told you that story. I was nineteen and dancing with a company out of San Diego. We performed at an artists' retreat at Darlen Mountain where Jimmy was in residency. At twenty-seven, he was already making a name for himself with his paintings.

"He was the most exciting man I'd ever met. Filled with great passion, you know. He'd talk for hours, waving his arms in all directions. I was flattered he noticed me. I left the dance company to live with him Los Angeles." Amy laughed a little. "We were together for three years before I got tired of sleeping on a mattress on the floor, sharing bathrooms with strangers in junky lofts.

"I hightailed it back East, moved in with my parents, got a job teaching ballet, and discovered I was three months pregnant. Then I met Stan when he brought little Katherine in for lessons as a way to distract her from her mother's death, and the rest is history. It turns out I didn't want wild and crazy. I wanted steady. That's what my Stan is, steady. He never minded a bit that my baby wasn't his biological child. We married and made a family and a life together."

Jillian shook her head in wonder. "How did your parents deal with all that?"

"Well, times being what they were, reactions were mixed. While glad to have the prodigal child home safe where they could keep an eye on me, they were concerned about the neighbors' reactions to me being pregnant, then marrying a black man with a four-year-old child. Probably relieved I wasn't planning to raise a child in their home too.

"It all happened very fast, you know. So, we went from 'glad you're here,' to 'how could you have been so irresponsible,' to 'you barely know this man' in three month's time. Once they met Stan and got over the initial shock, they were okay with it. Stan was very open about learning to appreciate every day since his first wife Kendra's illness and death. Katherine helped too. She was a precious child, gave the sweetest hugs. Stan's a good daddy, and he's a great husband. Reliable, kind, supportive, and steady."

"I believe that. I love his big smile and his laugh. Who couldn't love Stan? 'Heh, heh, heh.'" Jillian imitated Stan's low, slow laughter. Both women giggled. "How does an artist colony work?"

"Well, I don't know all the ins and outs, but I've been to workshops at a few over the years. Basically, they provide studio space and living quarters so artists have open access to studios without worrying about mundane things like supplies, food, and laundry. Well, they may do their own laundry, but food has been provided at every one I've ever visited.

"Jimmy was at Darlen for eight months. Some places have week-long workshops. Others, artists are in residence. Many offer scholarships, but I guess some people pay for the experience. If art studios are too expensive, you could offer a writers' retreat at the house in Belford."

"That might work better," Jillian mused. "I have no idea how we're going to pay for any of it."

"Trust the process," Amy said. "Life has a way of working out."

JILLIAN COMPLETED SOME WEEKEND CHORES and thought about Amy's invitation, wondering how to broach it with Andy. She couldn't tell him she wanted a second opinion. Should she admit she didn't trust her judgment when it came to men? No, that seemed weird. Maybe she'd just tell him the truth, however limited, and say it was Amy's idea. Now confident of her approach, Jillian made the call.

"Hey, I was about to call you," Andy said. "I just accepted a dinner invitation from your friend Amy Taylor. At least I hope she's your friend. She said she was, and I said we'd be there."

Jillian rolled her eyes. Of course Amy would invite him. Elaine called Amy's forthright approach to people the "take no prisoners" method, but Jillian appreciated her directness. In her childhood and in her marriage, Jillian had often encountered statements wrapped in innuendo and insinuation. In her opinion, being open, even if that meant being blunt, was better.

"That's why I was calling, Andy. I'm glad you accepted. I think you'll enjoy meeting Amy and Stan. You already know Elaine. She and her husband Larry will be there too."

"I'm looking forward to it. It'll be good to meet some more people in Newton. Do I need to bring anything? I mean, Amy said no, but what do you think? Food, drink, chairs?"

"Well, Stan loves beer. I'm bringing a couple side dishes. Why don't you come over after work? We'll walk to the Taylor's through the yard."

Andy agreed but reminded Jillian that he would be working from home for a few days and had a meeting scheduled Wednesday afternoon.

JILLIAN WAS ALSO WORKING FROM HOME on Monday because Willie's annual checkup was scheduled that afternoon. After several hours researching listings and choosing furniture for two homes she was staging, she decided to treat herself to an early lunch at Bruno's. The weather was beautiful, so Jillian and Willie walked the half mile from the main lot to the restaurant, where she scanned the patio for a seat. *Oh no. Seems like everyone had the same idea.*

"Jillian, we've got an extra seat if you care to join us," Clark Grebe called from across the patio, where he was seated with an older couple she did not know.

Jillian walked over to the table with Willie. "Thanks, Clark. I wasn't expecting such a crowd. Are you sure I won't be interfering?"

"Not at all," the woman said, introducing herself and her husband. "Clark's been showing us some houses. He mentioned you're also a realtor."

Jillian said she was and explained about Willie's vet appointment. The server offered Willie some water, and Jillian requested a small Doggie Delight, which featured a spoonful of Greek Yogurt topped with blueberries and pears, served with a dog biscuit.

As they ate, Jillian asked about the houses they'd viewed and, at Clark's suggestion, mentioned a few others they might like to see. Clark was friendly but not flirty. He didn't mention exercise or diet and insisted on paying the bill. *I think Clark has finally realized we're just colleagues.*

―――― ∞ ――――

JILLIAN LOOKED FORWARD to introducing Andy to her friends. Tall and willowy, Amy was Jillian's closest confidant and best friend. Her preferred bohemian clothing style sometimes seemed at odds with her blunt opinions. She didn't suffer fools lightly. Amy's husband Stan was in many ways her opposite. Short, stout, and about ten years older, he had spent many years as a mental health counselor but now preferred staying at home, reading books or working on his retirement hobby of metal art.

On the surface, Elaine and Amy didn't seem to have much in common, but they'd found common ground in Jillian. Elaine had joined Harrison's Realty several years after she and Jillian had first met. Now in her late sixties, Elaine was a true friend with a heart of gold, generous with her time, encouragement, and gentle goading of anyone who needed a push in what she believed to be the right direction. Elaine seemed to know and look for the best in everyone in town.

Wednesday evening, after a quick shower and change of clothes, Jillian packed the food she'd prepared in a cooler for easy transport. She fed Willie, then found him a chew toy in case he needed some incentive to behave. "I'm a little nervous," Jillian said as her little dog followed her from room to room. "I hope everyone likes Andy as much as I do, but if they don't, I want them to be honest."

Before long Andy arrived with a custom variety pack of microbrews and a bouquet of flowers. "Too much?" he asked as Jillian exclaimed over how pretty the flowers were.

"No, I'm sure Amy will appreciate them." Jillian walked into the kitchen where Andy added the beer to the cooler. "Ready to meet the neighbors?"

"Sure. I feel almost like a teenager meeting my date's parents. I hope they like me," he joked, unknowingly mimicking Jillian's thoughts.

Willie barked joyfully as they approached the back gate. Larry and Stan were standing around the grill but turned as Andy and Jillian walked into the yard.

Jillian kissed Stan's cheek, then patted Larry's arm, not knowing him as well. "Larry, it's good to see you again. This is Andy Harrison. Andy, Larry Parker and Stan Taylor."

"Amy says it'll be too dark to eat out here, Jillian. Need any help getting that cooler inside?" Stan asked as Andy pulled out the six-pack and offered beers to the men.

"No, I'll manage, but keep an eye on Willie, okay? Back in a bit."

Inside, Jillian greeted Elaine, handed Amy the flowers, and added her dishes to the table, which held a platter of sliced tomatoes, lettuce, onion, cheese, and pickles, as well as a pan of baked beans.

"Everything looks great, Amy. Thanks for putting this together so quickly."

"Well, it's no bother, Jillian, but let's go on outside until we're ready to eat. If I'm going to offer an opinion on Andy, I need to meet him."

"He'll be the one with the ponytail, not the pot belly," Elaine joked.

Jillian saw Stan standing close to Andy with one hand on his shoulder. Andy's head was bowed, and he appeared to be listening intently. Both men looked up as the women came outdoors.

Andy walked toward them. "You must be Amy. Thanks for putting this together. Stan was telling me you knew my dad."

"We did, Andy. We were awfully sorry to hear about Ben. The flowers are lovely, thank you." Amy motioned to the patio chairs. "Shall we sit?"

As everyone moved that way, Andy said, "Elaine, it's good to see you again so soon. I look forward to working more closely with you."

Elaine laughed at Jillian's evident confusion, then explained, "Tom's decided that I will mentor Andy on sales and leases, rental homes, and commercial sites. We found out today in a meeting Tom set up off site."

"Oh." Jillian nodded. "Exclusively commercial?"

"No, no. I'll keep my current listings. Residential listings are new to Andy too, but with the market downturn, we need to boost our commercial holdings."

"Jillian's been telling us about the house at Blackwater Pond." Amy changed the subject.

Andy looked at Jillian and raised his eyebrows. "Did she tell you she thinks it's haunted?" Everyone laughed as Andy told the story of how Jillian had enlisted Barb's help in tracking down rumors of paranormal activity.

Larry nodded. "My son-in-law is part of that group that goes looking for ghosts."

"And bigfoot," Elaine added. "That boy's got a screw loose if you ask me."

"To each his own," Stan said, his deep voice rumbling. "I'm more interested in Ben's connection to Belford. I wonder why he bought that house." He got up to check the burgers. "He never mentioned it." Stan and Ben had attended the same men's group at church.

When Elaine started talking about how much she'd like to see the house, Andy turned to Jillian and quietly said, "You didn't tell them?"

Jillian shook her head. "It's not my story to tell, Andy. They know we inherited the house. I told Amy there's a family connection. That's all."

Stan announced the burgers would be ready in five minutes, so the party moved indoors, and Willie settled in the kitchen with his chew toy, eyeing the entrance to the dining room. Had they eaten outdoors, he could've expected some clandestine treats, but Willie knew better than to beg from the table. Well, Amy's table anyway. As the friends shared burgers and sides, the conversation moved to Andy's job and life in Philadelphia.

"I'm able to work remotely a good bit, and having the boys in boarding school makes shared custody arrangements somewhat easier than they'd be otherwise," Andy said. "East Tennessee is beautiful, and I'm loving the easier commute. Actually considering a permanent move. Newton has its attractions," he added, winking at Jillian. "Are you all native Newtonians?"

Amy pulled the pie from the refrigerator and passed it around as everyone answered.

Stan had always lived in Newton, but the others had moved to the small city from elsewhere: Elaine from New York, Larry and Jillian from Georgia, and Amy from California.

"I moved to Newton with my parents as a teenager," Amy explained. "Went to California with a dance company. When I left Jimmy, I came back to Newton."

"Ed and I moved here after the boys were grown. We wanted out of the city," Elaine said.

"I'm from Nashville, Tara was from Orlando," Larry said of his first wife. "We met in high school after our fathers transferred to Newton. I guess we've all been married to other people."

Stan nodded. "And I was the only born here. Guess I'll stay, wagging my tail in the mud."

Everyone, except Jillian and Amy who'd heard it before, laughed in confusion. "What?"

"Oh, it's an old story, a parable of Zen that tells of a hermit priest offered a chance to move to the palace. He mentions a turtle shell carved and hanging on the palace wall. The hermit asks where the turtle would be happier, the palace or the pond."

Stan looked around. "The answer's the pond, of course. That's me, happy to be a big turtle in a small pond. I'll keep wagging my tail in the mud."

"You're almost as wise as Miss Nola, Stan." Andy laughed. "I'm going to remember that."

"Well, turtles do often represent wisdom, patience, and determination, so if she's wise as I am, Miss Nola must be special indeed. Heh, heh, heh," Stan laughed. "Tell us more."

"Well, she's about ninety, wise, and quite the historian." Andy laughed.

Amy, who'd had enough talk of turtles, stood. "Why don't we move back outside for awhile? Leave all the dishes. We'll take care of them later. I'd like to hear about Nola and what she had to say, but some of you don't have the luxury of sleeping late."

Jillian glanced at Andy, worrying that he might feel pressured to share his story. She stood. "Another time, if you don't mind, Amy. This has been lovely, but we do have to work tomorrow."

Andy glanced curiously at Jillian, then turned to the others. "Tonight was a lot of fun. I appreciate being included. Why don't we continue the party at my house—well, my mother's house—on Friday? I'll grill some steaks, bake some potatoes. We can tell you more about Belford then."

Plans were made and goodbyes were said. Andy and Jillian walked back through the garden gate without speaking. Darkness had fallen, but the path was clearly lit.

What is he thinking? He hasn't touched me all evening. No hello kiss, no hand holding, no hand at my back, or even a brush of our arms. I have to say something. Jillian's steps slowed.

"Jillian? You're awfully quiet. What's wrong?" Andy said, stopping beside her.

"I was just asking myself the same thing. You haven't touched me all evening. Are you upset about something?"

Andy put down the cooler and pulled her close. "No, not at all. I just wasn't sure what or how much you'd told your friends about us. I didn't know if we were public yet." Andy kissed her lips softly. "I love you, Jillian. Maybe it's too early to say that, but that's how I feel."

Jillian's pulse quickened. *Was it too early?*

Andy said, "We left Amy's dinner party rather suddenly. Are *you* upset about anything?"

"No," Jillian said, kissing him. "I just didn't want you to feel obligated to share your story if you weren't ready, but we can talk about that later." Jillian kissed him again, put her arms around his neck, and whispered, "I feel the same way."

Andy drew her even closer. "Yes, we'll talk later," Andy agreed. "This is better."

Chapter Fifteen

The next morning, Barb waved a stack of messages. "You're later than usual," she observed.

Jillian blushed but thanked Barb without further comment and walked toward her office, thinking of the private moments she and Andy had shared after leaving the Taylors' last evening.

Jillian flipped through her messages. *Mike Chapin! Maybe the inspection's back.* She called him right away. "Mike? Jillian Peters. I'm hoping for good news."

"Yes, ma'am. The report's finalized. I mailed the official copy yesterday. If you'll verify your email, I'll shoot one over to you now."

"Fabulous," Jillian said, giving him the address. She finished the call, then walked to the front office where Barb was shaking the printer's toner cartridge.

"It's almost out of ink, and I'm not sure we have another cartridge," Barb explained.

"Oh no. I'm trying to print an important document. Mr. Harrison will want to see it. Is he in?"

"I don't believe so. He seems to be running late too," Barb added pointedly.

It had been pretty late when Andy left her house last night, but that wasn't Barb's business.

When Barb reinstalled the cartridge, it began printing.

Jillian picked up the first page. "Thirty-two pages," she groaned. "I hope there's enough ink. Barb, I need to make some calls, but I'll be back in ten minutes. If you see Mr. Harrison, please ask him to find me."

Jillian hurried to her office and sent Andy a quick text: "Inspection printing now." Then she rifled through phone messages and saw one from an angry client. Adam Brown. Again.

I'm falling behind, worrying about Belford. I have to do better. I'll review all my active listings and see how I can help.

"It's about time," Adam's irate voice echoed through the speaker phone. "What's it going to take to get the house sold? Were there any showings this weekend?"

"No, I'm afraid there weren't, Adam. If there had been, I'd have told you," Jillian said calmly. "As we've discussed, choosing to list at the upper end of the market eliminates many buyers, particularly as interest rates climb."

"I don't get it. A friend of ours sold their house in three weeks. We've been on the market for months. Maybe we should go with their realtor."

Jillian looked over Adam's file as he complained. "I know it's frustrating, Adam, particularly since you've already moved out of state." Jillian walked her client through his options and made suggestions about dropping the price, repainting, or staging the home—suggestions she had made before. "Your home has some unique features, which not everyone appreciates. Buyers may have difficulty visualizing how to use the space. Think it over, and let me know your decision."

Jillian ended the call and took a deep breath. She made a note on her calendar and stood, eager to see the report. She rushed out the door as Andy strode in.

"Whoa, there. You about ran me over. What's your hurry?" Andy asked, walking her gently back into the room before stealing a kiss.

"The inspection's back. I was too nervous to sit and watch it print, so I returned a phone call. I'm going to get it," Jillian explained.

"You mean this report?" Andy teased holding it above her head. "How badly do you want it?"

"Please put me out of my misery. Let's see if this renovation is doable."

"Yes, ma'am. Your place or mine?" Andy asked.

"Yours!" Jillian quickly pulled Andy across the hall into the conference room.

Andy spread the report on the conference table. "Structurally sound. That's good news," Andy said. "No cracks or crumbling noted in the foundation. No evidence of termite infestation. Roof appears in good shape. Mike recommends replacing it because of its age and some curling shingles, but no sign of leaks. Some dampness in the basement, but nothing significant. I was a little worried about that with the creek and pond," Andy admitted. "I guess the soil drains well enough to prevent problems. Minor cracking at arch downstairs, probably due to house settling. Again, nothing major. This is sounding too good to be true."

"That's what scares me." Jillian continued reading. "Really, the only problem I see is the wiring. What does Mike say?"

"Replace the whole shebang," Andy said, flipping to the recommendations page.

"I was afraid of that. It's going to cost a fortune. Can we afford a total rewiring and the new plumbing Mike recommended earlier?" Jillian asked, feeling a little deflated.

"Yeah, I think so." Andy stopped and then started again. "Financing is my job. Yours is aesthetics, remember? Dad made some arrangements for financing the renovations."

"Like what?"

"Well, partly the rental property Elaine and I've been trying to move. Slow progress there, by the way. Partly investments from some of those stocks I 'purchased' way back when Dad and I played our game. I didn't realize it then, but Dad invested in some of those stocks. Over the years, they accumulated interest, which he reinvested. If the rentals sell, there should be enough to bring Blackwater Manor back to its glory. Barring unforeseen complications, and depending on what we decide we need, that is."

"Good Lord! He actually bought stocks based on a teenager's recommendations?"

"Well, yeah." Andy shrugged. "I was winning, so it wasn't much of a risk. And Dad reinvested the proceeds in safer investments. You can stop gawping at me. I told you I was good at math."

Jillian hugged Andy. "That's amazing. You know Clark Grebe thought your dad was the savvy investor. He'd have a fit if he knew it was you."

"Hmm. Well, if I ever see ol' dagger eyes again, I'll try to work it into conversation. He's not still bothering you, is he?"

"Not really." Now that Clark had stopped hounding her for dates, she'd realized he was a pretty decent guy. A little insecure, but unexpectedly funny. Pushy, but thoughtful. He'd insisted on buying lunch for her and her 'little dog too' when she'd run into him on Monday, then asked how the Good Witch of the North was getting along with the tall man, meaning Elaine and Andy.

"Jillian? What does that mean?" Andy asked evenly.

"It means I can handle Clark. You don't need to worry about him."

Andy grew very still and quiet. "Are you still seeing him?"

"What? No. Of course not, Andy. Not socially anyway. I run into him now and again. That's all." *Seriously? He's jealous after all the kisses we shared last night? How about trusting me?*

Andy looked at Jillian for a long moment, frowning. Then he shook his head and continued. "Long story short, we can afford the rewiring. Mike also suggests we complete an electrical inventory, kind of map out what we need and where we want outlets, which would be a lot easier if we knew what we wanted to do with the house once it's renovated."

"Yes, it would." Jillian sighed. "I like all the ideas we've tossed around—B&B, private school, artists retreat, or wedding venue—but somehow, none seems exactly right."

"I agree. It's counter intuitive for me, but I'm not all that concerned with making a profit." He paused and looked at Jillian.

"How would you feel about some sort of philanthropic cause?"

Jillian's eyes widened in surprise.

Andy continued. "I don't know what exactly, but with Dad's cancer and my marriage falling apart, I've spent the last three years struggling, feeling like I've been to hell and back. Now, well, struggles are universal. Dad and Ellie had to move on after illness and loss. I've been so fortunate to raise my sons, to have loving parents." Andy took her hand. "To get a chance to love again.

"Somehow, I want to carry forward the legacy of all those folks associated with the house at Blackwater Pond. Let's talk to Miss Nola again, see what she has to say. Am I crazy? Would you be upset at potentially losing out on profit from a sale?"

"No, I'm just amazed at your generosity." *Has he made peace with his past?*

"Ah, well," Andy stammered, a little embarrassed. "Thanks. I'm fortunate. I know that. I want to do right by the house."

"It's like Nola said, death and loss sometimes bring gain. Maybe personal gain isn't what she meant."

"There's wisdom there." Andy nodded. "Let's finish looking at this report. The only heat source was an oil stove in the living room. I don't remember seeing that, do you?" Andy asked.

"No. Maybe it's been removed. So, new HVAC. Got it. What about plumbing?"

"All new. You know what? Let's pick a day to go to Belford. I want to do this. Hang the cost!" Andy said, somewhat recklessly. "I'm not fighting with destiny."

On Friday evening, as planned, the three couples gathered at Carol's house for dinner. Carol was still out of town, traipsing through graveyards on her genealogical tour, but Andy made everyone feel right at home with lights shining over the patio and citronella candles flickering on the table. Drinks and appetizers were set up outside. Jillian arrived early to bake potatoes and brown some rolls. Elaine brought a salad topped with strawberries and pecans, and Stan baked a chocolate cake.

"Everything looks great, Andy," Elaine said. "I don't remember Carol having lights out here."

"She didn't, but I thought we needed them if we were going to eat outside. It'll be dark pretty soon."

Andy removed his striped chef's apron and pronounced the steaks done. Everyone took their plates and claimed a spot at the outdoor dining table.

"So how are you liking the real estate business, Andy?" Larry asked. "I hope Elaine's not driving you crazy." He rubbed his wife's shoulder. "She's one hell of a realtor, but she sure is griping about the market these days."

Andy agreed there were some issues with prices rising and inventory falling. "I'm a little concerned about construction costs driving prices even higher. That could knock some buyers out of the market and slow things down even more."

"How will rising construction costs affect your renovations on

Blackwater Manor?" Amy asked.

"I guess that depends on how quickly we're able to move on any construction and renovation we have to do. We got the inspection back a couple days ago," Andy said.

"Mike Chapin wasn't able to squeeze us in any earlier because he had too many other folks wanting to close in a hurry before interest rates increase again," Jillian explained.

Amy asked about the inspection, but Andy said he'd like to tell the backstory first. "Last time, I told you the story of Jillian's master sleuth, Barb." Andy leaned back again and put his arm around Jillian. "This time, this pretty lady right here got our little ball of discovery rolling." Andy explained how Barb's notes had led to Jillian's phone call with the librarian and their meeting with Nola.

"She sounds delightful," Amy said. "I'd love to meet her and see the house. Did you notice any antique or junk shops in Belford?" Since retiring, Amy had started refinishing rickety old furniture. Far more talented than Jillian had ever been, she used chalk paint, stencils, and decoupage to add beauty and purpose to small throwaway pieces.

"There's a shop on Main Street," Jillian said. "We'll go when you come tour the house. Now that the boards are down, shedding a little light, we won't need flashlights."

"Speaking of shedding light," Andy said, "I haven't told you the most important part of our visit." He shared the story of discovering his birth certificate and Miss Nola's help in solving the mystery surrounding his birth. "So now, we're planning to drive up to Gentry sometime soon to track down more information on my birth parents."

As everyone exclaimed about Andy's revelations, Jillian noticed Stan sitting quietly, eyeing Andy with some concern. *Hmm. Wonder what he's thinking?*

"Well," Amy said, "that is exciting news, but I imagine it was quite a shock. Discovering you are an orphan must have caused some emotional turmoil."

Jillian gave her a sharp look. *Amy? Are you trying to provoke him?*

Andy looked a little surprised, but before he could speak, Stan broke in. "Think we could have another round of drinks, Andy? I'll help."

Andy stood and walked into the kitchen. Stan followed after placing a hand on his wife's shoulder and patting it gently.

Amy looked at Jillian, shrugged, then apologized to the others. "I'm sorry. Stan obviously thinks I've stepped in something stinky. He'll smooth things over. Shall we change the subject?"

So, it was a test. I hope Andy's not upset.

By the time Andy and Stan returned, Jillian was sharing more about the inspection and planned renovations. "We'll need to restore the windows, but one of the biggest expenses is bringing the wiring up to code. We'll do an electrical inventory, kind of plan out what we need where, which has to wait until we know how we'll use the house."

"The house may be too remote for a wedding venue," Elaine said.

"That was your idea!" Jillian said.

"I know, but it may be too far from Chattanooga to be profitable. You'd need caterers, waitstaff, setup crews, and maybe tents, musicians, gardeners, marketers, a website guru... A ton of people."

"It's a little premature to set up a booking site," Andy said with a forced laugh as he brought out the drinks.

"True, we haven't decided any particular use yet," Jillian agreed. "One of many ideas." She smiled at Andy, wondering if Amy's comments had offended him.

Stan mentioned the grounds and gardens again. Before long, he was describing his art installations of welded metal objects, many of which resembled large, ungainly birds. Andy rubbed Jillian's back and smiled at her reassuringly.

When Larry yawned rather loudly, Elaine suggested brunch at their home the following weekend. "And let's plan a trip to Belford. Maybe a picnic on the grounds?"

Everyone agreed that sounded wonderful, so they said their goodbyes.

"What an interesting evening," Andy said after they'd gone.

"Yes, I think everyone enjoyed it," Jillian said, removing the last of the drinks from the table. "Did Stan speak to you about anything special?"

"He did." Andy nodded slowly. "First, he said that Amy can be a bit tactless, but that she'd made a good point. Then he sort of suggested, or maybe he asked, if I was seeing anyone, talking to anyone." Andy shook his head. "I'm not seeing a therapist right now. I don't object to therapy. I went after I filed for divorce, but then, you know, everything got busy, trying to manage the boys, the divorce proceedings, Dad's illness, Mom's business concerns. I couldn't find the time, so I quit going." Andy started toward the kitchen again. "I think I'm doing okay, considering."

"Amy can be blunt," Jillian admitted, following him, "and I understand it's hard to fit counseling in your schedule. It's important though."

"Yeah, I know. I get it," Andy said tersely. "Stan offered to give me some names. I'll think about it. Right now, it's just one more demand on my time, and I'm pretty swamped already."

Jillian knew better than to push counseling on someone unready to participate fully, but she hoped Andy would make the time. His stress level was high, and his brief, angry outbursts sometimes lived close to the surface. Each time he grew sullen or worse, Jillian chose to leave, hoping all the while his anger would abate in time.

OVER THE NEXT FEW WEEKS, the three couples met again and again for dinner or brunch, getting to know each other. Andy seemed to mesh well with the group.

One Saturday evening though, Andy suggested a more intimate gathering. The three of them, Andy, Jillian, and Willie, snuggled on one of the loveseats at Jillian's house, laughing at the antics of the older cast of *The Best Exotic Marigold Hotel*.

I could get used to this. "We need to do this more often, Andy." Jillian let Willie out the back door.

"I agree." Andy took her in his arms. "Dinner with friends is great, but this is special." He kissed her softly. "I can't believe you hadn't seen that movie. It's pretty old."

Jillian returned his kisses, then let Willie inside. "Mmm, Sonny's advice about everything being all right at the end is pretty wise." *I don't want this night to end.*

"It is." Andy held Jillian close. "When the time is right, everything works out for the best. I'm counting on that," he added, kissing her again. When Willie barked, Andy murmured, "I should go," but continued to hold her close, kissing her neck.

Jillian leaned back and looked into Andy's eyes. "I'd like you to stay."

Andy's mouth curved in a slow grin. "Are you sure? Won't Willie object?"

"Willie's sleeping in the kitchen tonight," Jillian said as she took Andy's hand and led him down the hall.

Chapter Sixteen

One Monday a few weeks later, Jillian took special pains with her appearance, hoping to look attractive but somewhat demure. She and Andy had continued seeing each other outside the office, enjoying but not advertising their relationship. She settled for a pair of navy slacks with a long, loose white blouse and a flowered navy scarf.

They'd managed weekly dinners with friends and nights alone but had rescheduled the trip to Gentry several times, despite their eagerness to find more about Andy's biological family. Now that Adam Brown's house was finally under contract, after he'd heeded her advice, Jillian planned to call Gentry's librarian and ask about Ellen Harrison. It was time to put the ghosts to rest.

The small town library didn't open until eleven, so Jillian spent the morning making appointments and doing research for clients. She wasn't sure if Andy was in the office but didn't want to start the office rumor mill churning by asking. Jillian kept her door closed. The chemistry between them had to be obvious.

Shortly after eleven, Jillian called the library in Gentry. After introducing herself, Jillian said, "I'm hoping to find some information about a young woman who taught in Gentry in the late sixties, early seventies. Do you know anyone who could help me with that?"

"Have you tried calling the school?" the librarian asked.

"Not yet," Jillian admitted, "but I'm not looking for confirmation of employment."

"What's your interest in this woman?"

"It's a complicated situation, but I'm helping a friend do some family research. We believe there's a connection. Were you living in Gentry at that time, by chance?"

"I was. I've lived here all my life and know most everybody. What's the woman's name?"

"Ellen Harrison," Jillian said. "She taught at—"

"A. J. Dills Elementary," the librarian interrupted. "She was my third grade teacher. We thought she was so pretty. Oh, it was a terrible thing when she died that next year." She paused. "I'm sorry. Did you know she had passed?"

Jillian made a quick note on her yellow legal pad: "A. J. Dills! Confirmed by . . ." Then she said, "We did, yes. I'm sorry, what was your name?"

"Mrs. Nancy Wilson. Nancy Parks then. Miss Harrison was different from most of our teachers. She had long blonde hair and the prettiest green eyes. So young and full of life. I felt special being in her class. She taught us all about books. I credit her for me going to college. I truly do."

"Mrs. Wilson." Jillian added the name to her notes. "We're trying to track down the Raffertys mentioned in Ellen's obituary. Are they still in the area?"

"The Raffertys. My goodness. My sisters used to talk about those boys all the time. No, they don't live here anymore. Miss Harrison dated Andrew Rafferty, but I guess you knew that. He died in Vietnam. His poor mother." She sighed. "Randy Keith and my sister were in school together. He had a hard time of it too."

"I'm a little confused, Mrs. Wilson. Is Randy Keith a first and last name? Is he related to Beth Ann Rafferty? I'd assumed they were married."

"Oh my, no. Randy Keith is Beth Ann Rafferty's son. They're both still with us. Beth Ann's husband was Gene. He's been dead awhile now," Mrs. Wilson added. "Randy Keith and Andrew were twins, you know. They went by Randy and Andy until first grade. The story is that their teacher called out Andrew, which suited little Andy fine. When she said Randall, that little rascal piped up and said, 'My name ain't Randall, it's Randy Keith.' He's been known by both names ever since."

"Andrew's middle name is Keith too," Jillian said. "Is that a twin thing?"

"No. I'm not one to gossip, but Keith was their last name. Miss Beth Ann married that Mr. Rafferty when those boys were twelve or thirteen. He was their stepfather."

Jillian thought the librarian's tone had cooled as she spoke of Mr. Rafferty. She wondered why but chose not to ask. "Did you know Randy Keith or Andrew?"

"Well, everybody kind of knew of Randy Keith. He's a real friendly fellow, a heart of gold. He'd been held back a year or two, so I knew him from hanging around with my sister. Andrew was smart, real smart. He had big dreams. I believe that's why folks took his dying so hard."

"The obituary listed Randy Keith and Beth Ann Rafferty as special friends. There was no mention of Gene Rafferty."

"Well now, I don't know why that was. Beth Ann didn't lose her husband until long after Miss Harrison passed. That's when Randy Keith and his mama moved over to Kentucky," Mrs. Wilson said.

"Do you know how I could get in touch with them?" Jillian asked. "It's important."

"If you leave your name and number, I'll see that Randy Keith gets it. They can decide if they want to talk to you."

Excited to learn that Andy had living relatives but not wanting to reveal too much, Jillian told Mrs. Wilson that she and her friend Andy Harrison planned to visit Gentry to see the school where Ellen had taught and asked if they could come visit her. Jillian hoped Mrs. Wilson's curiosity would encourage her to pass along her name to Randy Keith.

Jillian opened her door and peeked in the hall. Harrison's Realty offices were shaped like a Monopoly board, with the entrance at Go and small offices lining the exterior walls. In the center of the building was a large conference room which opened onto every hallway. If Andy was in the office today, he'd either be in the conference room or Tom's office, one of two larger ones on the Jail and Free Parking side of the Monopoly board. Seeing the conference room doors closed, Jillian popped down the hall to Elaine's office.

"Got time for lunch?" Jillian asked.

"No, I've got a closing at two and need to get these papers in order."

"Do you want anything from Panera?"

"Going to Panera?" Andy asked, opening the conference room door. "Mind if I tag along?"

Jillian blushed but tried to play it cool. "That's fine. Will you join us, Elaine?"

Elaine's look said she wasn't fooled. "No thanks, hon. You two have fun. We'll catch up later."

Jillian turned. "I'll grab my purse and ask Barb to hold my messages. Meet you out front?"

"Sure." Andy tossed his keys in his hand and began soulfully whistling "You Send Me."

Jillian could hear Elaine cackling in her office.

When Jillian got in his car, Andy teased, "You've been avoiding me. Are you worried about sparks catching the place on fire?" He kissed her hand as they exited the parking lot. "Where do teenagers around here go to make out? We don't have to go to lunch," Andy said, then laughed. "You're blushing again, Jillian. I'm teasing you."

Jillian rolled her eyes. "I'm trying to avoid being a topic of the steady stream of gossip in our agency." Jillian squeezed his hand. "You know I feel the sparks flying, Andy. I'm feeling things I'd forgotten existed."

"Dang," Andy drawled. "Are you sure we need lunch?" He pulled into Panera's lot, looked around, and gave Jillian a quick kiss. "Are we still going to Gentry tomorrow?"

"Yes, I spoke with the librarian. I'll fill you in after we order."

"Good. Maybe tomorrow I can hold your hand in public."

As they walked through the crowded lot after their lunch, Jillian noticed a woman with long black hair leaning against Andy's car.

"Who is that?" Jillian pointed. "Do you know her?"

Andy swore. "That would be Leila. What the hell is she doing here?" Andy rubbed his face and glanced at Jillian. "Feel like meeting the ex?" He strode off, Jillian hurrying after him.

"Leila!" Andy shouted. "What are you doing here?"

Tall and almost model thin, Leila wore an orange shirt-dress and clunky jewelry over a pair of leggings, with heels higher than any in Jillian's closet. As Andy approached Leila, a younger man stepped out of a nearby car and extended his hand.

"Hey, old man. How's it going?"

Andy pointedly ignored the hand as he glared at his ex-wife. "Why are you here?"

"Simply passing through, man. It's cool."

"There's never anything simple where Leila's concerned, Chad. You should learn that if you're going to associate with her." Still looking at Leila, Andy demanded, "Where's my son?"

Uncertain whether she wanted to meet Leila, Jillian stood on the grassy median, watching the others. She assumed this was the same Chad from Andy's band. Shorter than Andy and quite a bit younger, Jillian saw Chad as a frat boy gone to seed. His dark brown hair was a little long, and his untucked white button-down shirt pulled tight across his belly.

"Don't be rude, Andy." Leila held Chad's arm. "We're on our way to pick up Seth. He'll be at the Atlanta airport early tomorrow. We thought we'd swing by and bring you some of BJ's things. I thought you'd do your son a favor and deliver his guitar and the books he requested. That's all."

Andy stared at Leila. "All?" he asked disbelievingly. "I don't understand. You said Seth would be in Atlanta with you. What happened to your mini-vacation plans? Why will Seth be at the airport?"

"He's flying back from Miami because I let him spend a few days with Peyton," Leila said defiantly, letting go of Chad and brushing her long black hair from her face.

"Leila! We talked about this. You said Seth would be with you over break. I trusted you." Andy's voice was anguished. "You had no right to let him go to Miami! I'd already said no."

"I had every right. I am his mother," Leila retorted, stepping closer to Andy. She pointed in his face. "You don't get to make all the decisions for our boys."

Jillian shrank as the voices raised. She noticed people looking in their direction.

"Some mother." Andy's voice rose. "I told you it wasn't a good situation. God, Leila, you are so irresponsible. What were you thinking? Letting a child go stay with a drunk." Andy gripped his hair in both hands and turned in a circle on the pavement. "Who do you suppose watched those boys, supervised them in the pool, made sure they ate, made sure they didn't sample Shelby's booze?"

"Shelby's not a drunk. She just likes to drink," Leila protested.

"Besides, Seth's hardly a child."

"He's eleven years old, for god's sake. Of course he's a child. He's too young to be on his own."

"Jake was there, Andy. I'm not an idiot," Leila said coldly.

Andy rounded in fury. "Oh, Jake. Well, that solves everything. Shelby drunk and her teenage boyfriend, Jake, babysitting while her husband goes to work? Great role model. Not at all confusing for an impressionable child. Is there a rule book for idiotic parenting in the cougar cheater club?"

"Hey, low blow, man. Chill out." Chad stepped in front of Leila and pointed a finger at Andy.

"Don't talk to me!" Andy spoke from behind clinched teeth, eyes flashing in anger. "Stay out of this."

"Fine. Have it your way. Yell your heads off." Chad walked toward Jillian. He winked at her. "I'll get to know this lovely lady over here." Chad moved closer.

I don't like this. Go away. Leave me alone. Jillian edged toward the car as Chad neared.

"Andy. Let's go, please. People are staring." *Please stop yelling. You're scaring me.*

The argument grew louder as Andy and Leila yelled at each other, and Jillian's protest went unheard. Chad stood nearby, grinning and watching the argument.

"Jake is twenty-six!"

"And screwing his stepmother."

"That has nothing to do with Seth."

"I'm trying to protect my son!"

"You're trying to control him. You did the same thing with me!"

The fight erupted into a lot of 'he said, she said,' which ended when Leila suddenly slapped Andy.

Jillian jumped and cried out, "No! Stop!" She was shocked to see Andy grab Lelia's hands and get in her face.

"Oh, no you don't. Not anymore," he said coldly.

Jillian's heart was racing. Andy looked angry enough to hit Leila. Jillian's awareness of the small group watching and listening from the nearby sidewalk faded.

"You're shaking." Chad moved close to Jillian. "Don't worry, these two are always going at it. Leila's a passionate woman, in and out of bed." He put his arm around Jillian. "How about you, pretty mama? Are you a passionate woman? Holding out on big Andy? Is that what's got him so riled up?"

Jillian wrenched away and looked at Chad in disgust. Suddenly Andy was there, grabbing Chad's shirt with his left hand and punching him in the face with his right, knocking Chad back into the car. Leila screamed. Jillian panicked, looking wildly around the parking lot, trying to find somewhere to hide. She ran across the street to a nearby Starbucks. In the background, the fight continued.

Jillian stopped running before she entered the coffee shop. She walked quickly to the restroom and locked herself in. "Amy! Come get me, please. I'm at Starbucks," she cried into her phone. Shaking uncontrollably, Jillian sobbed for several minutes before pulling herself together.

How could I have been so wrong about Andy?

Chapter Seventeen

Amy knocked on the restroom door. "Jillian? You ready, sugar?"

Jillian silently followed Amy to the car, where Amy took her hand. "You ready to talk?"

"No. Take me home, please. I left my keys and purse in Andy's car. Thank goodness I had my phone. Oh, Amy, it was awful." Jillian, crying again, gratefully accepted the tissues Amy handed her. "I can't believe Andy hit him. I just can't. Screaming and fighting in the parking lot! I can't believe it."

Amy pulled up in front of Jillian's house. "Come on, honey. Let's get you inside and put the kettle on. You need some tea and conversation."

Jillian sobbed. "I'll take the tea, but I can't talk about it. I can't go back to work either. I feel dirty." Jillian picked up her phone and texted the office, then rubbed her face with both hands. "Thanks for rescuing me, Amy. I couldn't, I can't face Andy."

Amy patted her shoulder. "We'll talk later. Take a shower. I'll start the tea and take care of Willie. It's going to be okay, Jillian. Whatever it is, it's going to be okay."

Jillian stepped out of the shower, wrapped her hair in a towel, and pulled on a bathrobe. She looked at her carefully chosen clothes. Knowing she'd never wear them again, Jillian balled them up and threw them away.

A steaming cup of chamomile tea and two pieces of dark chocolate waited on the counter. Jillian carried her tea into the living room and pulled Willie onto her lap. "It's been a rough afternoon, little buddy," she whispered. "I've been a fool, a fool in love." Willie snuggled as Jillian mindlessly drank her tea.

Willie heard the car before she did. He ran to the door, barking and wagging his tail. Jillian froze at Andy's knock. "Jillian, are you okay? Open up. Jillian, please. Let me in." He knocked again louder. "I'm sorry, Jillian. I'm really sorry. I shouldn't let her push my buttons, but I did. I hate that I lost control that way. Please talk to me. Please."

Jillian moved to the door and looked through the peephole at Andy's grief-stricken face.

"Sweetheart, please. At least let me know you made it home okay. I need to know that at least."

Jillian stifled a sob as Andy stood outside the door, bowed his head, and wiped his eyes. She sank in front of the door, unwilling to open it, crying quietly as Willie whined in her lap and licked away her tears.

Hearing her phone ding, Jillian picked herself up off the floor and walked into the kitchen. She looked at her phone. Nine missed calls from Andy. Seven texts. She didn't read them, but she didn't delete them either. *I'll worry about them later.* Jillian rinsed her cup and let Willie out in the yard.

Jillian's phone rang. She looked at the screen. *Oh, Amy. I'm not ready to talk. I'm so tired.*

A text came through: "Will bring purse to you later. Andy talking with Stan. Love you."

Jillian let Willie in, turned off her phone, and crawled into bed.

Surprisingly, Jillian fell asleep quickly, but dreams of losing her purse and being chased by Chad, who changed into a werewolf, disturbed her. Easily recognizing their source, she drifted back to sleep. A bit later though, she woke screaming Andy's name. Jillian could not shake the image of Andy's ashen face sinking beneath a lake's surface.

Just after four, I shouldn't have slept so long. Jillian let Willie out in the backyard again, then stood, staring at the refrigerator. A quiet knock preceded Amy's entrance.

"It's me. I heard Willie and figured you were up. How are you feeling?"

That was all it took for Jillian to break down again. Her feelings for Andy were deeper than she'd let herself believe. The fear of losing him had caused her to dream about him drowning.

Of course he's drowning. He just lost his father, found out he was adopted, and got divorced. Then he finds out about Ellie and Andrew, but they're dead too. Of course Andy's emotions are surface level. Ugh, that sleazy Chad. And Leila. And poor Seth. Of course Andy's angry and confused.

Amy held her as she cried, then said, "Go sit down. I'm making tea and toast. You look shaky."

Amy poured the tea. "Talk to me now, hon. What are you feeling?"

Jillian's eyes filled with tears again. "I'm afraid."

"Afraid of Andy?"

Jillian nodded. "And I'm afraid of losing him." She tore off a corner of the toast. "Why was Andy at your house? What did he say?"

"Well, he got a little panicky when he couldn't find you, Jillian. Elaine wasn't taking calls, so he raced over here. We were out back, as usual, and Stan heard Andy knocking and calling for you and told him you were home safe. Andy said he'd had a big, ugly fight with his ex-wife in the Panera parking lot. He admitted punching some guy at least twice before realizing you had disappeared."

Amy sipped her tea. "Once he noticed, Andy quit fighting. The guy, Chuck? No, Chad. Chad swung at him and clocked him pretty good, but stopped when he saw Andy wasn't fighting back. Andy left them standing there while he went looking for you, told the ex-wife he'd deal with her later."

Amy rubbed Jillian's arm. "Andy said you wouldn't open the door."

"I couldn't face him, Amy. It was horrible. Leila slapped him hard. I panicked. I could almost feel it. Then, Andy, I've never seen him so angry. Scary angry. I was afraid he might hit her. And that sleazebag, Chad. Andy hauled off and punched him in the face."

"Seems like Chad deserved it." At Jillian's protest, Amy continued, "Oh, I know that's not an enlightened attitude, but Chad sounds like an ass. He was out of line. I'm sure Andy wouldn't have defended your honor in that fashion if he hadn't been so angry at the ex-wife. She seems like a real piece of work."

"Yeah. She is. I still don't understand how any of this happened. We had such a nice weekend." Setting her cup down, Jillian turned to her friend. "Oh, Amy, the last several weeks have been wonderful. Andy's been kind and loving, and I've been imagining a future together. Then today, suddenly he's yelling and punching Chad. His anger, oh my God, it scared me so bad. I've been such a fool to start something with him." Jillian put her head in hands and wept.

"What? Honey, you did nothing wrong." Amy patted Jillian's back. "Sit up now. Your relationship with Andy and this fight are two separate things. Don't let that manipulative woman and her sleazy boyfriend ruin a good thing. You and Andy can talk this out."

"There's nothing to talk out, Amy." Jillian sniffed. "I cannot be with a man with that capacity for anger. It's not moral self-righteousness. It's survival. You saw me this afternoon. I was an absolute wreck. He wasn't even yelling at me, and I fell apart. I obviously have too many emotional scars from childhood and from Paul. I don't like feeling that way. I want to feel safe without crawling back into my shell. It took me a long time to learn to stand up for myself. I'm not going back." Jillian shook her head and crossed her arms. "Plus, Leila said Andy tried to control her and the boys. For what that's worth. She might be lying."

Amy stood, hugged Jillian, then looked seriously at her. "Jillian, we love you, and we support you. Just be sure that avoiding Andy isn't another way of crawling back into that shell."

Jillian didn't say anything. *I can't face him. I can't.*

Amy took her cup to the sink. "I get that you feel unsafe, but it seems to me that you need to face this, face Andy. I'm not suggesting you continue a romantic relationship, but eventually you'll have to talk to the man. You can't hide from him forever; you work together. When you're ready, ask Stan to sit with you if you're uncomfortable being alone with him."

Amy walked toward the door, then turned. "Andy talked to Stan a long time this afternoon. Leila called wanting to know what to do about his son's things and the younger boy, so Stan rode with Andy to get the boy's things. For moral support, you know. For what it's worth, Stan didn't like Leila or Chad much. Anyway, we got Andy cleaned up and calmed down before he left."

"Cleaned up?"

"He had a few scratches and a spot on his ear was bleeding a bit. Nothing major." Amy sighed. "He's driving to Atlanta to pick up his boy. Told those other two to go on their way and he'd see the child back to school safely. He said to tell you he won't be in the office for at least a week, maybe two or three, but he'll try calling again." With that assurance, Amy opened the door and left quietly.

An image of Andy's furious face flitted through Jillian's mind. She shook her head, and the tears flowed again. Jillian knew she'd have to face Andy at some point, listen to whatever he had to say. Maybe even forgive him for scaring her, but it wouldn't happen today.

"I won't be his whipping boy or his therapist," Jillian told Willie. "I can't rescue him only to drown myself. He's not ready for a relationship. Not if he flies off the handle like that. Not if Leila abused him. I have enough scars of my own. I don't need that chaos in my life."

Jillian walked toward the kitchen. *Maybe we can figure out a way to work on the Belford house.* "Maybe one day we can be friends again, Willie. If he keeps his temper under control."

Jillian fixed a mug of hot chocolate, curled up in her favorite chair, and picked up a mystery. She wasn't in the mood for romance. Before long, she threw the book across the room in disgust. *Is everyone on Andy's side? Don't I have a right to distance myself from an angry man?*

Willie jumped down and retrieved the book but didn't want to relinquish it. "Willie, leave it," Jillian commanded. "Good boy."

Jillian began reading again, this time absorbing the lead detective's calm explanation. "Acts of violence often result from emotional strain. When people feel threatened, feel themselves losing something of value, they react emotionally. In men, that emotion is often anger and is likely to be expressed with physical violence. Think about that when dealing with suspects, when solving crimes. Loss, whether an object, a person, or control of a situation, can cause an atypical outburst. Anger is an active emotion fueled by adrenaline. And at the root of anger is fear."

Jillian's tears started again. She believed Andy to be a good person. He didn't make a habit of punching people, and he had definitely suffered a lot of loss recently. His anger may have been warranted, but was not, Jillian thought, shaking her head slowly, not anything she could be around. She'd worked too hard on crawling out of her shell to go back.

Chapter Eighteen

Jillian had a hard time getting started the next morning. She was grateful Andy would not be at the office, even though he was constantly on her mind. *I swear I'm getting one of those big rubber bands to wear on my wrist and snap every time I think of him. I have got to get him out of my head.*

"Maybe I'll treat myself to a latte," Jillian thought before remembering Andy buying lattes for their first trip to Belford. She stopped for orange juice and a biscuit instead.

"Do you know where Mr. Harrison is?" Barb asked as Jillian walked through the door.

"No, I do not. Do I have any messages?" Jillian said. "Sorry, my head is killing me."

Jillian stalked to her office, wondering if everyone and everything would remind her of Andy today. She closed her door, determined to get some work done and avoid office gossip. When Barbara buzzed her later that morning saying Andy was on the phone, Jillian said she was in a meeting.

Andy must've taken the hint because he didn't call again. Jillian emerged from her office midday, right as Elaine was heading down the hall.

"Hey, girl. Can you check your calendar . . ." Elaine took Jillian's arm and led her back into her office and closed the door. "You look like death warmed over. What's going on?"

"Just a bad headache. What do you need?"

"Um. Let's try that again, Jillian. Something is obviously wrong. Let's have lunch and talk it out." Elaine crossed her arms and looked steadily at Jillian.

Jillian closed her eyes and blew out a breath. "Fine, but I'm driving separately. I'm viewing houses this afternoon. Pick something up and meet me behind the library. I have books to return."

Twenty minutes later, Jillian watched as Elaine made her way through the tall grass to one of four tables in a tiny, unkempt park behind the library. There were trade-offs for privacy.

"We have chicken sandwiches and fruit cups from Ruby's," Elaine mentioned a small sandwich shop near the office, "since you and Andy went to Panera yesterday."

And there it was. Jillian tossed her sandwich back on the picnic table and traced some initials carved in the table top with a finger. "Yes. Yes, we did. That's why I'm in this state." She raised her head and told Elaine the whole story.

Elaine sat, open mouthed. "Oh, honey. I'd never have expected that of Andy." Elaine sipped her drink. "And that ex-wife and her sleazy boyfriend. Ugh. They deserve each other!"

Jillian shrugged and picked up her sandwich. "I knew Andy was stressed. I knew he was having trouble controlling his anger. But this . . ." She shook her head. "That level of public aggression. It scared me, Elaine."

Elaine looked at Jillian and sat quietly as they nibbled their sandwiches. "Is it the public nature of the fight that troubles you most?"

"Maybe? Someone who acts that badly in public could behave much worse in private."

"Jillian, could this be about Paul?" Elaine asked, looking carefully at her friend.

"Oh yeah. It's probably a learned reaction to him and my mother, both of whom put on public shows of charm and courtesy, then were mean and hateful in private. I was definitely triggered by his anger and just can't put myself in that situation again." Jillian looked at Elaine, tears flowing again. "Despite how much it hurts to end things with Andy, I know that's what I need to do."

"I hate that, I really do." Elaine wrapped up her sandwich. "I'm going back to the office," she said in a clipped voice. "Maybe rethink this mentorship business."

Jillian dried her tears. "Oh, Elaine, don't. There's no point in creating problems where none exist. We all have to figure out a way to work with Andy."

"My problem is going to be keeping my mouth shut and not giving him a piece of my mind," Elaine snapped. "If he puts one toe out of line, I will let him have it."

Jillian smiled sadly. "I appreciate your support, Elaine, but don't let my relationship with Andy ruin yours, okay?" She stretched. "You were right to drag me out of the office. I feel better. What was it you wanted to ask me earlier?"

Elaine opened her datebook. "Check your calendar for April 13 and 20. I'm hosting an open house on Willow Street. Want to work it with me?"

"Sure. Are we staging?"

"No, the house is empty, but the owners don't want to expend any additional funds."

Open houses were often a hit-or-miss proposition, with twenty visitors in an hour or two in an afternoon. Harrison's Agency always had two agents on duty to provide better service to clients and safety for the agents. Jillian and Elaine worked well together and had similar approaches to showing homes. Traffic was generally higher when Jillian staged homes for sale by placing furniture to show the rooms to their advantage, but some clients didn't like paying to rent, transport, or arrange furnishings.

Jillian thanked Elaine, then inspected a few homes that might work for a particular client. As she reached the final home, another text from Andy arrived. Jillian scrolled through the apology and the other seven Andy had sent, all saying pretty much the same thing. "I'm sorry I lost control. I love you. Please talk to me."

Jillian sighed, then responded: "I accept your apology for your behavior. Moving forward, we should limit our relationship to business."

She stepped into the house, quickly looking through rooms as she watched her phone. Five minutes, then ten passed with three dots dancing on screen. Finally, four words: "I am not overjoyed."

Jillian sighed again. Was he referencing the song he'd played for her at the swimming area, or was his word choice coincidental?

Another text: "Please give me a chance to explain. Can I call you?"

"No. Nothing to explain," Jillian replied, then turned off the phone and went about her business. Somehow, this house wasn't right for her clients either.

Jillian managed to get through the next two weeks without having to resort to rubber band aversion therapy. She called the therapist she'd seen after her divorce and scheduled some sessions to work through her emotions. She immersed herself in work and walked with Willie along the river each evening, hoping the exercise would help her sleep. She had dreamed repeatedly about walking the halls of the house at Blackwater Pond, searching for someone she knew was Andy. He hadn't called or texted in fourteen days. Jillian's fear had lessened, but her feelings for Andy had not.

JILLIAN HEADED TO WORK with some trepidation. Andy was expected back in the office today, and she expected he'd want to talk to her. *I'll just cope the best I can.*

"Good morning, Barb. How was your weekend?"

"Pretty good, Jillian. Oh, welcome back, Mr. Harrison."

"Good morning, Barbara. Jillian, may I see you in the conference room?"

"Not right away, Mr. Harrison. Perhaps about ten?" Jillian tried to avoid Andy's eyes but saw surprise, then pain cross his face.

"See you then," he responded, narrowing his eyes and pursing his lips.

Jillian walked quickly to her office, closed the door, and breathed out slowly. She sat behind her desk and tried to work, though her heart was breaking.

At ten, Jillian picked up her Belford file and walked on trembling legs to the conference room. Through the open door, she could see Andy pacing the floor. She waited for him to notice her.

"Ms. Peters. Come in," Andy said. "Have a seat."

Jillian, eyes blurry with unshed tears, sat and opened the folder.

"I'm glad you brought the Belford file. Have you had any thoughts about going forward with the project." Andy sat beside her.

"No," she said quietly.

"No, you don't want to move forward or no you haven't had any thoughts?" Andy asked just as quietly, putting his hand on Jillian's back. When she flinched, Andy pulled away as if he'd been burned. "Jillian." His anguished voice shook. "Oh God, I hate this. I hate this wall between us. I hate that you're afraid of me."

Out of the corner of her eye, Jillian could see Andy lift his eyes upward and run his hand over his mouth. *He's trying not to cry.* The thought made her want to cry even more.

"I screwed up. I know that. But you won't look at me, you won't talk to me, you won't let me apologize. I don't know how to make this right."

"You've apologized. I accepted. We move on. Just, please don't touch me," Jillian said quietly, rising from her chair. "We can work together, but I cannot be involved with someone prone to violent outbursts." Jillian's voice was calm, but her heart was hurting. "Once

I've clarified my feelings on Belford, I'll email you."

Andy sat, a single tear trickling down his cheek. "I'm not, you know." He stood slowly, looking at her. "I'm not prone to violent outbursts, but I'll stay away. I know I scared you, and I'm so, so sorry. Maybe one day you'll hear my side of the story and maybe understand."

∞

JILLIAN AND ANDY SETTLED INTO A ROUTINE of polite civility over the next few days. Andy made no overtures of familiarity, didn't call or text or invite her to lunch, and rarely spoke to her beyond a simple greeting each morning. For her part, she relaxed her use of the more formal 'Mr. Harrison.'

Neither had spoken anymore about the house in Belford, so Jillian was surprised to hear Andy mention it outside her office door. His voice rose and fell as he paced the hall, talking on his phone.

"No, no. It's still under consideration. An unfortunate delay. I hear ya, man. I feel sure they are curious.

"Yeah, I'm sure. We'll hire local where possible. Roofers, plumbers, electricians, carpenters, painters, wallpaper hangers, gardeners, and ground crew.

"Yeah, it's a big job. We'll know soon.

"No, we haven't decided. Okay, Henry. Look, I appreciate you calling. I'll be in touch."

Jillian surprised herself by stepping into the hall. "Andy? I couldn't help overhearing. Are you still thinking of renovating the house at Blackwater Pond?"

"Yes. Are you not?" Andy shortened the distance between them.

"I don't know. I thought it might be dead in the water, after—"

"It doesn't have to be. We can move forward as business partners and friends, I hope," Andy said quietly. "The house won't leave me alone. It haunts my dreams." He paused. "I'm kind of grateful."

Jillian looked at him curiously. "You're grateful for haunted dreams?"

"Breaks up the monotony of the nightmares." Andy rubbed his neck. "Between the nightmares, worries about my kids, and confusion about family connections, I haven't been sleeping well."

Jillian backed toward her office, apologizing. "Oh, Andy. I'm sorry. I promise I'll have an answer soon," she said, closing her door. Jillian hadn't been sleeping very well either, but the dreams had changed. Lately, she seemed to be watching a young woman with blonde hair piled loosely on her head, dressed in white, searching fruitlessly.

Belford was haunting her as well.

Chapter Nineteen

On open house day, Jillian loaded her car with sales materials, cookie dough and pans, water bottles, and two open house signs. Elaine would place additional signs in town before meeting Jillian at the house. Hopefully, she'd bring some folding chairs. Jillian's expectations weren't high, given market conditions, but she was glad to help Elaine.

Jillian's phone rang as she started her car. Glancing at the dashboard display, she saw Elaine's name and answered on the speaker, hearing a siren's whoop and men's voices in the background. Jillian's voice rose in alarm. "Elaine? Are you okay? What's going on?"

Elaine answered in a rush. "I'm okay but my car's not. I can't make the open house. I tried Betsy, but she has plans. I'm really sorry, but it's too late to cancel, and I don't know what else to do."

"Calm down and tell me what happened, Elaine," Jillian said. "Is Larry with you?"

"He's on his way. I just hate putting this on you. Idiot driver!" Elaine sputtered. "Some guy paying more attention to his phone than his driving clipped my car hard enough to spin it. I was putting up a sign along the main road leading to the subdivision. I swear I was off the road, completely on the shoulder." Elaine's voice slowed. "It's going to take a while to deal with this, and I'm too flustered to be of any use anyway. I know you're still uneasy around Andy, but I don't have another choice."

Jillian exhaled sharply. "Whoa, hold on. Andy's working the open house? With me?"

"Well, he told me he could handle it on his own. You don't have to stay."

Jillian thought about that for a minute. "I assumed he was in Philadelphia."

"No, he's been working from home to give you both some space," Elaine said.

"Oh," Jillian said quietly. "Has he ever worked an open house?"

"Well, no, but I don't know what else to do. I'm open to suggestions." Elaine paused. "At the very least, he can pass out some fliers if anyone shows up. You know how these things go. I just don't want people showing up and no one being there. That makes us look bad."

Jillian agreed, wondering what she should do. She had been avoiding Andy, but her discomfort was more rooted in her feelings for him than in fear. "It's okay, Elaine. You take care of yourself. I'll go to the open house and be sure Andy knows what he's doing. I may leave early, but honestly, I know I need to talk to him."

"Oh, hon. Thank you. I owe you breakfast."

"Yeah, we'll talk about that later."

Jillian gave herself a pep talk as she drove the rest of the way to the open house. She could do this. She would do this. Better to talk in neutral territory than at the office. Chances were they'd have plenty of uninterrupted time. She could listen, devise a plan for moving forward.

When she opened the door, a familiar voice called out, "Hello, welcome. Come on in."

Jillian's footsteps echoed through the empty living room as she walked toward the kitchen, where Andy was setting up a card table. "Hi."

Andy looked up in surprise. "Jillian? I didn't expect to see you."

"Elaine called. I thought I'd help you get set up."

"Oh yeah, I'd appreciate that. I'm definitely out of my comfort zone. First time, you know," Andy said, flipping the table on its legs. "I had to borrow mom's car to get everything over here."

Jillian nodded and put her bag on the counter. She washed her hands and said, "I'll get some cookies started. You didn't happen to bring any coffee, did you?"

"I did. I'll go get it."

Jillian watched Andy go. She wasn't as nervous as she'd anticipated.

Andy returned carrying a box with a coffee maker, coffee, creamer, sugar, and cups. He stepped around her and set it on the counter. "I'll just go get the chairs and info sheets."

Jillian started the coffee brewing and checked on the cookies. Then she started turning on lights, making sure the house was ready to show. By the time she got back to the kitchen, Andy had organized the sales data and was asking a couple of visitors to sign in.

"We're just nosy neighbors," the woman explained.

"Nothing wrong with that," Andy assured them, handing them a sales flier. "You might be surprised what homes in the neighborhood are going for. Look around and let us know if we can help."

Jillian smiled at the couple and added, "Stop back by for some cookies."

She turned to Andy. "When they leave, you should look around and notice any special features of the home so you'll be ready to answer questions about the appliances, square footage, school districts, and so on."

Andy nodded. "Good suggestions. That'll help me look like I know what I'm doing."

After the couple left, taking a few cookies with them, Andy toured the home, then joined Jillian in the kitchen, where she sat sipping her coffee.

"Great basement space. Wonderful view of the wooded backyard from the large screened porch. New HVAC. Appliances in good condition." He paused. "How'd I do?"

"Pretty well. Don't forget the two-car garage. A lot of these older homes don't have garages."

"Good advice." He poured himself a cup of coffee and motioned at the chair as if seeking permission to sit down. "Uh, I'm feeling a little awkward. How have you been?"

"Okay, I guess." Jillian shrugged. "It is awkward. I know we need to talk. I'm sorry it's taken me so long, Andy, but I was scared. I've reconnected with my therapist, and I'm ready to listen to whatever you have to say so we can figure out how to move forward."

"I'm so glad to hear that," Andy said, leaning forward. "I'm sorry my behavior caused this rift between us. Every excruciating minute of that afternoon is seared in my memory." Andy grimaced. "I'm not excusing my behavior, but please know that what happened isn't typical. My emotions have been riding close to the surface for a while now. I'm working on it, truly. I'd like to explain why things escalated so quickly with Leila."

"Go ahead."

"Well, you know about Leila's unfaithfulness. Chad's the one I caught in my bed with her, which brought me to my senses and made me realize she was never going to change. Maybe I should've thanked him for taking Leila off my hands instead of punching him for what he said to you." Andy reached for her hand but pulled back. "I didn't hit Chad because of Leila. It's you I was worried about. Not Chad, not Leila, Jillian. You. I lost it when I saw how uncomfortable he was making you."

Andy rubbed his forehead. "Chad was in my band and met Leila through me. He's a real jerk but a decent drummer with good connections to line up gigs, so we let him join. It didn't take the band long to realize he's lazy and arrogant with no sense of decency. Honestly, Leila probably chose Chad because I can't stand him."

Andy twisted his mouth. "I don't hate Leila, but neither do I respect or trust her. She's punishing me. She's gotten really vindictive in the last decade. Anything I care about, she finds a way to destroy." Andy looked out the window, then at Jillian. "Maybe I'm being paranoid, but the accountant she had a fling with? We played racquetball together. I swear she wants to drive me crazy. She's being pretty successful." Andy trailed off and was quiet for a minute.

"Leila knows that my boys are the most important, most precious things to me. I'm very guarded in what I say to her about them because I'm afraid she'll use it against me. Involve them in getting back at me. Maybe I'm imagining evils that aren't there, but there's a pattern.

"Chad's a decade younger than Leila, and he's rich. Trust fund rich. Leila likes his money and his lifestyle and his friends. You know she let Seth go to Florida with his school friend Peyton. We met Peyton and his mother, Shelby, at a pool party at Chad's about three years ago. Shelby's married to a much older guy, and Peyton is his only biological child. There's a—" Andy broke off as he noticed people coming up the walk. He stood to greet them.

"Good afternoon, folks. Thanks for coming by," Andy said as a family of six came in. "Here's some information about the house."

Jillian wandered out to the screened porch. She was confused by much Andy had said, but his reasons for hitting Chad were clear. He hadn't been angry about Chad being with Leila. He'd been mad that Chad was talking to her—someone else he cared about. And he'd been furious that Leila was involving Seth in her plan for vengeance. Still, Jillian wondered why Leila would want to punish Andy.

Jillian returned to the kitchen and helped Andy answer questions about the neighborhood and town. She smiled as the family left. "You did pretty well there. I think they liked the house."

"Thanks. Elaine will be encouraged. She hasn't had many viewers."

"It only takes one."

"Yeah, that's true." Sitting back down at the table, Andy asked, "Ready to hear more?"

"Peyton is the boy Seth was visiting in Florida, right?"

"Yes. They reconnected at school. I'm not crazy about it, but I don't want to blame the kid for his mother's problems. Peyton's mother has a very young boyfriend on the side, and they party quite a bit. The whole situation's unhealthy. I don't want Seth around it, which I'm sure is why Leila allowed it."

Andy walked toward the window. "Her attitude toward Seth makes me crazy. He is a child, and in a lot of ways, less mature than his brothers were at eleven. I worry that he's too easily led. He's been fighting for attention since he was born." Andy shook his head and turned back to Jillian. "The whole situation is wrong."

Jillian glanced at the clock and began cleaning up the coffee and cookies. "I understand your concern, Andy. The situation isn't healthy. How was Seth?"

"Okay. The boys flew back to Atlanta together. Peyton's spending Easter with his grandmother." Andy noticed Jillian cleaning and started replacing the sales materials into files. "Seth said he got tired of Peyton's bragging and bossing, so I hope the friendship will cool. Seth seems to understand now that he needs approval from both parents for any future visits. His brothers support me there, which helps tremendously." Andy folded the table and asked, "Do you think we're done here?"

"Pretty much. I'll close up downstairs. If anyone comes during these last fifteen minutes, I can always turn the lights back on."

When Jillian returned, she noticed Andy had taken the table and chairs to his car and boxed up all of her belongings. She walked back to the screened porch and stood, looking a little lost.

"Are you all right?" Andy asked from the doorway.

Jillian shrugged her shoulders. "I don't know. I have some difficult questions."

Andy nodded. "Okay."

"When Leila slapped you, you said, 'not anymore.' Had she done that previously?"

Andy blew out a breath. "Yeah." He rubbed the back of his neck and avoided looking at her. "A few times. Four, maybe five times over the years."

"Have you ever hit her?"

"No!" Andy said quickly. "No, I've never hit her, never hit our sons, never hit anyone but Chad and Micky Wells in third grade when he tried to steal my bike."

"Leila said you tried to control her."

Andy rubbed his eyes. "Shortly after the first affair, we decided a third child would help us heal. Leila realized she was pregnant about the same time we each were offered some pretty exciting opportunities for advancement at work. Mine paid a lot more and hers involved travel, so with a new baby on the way, it made more sense to focus on my career. I accepted the promotion against her wishes."

Andy looked Jillian in the eye. "Leila says my decision was a play for control of her career. It wasn't, but I didn't listen to or respect her feelings, and I didn't tell her how angry and hurt I had been about the affair, so I didn't give her a chance to listen to or respect mine." Andy paused. "That's why she's punishing me."

Jillian walked back into the kitchen and leaned against the counter. "That helps me understand a little better, Andy, but I'm still confused why Leila and Chad were in town."

Andy sighed heavily. "Leila thrives on drama. Rather than the mini-vacation in Atlanta she'd told me about, Leila allowed Seth to go to Miami for most of the week, planning to visit the aquarium and the Coca Cola Museum when he got back to Atlanta. Like I said, nothing's ever easy with her. I think the whole 'we're bringing you some of BJ's things' was a way to rub my nose in the fact that she'd allowed Seth to go to Miami. She could have called, but she used the tracker app on my phone to surprise me. Another power play." Andy shrugged. "Anything else you want to know?"

"No. Not now anyway."

Andy picked up the box of sales material. "So, are we good now?"

"Sure, it's four o'clock; I think we can leave." Jillian began turning out lights. "I'll get the sign out of the yard and lock up. Don't forget to retrieve all the other signs."

"Jillian. That's not what I meant." Andy put the box down and motioned from himself to Jillian. "Are *we* good? Can we go back to where we were before Leila and Chad came to town?"

Jillian's eyes brimmed with tears as she shook her head slowly. "Maybe just friends." Jillian moved down the hall quickly.

Chapter Twenty

After the open house, Jillian called Elaine. "Have you calmed down?"

"A little," Elaine said, "but honestly, I keep thinking 'what if.' What if I'd been in my car or closer to it? I could have been hit!"

"It is scary, Elaine. Just keep reminding yourself that you're safe and none of that happened. How's the car?"

Elaine explained about damage to the rear and side of her car, then asked about the open house. Jillian said it had gone well and suggested she follow up with the last family. "We think they really liked it."

"'We,' huh? How'd it go with Andy?"

"Honestly? It wasn't as awkward as I'd expected. We were both a little nervous, but we managed a good talk in between viewers."

"I'm so glad, Jillian. I was really worried I'd done the wrong thing."

"Well, it's not like you had much choice."

Elaine paused. "To be honest, I did. Betsy was willing to change her plans, but I thought this might nudge you two a little closer."

"Elaine! Your nudge could have backfired."

"It could have, but I had a feeling, a strong feeling that someone needed to act, so I did. You two have been pussyfooting around each other for weeks. The accident seemed almost providential."

"So, you're saying you stepped out in faith?"

"Eh, that may be a bit much. Intuition, maybe. Hey, it worked out."

Jillian thought for a moment. "I'm not exactly happy at being nudged, but I did need to talk to Andy, so I guess I owe you breakfast."

"No, I shouldn't have interfered, so I owe you breakfast. How about tomorrow?"

"True. Okay, are you cooking or will you deliver?"

Elaine, who rarely cooked, cackled. "Now I know I'm forgiven. See you at nine."

"Make it eight. I've missed church too often lately, for one reason or another," Jillian said, remembering all the recent Sunday mornings she'd spent with Andy or avoiding Andy.

Jillian and Elaine had a long-standing tradition of calling each other out if they felt the other deserved it. To ease the blow, the one who did the calling had to provide breakfast. Rebukes and recriminations were best served with carbs, after all.

Elaine had been wrong to interfere, but Jillian accepted that she needed to talk things through with Andy. She'd intended to do so all along but had been giving herself some time and space. Screaming, slapping, and fist fighting might not be a deal breaker for everyone, but Jillian had reasons not to associate with that kind of behavior. She forgave Elaine but planned to keep her distance from Andy until her attraction had faded. She didn't want to be tempted to resume a relationship she believed wrong for her.

On Sunday morning, Jillian carried table settings and orange juice outside. Willie made every trip back and forth with her, wagging his tail constantly. Willie loved eating on the patio, where he always managed to get an extra bite or two.

Elaine arrived with a large bag from Panera. "Here you go. Bagels, two flavors of cream cheese, and a healthy fruit cup."

Jillian looked at Elaine. "I'll pretend you did not purposefully return to the scene of the crime."

Elaine paled. "I swear it didn't cross my mind. That was thoughtless of me."

"I'm kidding, Elaine. Mostly, anyway. I can't avoid everything that reminds me of Andy, and it has been weeks." They walked through the kitchen. "We're eating outside. Do you want coffee?"

"No, juice is good. Thanks for calling, hon. I was worried I'd messed up."

Jillian unpacked the food. "You didn't mess up. You gave me a much-needed kick in the seat of the pants. I want to restore the house at Blackwater Pond, so I have to be able to talk to Andy." Jillian chose a bagel. "The fight was bad, and I reverted back to a scared child. Not my finest moment."

"Nor was it Andy's. He told me what happened." Elaine took a bite of her cinnamon crunch bagel. "Yum. I love these things." She patted Jillian's arm. "So, I guess you two are all lovey-dovey, goo-goo eyes again."

Jillian shook her head. "No, his anger scared me, and my reaction to his anger scared me more. I can work with him, but I can't hang out with him right now."

Elaine's eyes grew large as she stopped eating. "Jillian, are you afraid of him? Do you think he might hit you?"

"No, I'm sure he wouldn't. But it was Dr. Jekyll and Mr. Hyde that day. Dr. Jekyll and I had a fun, flirtatious lunch and made plans to go to Gentry. Then, bam! Suddenly, he's a different person. Who's to say when Mr. Hyde might show up again? A business relationship is safer."

"But surely you could be friends."

Jillian shook her head slowly. "Not when I'm in love with Dr. Jekyll. I can't trust myself around him. Maybe when I've learned to un-love him."

"You poor dear. I knew you still cared." Elaine grinned. "Do you want to know what Dr. J's doing today?"

Jillian looked at Elaine curiously. "Since when do you keep up with his schedule?"

"All part of the mentorship. Besides, somebody has to talk to the poor fella. You've ignored his calls for practically a month and had your door closed all week. Andy's driving to Gentry today."

Jillian looked up sharply. "Alone? Really? Hmm."

"What?"

"Well, I'm kind of, I don't know, disappointed. I know that makes no sense. I just . . ." Jillian paused. "Stop laughing, Elaine. It's fine. Andy should take the initiative. It's his story." Jillian huffed. "Just let me know what he finds out, okay?"

A FEW DAYS LATER, Jillian arrived at the office after a showing. She waved at Elaine and Andy, who were in the parking lot, and hurried inside. *Wonder where they've been. Elaine still owes me the scoop on Gentry.* Jillian's resolve to stay away from Andy was weakening. Her curiosity was getting the better of her, but she feared a friendship would lead to a relationship, and she was still distrustful of Andy's anger.

Jillian heard Elaine's cackle in the hall. When Elaine didn't immediately appear in her office, Jillian sat, contemplating excuses for going to see her. *Oh, this is ridiculous. She knows I'm curious. She'll see through any ruse I come up with. I may as well be honest and let her laugh.*

Jillian walked down the hall and closed the door to Elaine's office. "Well?"

"Well, that didn't take long." Elaine smiled. "Curiosity got the better of you, eh?"

"You know it has. You can gloat later. Dish."

Jillian sat down, and Elaine leaned back in her chair. "Well, it was a rather disappointing trip for young Andy, I'm afraid. Small towns mostly close up shop on Sundays. The library was closed, school closed, of course, so he wandered around downtown. A hardware store was open, but the cashier didn't remember anything about a teacher dying young. He remembered the name Randy Keith but had no idea what had happened to him."

"So, that's it? That's all he could find out?"

"There's a bit more. Andy stopped at a gas station on the outskirts of town and asked the same questions. The attendants were too young to know anything, but one of the mechanics heard him asking about Andrew Rafferty and said he remembered him. Andy told the guy that he was Andrew's son. The man said, 'No way.' He'd lived in Gentry all his life, Andrew died in Vietnam, and there had never been a whisper of him having a kid. Andy tried to explain, but the man kept shaking his head. He wouldn't say anything more, so Andy left."

"Do you ever feel like you're being pushed toward something? I'm reluctant to be alone with him, yet I want to help Andy find his family. I've kept him at a distance, yet I love him. It's like I'm standing in the middle of rushing water, trying to resist moving. I'm finding it hard to keep my balance."

"Then step forward, honey. Walk out in faith."

"I hate it when you use my words against me." Jillian glared, closing the door behind her.

Jillian gathered her things, told Barb she'd be out for an hour or so, then drove to the river. She walked to her favorite bench.

The simple truth was that she missed Andy. He'd respected her wishes and given her space since the open house. Since the fight, really. She loved Andy. Could she trust him? Could she forgive him? What was it the Bible said about forgiveness? Seventy times seven? She'd have to think about that.

When Jillian let Willie outside that evening, he was very interested in something near the back fence. Deciding she'd better investigate, Jillian walked across her yard and heard Stan's laugh, "Heh, heh. Yeah." Seeing that Willie was worrying a turtle, she moved it under a bush near the Taylors' fence and turned to go inside. Jillian heard Andy's voice and stopped walking.

"These are cool, Stan. I'd like to commission a wall hanging. Can you do something like this?"

"Ko-Ko-Pel-li," Stan said slowly. "With the guitar? How big?"

Andy's showing Stan his tattoo. Jillian was embarrassed to eavesdrop but continued to listen.

"I'd probably use some spoons for hair. You cool with that?" Stan asked.

"Sure. You're the artist."

"And you're the musician. Ready to play that sad song you've been working on?"

A song? Should I listen? Jillian couldn't seem to move away. She crouched near the fence as they walked away. Soon, she heard Andy strum his guitar and start to sing.

"I'm so afraid of losing you, I just don't know what I can do,

How can I make you see that I would never want to make you cry?

Don't make me say goodbye to you, ooh-ooh."

Andy's voice faded into muffled words, then grew louder.

"Whatever happened to not living in fear?

When you're ready for love, I'll be here."

Tears streamed down Jillian's face. She had been living in fear.

Even though she was afraid to face Andy, to face the depth of her own feelings, Jillian knew she had to.

"Whatever happened to the girl I knew?

Give me a chance and I'll be true."

When the song ended, Andy said, "It's rough, different from my usual stuff, but what do you think, Stan?"

"Hell, I'd take you back, and I don't even know you that well. Heh, heh, heh."

Jillian hurried back inside. Overcome with emotion, she texted Amy. "Can you come over w/o A&S seeing you?"

"There in five."

Everyone seemed to feel she and Andy belonged together. Did they? Was she being foolish? Was she living in fear? Jillian opened the front door as Amy walked up the sidewalk.

"Okay, I'm here. Why are you crying? Why the subterfuge?"

"Andy's song. He's right. I am scared. I don't know how to stop being afraid of being afraid."

"I've heard there's therapy for that," Amy said bluntly. "What on earth are you talking about?" Amy flopped down on a loveseat.

"The song Andy sang for Stan," Jillian said, sitting across from her.

"What? Start over, please. You've lost me. Last I saw, Stan was showing Andy his installations in the backyard."

Jillian paced as she told Amy about Willie, her eavesdropping, and Andy's song. "I think I made a mistake in avoiding Andy all these weeks. I've hurt him trying to protect myself. I have been living in fear. I crawled back in my shell and cut myself off from good things because I was afraid. But maybe I don't have to be. I'm not a child anymore. Maybe we can work things out."

"If you're afraid of him, he's not right for you."

"But Amy, I've realized my reaction, my fear, was rooted in childhood trauma, not anything Andy actually did or said to me. I do love him, and I don't want to live in fear."

Amy considered this. "Makes sense to me. What are you going to do?"

"I can't jump back in where we were, but I can at least listen. I'm making tea. Do you want some?" Jillian walked into the kitchen. "I'll talk to Andy, see what he thinks about taking things slow, about beginning again."

"That's reasonable. Life's too short not to take a chance on love. I'll skip the tea and send him over now," Amy said as she followed Jillian to the kitchen.

Jillian jumped and stared at Amy. "What? No. That's too soon. I need to prepare."

"Prepare what? You need to be open and honest with each other, not repeat rehearsed speeches. Tell the man how you feel. If he's still at my house, I'm sending him over."

Jillian gulped. "Give me ten minutes."

Jillian opened the door. "Come in." She motioned to the loveseats. "I want to talk to you."

Andy sat and waited. Jillian almost expected him to react sarcastically as Paul would've, saying, "About time," but he waited silently.

"I heard your song, Andy, parts of it anyway. I was in the yard with Willie and heard you and Stan talking. I should apologize for eavesdropping, but I'm glad I heard it."

"I don't mind. It's rough, but it's your song," Andy said cautiously.

"What you said about living in fear resonated with me. That's been my mantra for the last five or six years." Jillian brushed tears from her face and threw out her hands. "I have issues, Andy. I try not to live in fear because I've been afraid so much of my life."

"What are you afraid of, Jillian?" Andy asked quietly.

"Of making people angry, of people not liking me." Jillian shook her head in exasperation. "I'm afraid of fear. Shutting down. Total incapacitation. Panic attacks. Mostly, I'm afraid of being afraid."

"Oh, honey, I am so sorry." Andy paused. "I didn't mean to scare you, but I know I did."

Jillian bit her lip. "You did. Your anger did. The rage with Leila and Chad. The slapping and hitting caused me to panic and run. I've had a hard time forgetting those feelings."

Andy leaned forward and put his elbows on his knees. "I don't know what to say. I never wanted to scare you, hurt you. Jillian, I was wrong to engage with Leila and Chad. I'm truly sorry I lost control." He straightened. "I've been seeing someone, talking it all out. Stan recommended the guy."

"I'm glad, Andy. I know your situation is crazy, and it's not surprising your emotions are haywire. I can't blame you for being mad. Your feelings are understandable." Jillian let out a deep breath. "Feelings—but not the actions, the yelling and fighting. I can't stand to be around violence because of my childhood. I won't be around yelling and fighting. I won't. You have to understand that."

Jillian closed her eyes for a moment. "I thought I'd worked all this out in therapy after my divorce. My mother yelled and slapped. Being around screaming and violent behavior sends me back in time to being a scared little girl."

She opened her eyes and looked at Andy. "Nothing I ever did was good enough. I tried hard to please her, to stay out of her way, to make her happy. I was ten when my father first saw her slap me. How he'd missed it all those other times, I don't know, but this time he came to my defense, and she slapped him. He slapped her back. They yelled and screamed and threw things all night. I hid under the table, shaking and crying, unable to move."

Andy was very still as he listened. "That, that sounds rough. What an awful thing to experience. I'm sorry, Jillian. I'm sure it was scary." Andy rubbed his chin. "And the parking lot fiasco brought all those feelings back to the surface."

Jillian nodded and took a deep breath. "My reaction to your fight was a reaction to panic caused by childhood trauma. My shutting you out was a response to trying to avoid fear. It wasn't a healthy response though. I'm not a child. I have more options than hiding or running."

Jillian sat quietly watching Andy as she thought about those options. Andy held her gaze. Perhaps he was running through them as well. Jillian's heart pounded. She could tell him to leave, to forget about a personal relationship, to forget about Belford. She could go back to her quiet little life, which once had seemed enough but now seemed very lonely. They could continue an awkward sort of friendship and hope the rough edges would smooth out over time. Or she could take a step across the chasm between them, a step over the bridge Andy's song had created.

"Your song helped me see that my fear was hurting us both. I owe you breakfast."

Andy blinked. "What?"

"Breakfast. Your song called me out, so I owe you breakfast. It's a thing Elaine and I do," Jillian explained, laughing a little. "Want to collect tomorrow?"

"Uh, sure. What exactly does this mean?" Andy asked uncertainly.

"It means I've recovered my equilibrium." Jillian shrugged. "I'm not running away, running from what we started, running from us. I need appropriate boundaries and behaviors, but I'm not running from my feelings, Andy. I'll need time, and we both have work to do, but can we start over?"

Andy breathed deeply. "Yes. My God, I wasn't expecting this at all. Yes, we can start over. Can I kiss you?"

Jillian smiled, a little sadly. "Maybe just a hug. I'm serious about moving slowly."

Andy stood up and reached out a hand to Jillian. They held each other a long time before Andy asked, "Are you really all right?"

Jillian nodded. "I will be. I know I've gone from tears to laughter in about sixty seconds flat, but I'm okay. I'm not that child cowering under the table any longer. Thanks for reminding me to not live in fear. I would've crawled out of my shell eventually, but this is better.

I've missed your hugs."

"I've missed you," Andy said, still holding her. "Thanks for telling me about your childhood. The past haunts us all, I guess. Let me know if I start scaring you again or moving too fast. And can you explain about breakfast? I think I missed something."

Chapter Twenty-One

Andy and Jillian proceeded cautiously, each a little wary of setting the other off. Gradually, they relaxed, sharing more casual conversation, deep talks, and lots of kisses and caresses. They attended church together and ate out afterwards, alone and with friends. Andy made good progress with his counselor and went running along the river every morning. To relieve even more pressure, they extended the decision deadline regarding the house at Blackwater Pond. Work was too busy to see each other much there, so they ate together each night at Jillian's home. Little by little, they were learning to trust again.

One evening as they sat in the living room sharing dating histories, Andy asked, "Have you dated much since your divorce?"

"No. Honestly, meeting eligible men isn't easy."

"Really? I'd think they'd be lined up at the door." Andy brushed her hair from her shoulders.

"Well, I don't have a sign that says, 'Here I am. Pick me,'" Jillian countered. "Not many single men my age buy houses. A few guys at church seemed interested, but I didn't encourage them."

"Did you ever try online dating?" Andy asked, moving closer and kissing her hair.

"For a very short while. It's weird, shopping for men. At first it was exciting to see who was interested, but some were in a rush to remarry and I wasn't. Others were creepy. The whole experience was depressing and confusing.

"Elaine often tried to fix me up, but I didn't usually go. I probably gave off the wrong vibes anyway. I like my life. I haven't exactly been desperate to find a man."

"And now?" Andy asked, moving so he was facing her and nuzzling her cheek.

Jillian smiled. "And now I'm enjoying spending time with you, remembering what I was missing all those years." Jillian cupped Andy's face. "My emotional state before you came into my life was more acceptance than happiness. It was good to be alone, to let go of expectations and accept my situation. I'm glad we started over. I can move forward now."

Jillian kissed Andy softly. He returned her kisses with increasing ardor until Jillian pressed her hand against his chest. He leaned his forehead against hers, then sat back.

They sat in silence awhile, content in each others arms, until Jillian reminded Andy that it was his time to share. "Start with that girl in high school. What was her name, Marie?"

Andy stretched his legs out before sharing that he'd dated quite a few women. "During college and grad school, I wasn't interested in settling down. I had a band, we played in bars, and I met a lot of women. Once I graduated and moved to Philadelphia, I met Paige and moved in with her pretty quickly. We were together for four years but, uh, discovered we wanted different things." Shortly after their split, Andy had met Leila at a party and soon had the sons he'd hoped for.

"Being a good father is a top priority. My sons mean everything to me. Even though they're away from home, in school, we're close. I talk to the younger ones daily and Beej weekly. I'm proud of their accomplishments and love seeing them interested in things that interest me.

"Dad and I never had that much in common. He was all about football, less interested in music. Our stock thing was about our only shared interest. I liked reading that Ellie played guitar."

Andy put his arm around Jillian, pulling her close. "Enough talk about the past. I'd rather forge a connection with you." Andy kissed her, but Willie started barking. "Okay, okay, I get the message, boy. I'll leave your mama alone." Andy bent down and picked up the small dog, placing him in his lap.

"So, Miss Jillian, what do your children think about our very strange inheritance?"

"Well, they were pretty shocked. I haven't said much since. Waiting until we know more."

"What are your thoughts?"

"I'm intrigued. Renovating a period house is a dream come true. It's intimidating, but I'm drawn to it. What do you think?"

"The house and the history are calling my name. I want to go to Gentry again. Will you come with me?"

"Yes, Andy, I will," Jillian said, knowing in her heart she would go anywhere with him.

After sharing a few more lingering kisses, they parted ways for the night.

I love him. It's time I relax and enjoy it. I need to tell the kids. Nine o'clock. That's not too late. We won't talk long. Wonder how they'll react to their mother having a boyfriend. Boyfriend. There should be another term— significant other, lover, partner.

"Mom? You don't normally call this late. Is everything okay?" Elizabeth asked.

"Yes, I just wanted to update you about the house."

"Hang on, I'll put you on speaker so Sarah can hear."

"Well, we're still not sure exactly what we'll do with it, but we're going forward with renovations on Blackwater Manor."

"That's fabulous, Mom. Not just that you're getting to renovate a period home, but also that you'll continue working with Andy Harrison," Elizabeth said. "You like him, don't you?"

Jillian blushed, grateful her daughters couldn't see her reddened cheeks. "I do, yes. I love him, actually. We've been seeing each other a while now."

"We knew it," Sarah said. "Good for you, Mom."

"So it's not weird for your old mom to have a boyfriend?"

"Mom, you do you," Elizabeth said. "We're happy for you, and James will be too. We need to meet this guy."

"And see the house!" Sarah added.

"How about Saturday?" Jillian asked. "Amy and Elaine have been hinting. Elizabeth, I'll need your expertise on wallpaper and furnishings and so forth."

Sarah said her goodbyes as the conversation turned to interior decorating, but Jillian didn't talk long, knowing she had other calls to make. Before she chickened out, she called her parents.

"Hello, Mother. How are you?

"Rather busy, getting ready for a planning session tomorrow. What is it?"

Jillian sighed. Her mother was difficult on her best days. Jillian no longer expected support or praise from her mother. "I wanted to share some news. As you probably remember, I inherited . . ."

"Yes, yes, spit it out, Jillian. I really am busy."

"Okay, then. We've decided to renovate the house in Belford, and I've fallen in love with Andy Harrison."

"I see. Well, I hope this relationship lasts. Maybe you won't turn into one of those divorced women who chases after every available man after all. Here's your dad."

Sometimes I don't know why I bother. At least I tried. I told her.

"Hi, sugar. What's going on?"

Jillian shared their decision about the house, then said, "Andy Harrison and I developed a friendship that turned into more, Daddy. I love him."

"Well, that's special, sugar. I'm happy for you."

"When would be a good time for you and Mother to meet him?"

"Oh, now, I couldn't say. Your mother's quite busy, and it's a long drive. You're not a spring chicken, sugar. He doesn't need my approval."

"I know that, Daddy, but I'd like for you to meet him. Get to know someone important to me." Jillian held her breath in the silence.

"We'll meet him soon enough, Jillian. Your mother, well, it's not the best time."

After a few awkward minutes, they said goodbye. While she might wish for a different relationship with her parents, this was what she had. Jillian sighed, then called James.

"Hi, son. How was the play?"

"Pretty good for a high school performance," James said. "Cheap entertainment anyway. How's your week going?"

"Good. I have some news."

"Hang on, I'll get Meg so you can tell us both."

After saying hello to Meg, Jillian started again. "I've told the girls, so it's time to share my good news with you two."

"You're in love, aren't you?" Meg said. "I can tell."

"What? In love with who?" James asked.

Jillian laughed. "Well, yes, Meg. I'm in love with Andy Harrison. We've been working closely together, and our friendship has grown into something more." Jillian could almost see the frown on James's face as he processed her news.

"So, is it serious?" James asked. "Like, do I need to talk to this guy? What are his intentions?"

"No need to worry, James," Jillian said. "We're not rushing into anything."

Jillian invited them to tour the house on Saturday, but they had plans, so they agreed to meet Andy another time. After seeing to Willie's needs, Jillian turned in and dreamed of Andy's kisses.

Chapter Twenty-Two

Jillian was excited to spend the day finding answers about Andy's past and had expected to immediately head out to his car. But when she saw Andy standing in her doorway, smiling at her almost shyly, Jillian took his hand and pulled him inside. Confessing her love had made her bold.

Andy looked at her curiously but didn't say a word as Jillian reached for his face, drawing his lips to hers. She kissed him deeply, passionately.

"Whoa, wow. What's all this about?" Andy asked when she finally stepped away.

Jillian bit her lip. "Uh, it wasn't planned." Jillian blushed. "Oh, Andy. I just miss you, miss the physical passion we shared, but . . ." Jillian leaned back in his arms, looking into his eyes. "I don't mean to tease you, Andy. Physically, I'm ready, but mentally, I'm just not." Jillian blushed again. "I love you, so much, but I shouldn't have started something I wasn't ready to finish. I'm sorry, please be patient."

"Jillian, don't be embarrassed. Your advances are very welcome. I love you and miss you, but this is your call, sweetheart." Andy cupped her face and kissed her softly. "I dream of our love making and wake up wanting you, but I won't push you. You'll know when the time is right, and I'm a patient man. We're worth waiting for."

THEY HELD HANDS much of the hour-long drive to Gentry. Andy slowed as they neared the town limits, passing a small manufacturing plant adjacent to a large body shop and fenced auto junkyard. An older home converted to an antiques store spilled its wares onto the front porch. Across the street a small grocery store with a dozen or so cars in front shared a parking lot with a bank.

Andy turned onto the main street lined by a row of brick buildings housing offices and stores. As they crossed the railroad tracks, they saw A.J. Dills Elementary school.

"School or library first?" Andy asked, slowing.

"We're here. We may as well go in."

After parking in the circle drive, they walked through a covered portico across from the requisite flag pole. Andy took a deep breath. "Okay, I think I'm ready."

They waited in the office behind parents checking their children in late to school. When they reached the desk, Andy explained about his mother and their hopes of finding pictures or information. The receptionist consulted the principal, who escorted them to the library after hearing their story.

"We've never had yearbooks due to the expense, but the archives may have photographs or newspaper clippings from the time your mother was here," Principal Wellington said.

"Thank you," Andy said. "Both my parents had ties to Gentry. I'd love to find pictures."

In the library, an older woman, not much taller than some of the students, approached them. The principal introduced them, saying, "Mrs. Stevens, meet Mr. and Mrs. Harrison," then explained the situation. "Please help them with the archives."

Jillian's mouth flew open at the introduction, but she didn't object.

Andy squeezed her hand, then spoke. "We've recently learned that my mother taught here from 1968 to 1971. I never knew her, so I'm hoping to find photographs or information about her."

"Hmm. You're welcome to go through the archives. I'll be right back."

Andy whispered, "Okay there, Mrs. Harrison?"

Jillian muttered, "Fine," as Andy followed Mrs. Stevens to a storage room.

"The archives are labeled by date. You'll need 1965 to '69 and 1970 to '74. On the bottom, naturally. Just stack the other boxes here, and carry the ones you need to any table," Mrs. Stevens instructed. "Help yourself, but use these markers in places where you remove things." She handed him a stack of laminated red cards. "Anything you want copied, lay aside."

"Let's work together, Jillian. It'll take longer, but I don't want to miss anything."

They sat down and dug into the first box, removing and scanning each artifact quickly for any reference to Andy's mother. About a quarter of the way through the box, Jillian said, "Here's the article from the *Gentry Observer* about the new teachers."

"Cool, let's copy anything we find. We'll read and sort through it all later."

They continued looking through newspaper clippings, photographs, mimeographed sheets of school news, and the occasional handwritten note. They decided against copying staff photos or 'news items' about Miss Harrison's class fieldtrips.

They set aside three more artifacts from the first box. A photograph of Ellie playing the guitar for a group of students was clipped to a handwritten article about "The Singing Teacher." A second photograph of teachers staffing a carnival booth featured Ellie laughing and tying a student's blindfold in preparation for some long-forgotten game. A mimeographed newsletter from 1968 contained a photograph of Ellie and a student pointing to a map alongside an article titled "Learning about Vietnam."

Andy stared hungrily at each photograph. "Look, Jillian. There's her guitar."

"I think you've got her smile," Jillian said, rubbing his back.

Andy grinned and nodded slowly, looking back through the photographs.

Jillian picked up the newsletter. "I had forgotten about dittos. Do you remember the smell?"

"What's a ditto?"

"These purple copies. Mimeographed pages. We called them dittos. The copies felt damp, and we all smelled the inks," Jillian explained, mimicking smelling the pages. "Don't laugh; it was a thing."

"I think we just had regular copies by the time I was in school. Let's get back to work, old woman."

Jillian poked him playfully. "You'd better behave or we'll get in trouble."

The second box yielded fewer results, but they quickly spotted a photograph of a rather listless Ellie with her third grade class standing beside a large pile of newspapers. The bottom of the Polaroid photo was marked "Winners of the Paper Drive, October 1969."

"I was three months old when this was taken. She looks sad, doesn't she?"

"Yes, sad and unhealthy. Her clothes are baggy, and her hair's different. She'd had a rough time," Jillian commented, setting aside the photograph.

As they looked at the staff photo for 1970, Jillian asked, "Was Ellie in the 1969 picture?"

They flipped back and examined it more closely. "She's not here," Andy said.

"Maybe she started school late that year. She'd have kept quiet about the baby of course, but might've been 'sick.'" Jillian added air quotes. "Or, if they knew about Andrew Rafferty's death, which I'm sure they did, maybe they gave her a little extra time."

The box yielded few mentions of Miss Harrison in the spring of 1971. In the 1972 staff photo, she appeared thinner and had crutches. "There's no cast or anything," Jillian said. "Maybe she was experiencing weakness from her polio. Can that happen?"

"I don't know. Maybe. We're getting close to her death date. I'm almost afraid to open this." Andy held up a large brown envelope.

Jillian took it from him gently and pulled out a handful of notes from students. "These are expressions of condolence. I'm surprised they're in the archives." She chose one. "'Miss Harrison, you're my favorite teacher. I miss you. Love, Hilda.'" Jillian looked at Andy as he sifted through the letters, shaking his head. She laid her hand on his arm and asked, "Do you want copies?"

He stuffed the cards back in the envelope. "Let's finish the box. These letters make it more real than the pictures. I don't understand why that is." Andy took a deep breath. He picked up a file but handed it to Jillian. "Would you look? See what's in there."

Jillian took the file and flipped through a few pages. "There's a copy of the obituary." She set it aside. "And a parent notification letter." Skimming it quickly, she added, "It explains that Miss Harrison died suddenly and says Mrs. Watson is coming out of retirement to take over the class until a new teacher can be hired." Continuing through the file, Jillian pulled out a stapled mimeographed student newspaper. "Look at this, Andy. The paper is called the 'Pickle Jar.'"

Andy snorted. "A. J. Dills's Pickle Jar." He took the paper from her. "We had a school paper in sixth or seventh grade. I wrote articles about the football team and the science fair. We typed them though. These poor kids wrote everything by hand. Here's a fall festival article. And," Andy's voice slowed, "an article about my mother. 'Goodbye, Miss Harrison' by Nancy Parks."

"Nancy Parks? She's the city librarian. Now Mrs. Wilson. Ellie taught her. What does it say?"

"Miss Ellen Harrison passed away suddenly. She taught at A. J. Dills for three years. We will all miss her very much. She loved to sing and play guitar. She taught us to love books and to be nice to each other. She was very pretty. Miss Harrison made me want to be a teacher."

"Sweet. Let's add that to the copy pile and go see her. Where's Mrs. Stevens?"

"Right behind you," the librarian said as Jillian jumped. "Are you finished?"

"Yes, thanks. We'd like to copy these. Andy, what did you decide about the cards and letters?"

"Cards and letters?" Mrs. Stevens asked.

"Yes, these are condolence cards and letters from students about Andy's mother."

"Oh, please take those with you. They should've been given to family long ago."

Once they had their copies, Andy restacked the boxes while Jillian got directions to a nearby food counter. They wanted to fortify themselves before their next trip down memory lane.

Chapter Twenty-Three

The drugstore was surprisingly large for a small town but didn't appear to have changed since the 1940s. On the right side of the store stood a food-service area with red vinyl bar stools in front of a shiny aluminum counter top. The menu board listed burgers and grilled cheese sandwiches, with a meatloaf plate as the special of the day.

"I'll have the meatloaf plate," Andy said. "What would you like?"

"Grilled cheese, fries, and a coke. That's my standard order in diners, drugstores, and any other unfamiliar restaurant."

"Really? I almost always get the special," Andy said. "I guess it's hard to mess up a grilled cheese. Not a lot of variation from place to place."

"Oh, I was surprised the first time I ordered one in Tennessee. I hadn't expected lettuce and tomato."

"Huh, that's different." They moved to a booth in the back corner.

"Be honest now, Andy. Have you ever eaten in a drugstore?"

Andy grinned. "I don't think so. I have, however, eaten at the Wawa."

Now it was Jillian's turn to laugh. "The what?"

"The Wawa. You heard me right. There's a chain of Wawa stores throughout Pennsylvania and other Northeastern states. It's the sound a goose makes: wawa. They sell sandwiches and stuff." Andy looked around. "Weird. If my parents hadn't died, I might've grown up in Gentry, bringing girls here on dates."

"It is strange to think how different our lives would have been in different circumstances."

Andy rubbed his chin. "Would I have gone to college? Seen the world? Met Leila and had the boys? Would I even be me?"

Jillian reached out and took Andy's hand. "Did you ever read *Grapes of Wrath*?"

"By Steinbeck? Yeah." Andy looked at Jillian curiously.

"I read it in high school at a time I was feeling quite unsure about my future. I remember a line the mother said about the possibility of a thousand lives we might live, but in the end, it comes down to just the one we do. That stuck with me. Our choices, coupled with things beyond our control, lead us toward the life, through the life, I guess, that we're meant to live.

"If your parents had lived, Andy, you would've had a different life, maybe one without boarding school and world travel, but you'd still be you. Your essence wouldn't change."

"You're a formidable combination, Jillian Peters. Sexy and smart. I appreciate your words of wisdom. I'm in a strange place, sweetheart, but somehow it's better with you beside me." Andy reached out and squeezed Jillian's shoulder.

Their food arrived. Jillian smiled her thanks, and Andy's mood lightened as they enjoyed their meal and the hand-dipped chocolate shake they shared.

"Ready to face another librarian?" Andy asked, leaving a generous tip on the table.

"Yep. Let's go meet Mrs. Nancy Wilson and see what she can tell us about Ellen Harrison."

~~~

SINCE THE LIBRARY WAS WITHIN WALKING DISTANCE of the drugstore, they strolled down the street looking in shop windows as they passed. No one was at the front desk, so they looked through the stacks. "Hello?" Jillian called out as the back door opened.

"Oh my goodness, you startled me," a gray-haired woman exclaimed. "I nearly dropped my lunch!"

"I'm so sorry," Jillian said. "We were surprised no one was around when we came in."

"That's all right. I'm never gone but a minute, so I leave the door open. I'm the librarian, Nancy Wilson. May I help you?"

"I'm Jillian Peters, and this is Andy Harrison. We spoke on the phone several weeks ago."

"Yes, I remember." Mrs. Wilson looked at Andy. Her hand flew to her mouth. "My goodness."

"Is everything all right?" Andy asked.

"Yes, yes. Please sit down. It's just that when I heard your name then, I never expected . . ." Mrs. Wilson paused, closing her eyes. "I'm babbling. It's nice to meet you. How can I help?"

Jillian said, "We visited the school this morning, Mrs. Wilson, and found several pictures of Ellen Harrison. I believe she was your teacher? Perhaps you hadn't realized Andy is her son."

"So I see," Mrs. Wilson said, nodding. "You bear a remarkable likeness to Miss Harrison. Mrs. Wilson looked at Jillian. "After our phone call, I pulled out my box of school memorabilia. I kept copies of all those little newsletters we wrote. Several pictured Miss Harrison, probably the same ones you saw earlier." She looked at Andy. "Her hair and eyes were just the color of yours. We never knew though. I still don't understand. Miss Harrison died almost fifty years ago. How is it possible? She . . ."

Mrs. Wilson paused, seeming to put things together. Jillian decided to be blunt. "Andrew Rafferty was Andy's father. When Ellen heard about his death, she went into labor prematurely. Andy was born in July 1969 and adopted by Ellie's brother and his wife. We've been piecing together the story since Andy's dad, his adoptive father, died last December."

"Can you, can you tell me something about her?" Andy broke in. "What she was like, what kind of person she was, anything?"

Jillian reached for Andy's hand as Mrs. Wilson smiled at him and leaned back in her chair.

"She was the best teacher I ever had, and I mean that. Just a breath of fresh air, full of new ideas, a new way of teaching, a new way of thinking. She made us all feel so special, full of hope and possibility. Why, she'd bring that guitar to class and sing for us, a lovely clear high voice, like those folk singers." Mrs. Wilson smiled. "Before the year was out, most of us girls were growing our hair long and wanting to wear miniskirts or what my Daddy called hippie clothes, those loose flowing smock tops and caftans, like Miss Harrison had started wearing.

"We knew she had a boyfriend. I felt quite special that my sister was friends with her boyfriend's brother." Mrs. Wilson laughed. "We'd see them at the football games and around town some. It seems silly now, but I felt like I knew the queen or something. She'd started teaching at A. J. Dills the year before, so I'd looked forward to being in her class for a whole year. When Andrew went off to war, it seemed very tragic but almost romantic somehow. I realize now it wasn't."

Mrs. Wilson jumped up suddenly. "I'm sorry for your loss. Will you excuse me, please? I need to make a phone call." She disappeared into an office, shutting the door behind her.

"What on earth?" Jillian looked at the office door.

"Maybe she's alerting the town gossips."

"Maybe. She—" Jillian broke off as Mrs. Wilson returned.

"I called the Raffertys. Randy Keith always was sweet on my sister Judy's best friend, so I remember him more than Andrew. The three of them, Judy, Kelly, and Randy Keith, were classmates. Randy Keith had seizures that caused some learning problems, so he was a couple years behind Andrew. Randy Keith and Kelly married, but she passed quite young. He didn't remarry, lives with his mama now. Judy still carries them food over to Kentucky once a week."

Andy and Jillian exchanged confused looks.

"I'm sorry. I'm babbling again. You don't need to hear all that." Mrs. Wilson took a deep breath. "I asked Randy Keith if they'd like to meet you. He does but wanted to check with Beth Ann."

"That'll be him now," Mrs. Wilson said as the phone rang.

Jillian rubbed Andy's back as Mrs. Wilson went to answer the phone. "Are you okay? You're looking a little shell-shocked."

"Yeah, I guess. I'm freaking out a little. Do you think she means today? Now?"

Mrs. Wilson came back with a slip of paper in her hands. "This is Miss Beth Ann's number and address. She says you can come today if you want. She'd like to meet you. Maple Branch is not but a thirty minute drive from here. If you care to go, I'll tell her to expect you."

Andy looked at Jillian, shrugged his shoulders, and turned to Mrs. Wilson. "Yes, please let her know we're coming. Thank you for your help."

To Jillian's surprise, Mrs. Wilson turned red and looked at the floor. "I have a confession to make. The first time you called and left your number, I didn't pass it along. I thought maybe you weren't who you claimed to be. I couldn't imagine what you wanted with the Raffertys but thought they'd be better off not contacting you. I'm sorry."

Jillian started to respond, but Andy got there first. "Don't apologize, Mrs. Wilson. It's understandable wanting to protect friends from strangers."

"I'm still sorry. I shouldn't have made that decision for them." Mrs. Wilson straightened. "I truly enjoyed having your mama as a teacher. She was a remarkable young woman. God moves in mysterious ways. You all best get on now. Drive carefully." She shooed them out the door.

Chapter Twenty-Four

"Are you ready for this?" Jillian asked as Andy pulled up directions on his phone.

Andy nodded. "I think so, yeah. Pretty wild, isn't it? I'm off to meet my grandmother and uncle for the first time."

Reception was a little spotty as they traveled the twisty roads in a remote area of Appalachia, but they reached the town limits in about thirty minutes. "Maple Branch isn't much of a town," Andy said as they passed a convenience store, a resale shop, a hardware store, and a church. "There's not even a school."

Soon, they turned into the common driveway of three yellow-brick duplexes from the 1960s that Jillian felt sure were rent-subsidized housing. The Raffertys lived in the unit on the far left.

Exiting the car, Andy held out his hand to Jillian. "Let's go meet the family." They walked toward the front porch, where a wiry older man wearing faded work pants and a plaid shirt stood to meet them. He grinned broadly. "Come on in here, young fella. I'm Randy Keith. Proud to meet you." After shaking Andy's hand, he said, "Aw, hell," and pulled Andy in for a hug. He turned to Jillian and gave a little bow. "Ma'am."

He opened the screen door. "We'll set in the kitchen. Ma's pulled out some pictures for you to look at. Come thisaway."

Jillian and Andy followed Randy Keith through a small living area to a kitchen table spread with framed pictures and photo albums. "This here's your grandma." Randy Keith gestured. Beth Ann Rafferty used a cane to stand. A little plumper than her son, she wore a faded house dress.

"Let me look at you, Andy." Tears rolled down her cheeks. "I didn't know what to think when Nancy called. I wished I'd a known I had a grandson all these years."

Andy moved to Beth Ann and took her hand. "I'm glad to meet you. We've both missed out on a lot. This is my friend Jillian. Thanks for letting us come see you today. I'd like to hear about my parents. I believe you knew my mother as well as anyone, and you obviously knew my father."

"Randy Keith, hand me that red album. Let's start there." Beth Ann opened the album with photographs of her infant sons and their growing years. "My boys was twins, but different as could be," Beth Ann confided. "Andrew took things apart and Randy Keith put them together, so it all worked out pretty good. Andrew was always a singin' and Randy Keith banging on something." Beth Ann pointed to a picture of Andrew holding a new guitar and Randy Keith playing a drum set.

"This was the first Christmas after Gene and I married. He bought them things and then got mad at the noise!" She laughed. "I don't know what he thought was going to happen. They wasn't going to just look at them."

"Do you know how my parents met?" Andy asked.

"Why, yes. Your mama moved up to Gentry to teach at the school. She was driving some ol' rattletrap car that barely made it. Andrew worked on it down at the garage. He came home that night talking about how this pretty girl had sang for him while he fixed her car. He'd seen her guitar laying atop of everything she owned and asked about it, you see. They started keeping company right away.

"That very night, Andrew said she was the girl for him. No matter that she was a bit older and a college girl. They found each other and that was that."

Beth Ann turned a page and pointed to pictures of Andy's parents together—playing music, floating down the river on inner tubes, and dressed up for a school dance. "Look-a-here. This is right before he went over there." Andy looked at his father, dressed in civilian clothes, but with the bootcamp haircut, arm around his mother. "Everybody knew they'd get married. They brought each other a lot of joy. Soulmates, like," Beth Ann said. "Andrew joined up, then spent eight weeks in Louisiana for basic training. Where was it, Randy Keith?"

"Fort Polk." Randy Keith leaned against the counter.

"That's right. We drove down for graduation. Ellie went with us. It was the first time we'd been there. My goodness, it was hot. My boy was handsome and right proud to be a soldier. He studied helicopters next."

"Was he a pilot?" Andy asked.

"Maintenance. He was at Fort Eustis, in Virginia, to learn that. He come home for Christmas. We had a good time. Then he had to go." Randy Keith turned and walked out to the front porch.

Jillian's eyes followed him. She turned to Andy with concern and confusion. Andy shrugged.

Beth Ann sighed. "Randy Keith always felt bad he couldn't serve because of the seizures. He just fell in on himself when his brother died. We both did. He's smart, not a machine he can't fix, but Andrew was something special. Everybody knew it. His passing hurt us bad."

She returned to the photo album. "This is your daddy in his uniform. After he left for Vietnam, Ellie didn't come round for awhile. We had us a bad winter, and she kept getting sick." Beth Ann shook her head. "I thought she was missing my boy, had no idea she was expecting. She visited some in the spring. We'd share news of Andrew, best we could. Thinking back, maybe I should've known. She'd always been real thin. We teased her about filling out some."

Beth Ann looked at Jillian. "Women carry different, you know. I feel right ignorant to have missed it. Maybe we don't see what we're not looking for."

"My pregnancies were obvious by five months, but I had a cousin who barely showed at seven." Jillian patted her hand. "Andy was a preemie, so Ellen wouldn't have been that far along in the spring."

Beth Ann laid a wrinkly hand on her bosom. "Maybe so. I surely wish she'd a told us. It was Easter thereabouts when she told us she was going to spend the summer back at that home where she'd grown up. Said since Andrew wasn't here, she might as well earn a little extra money. I wanted her to stay in town and rest. She was so wore out all the time."

Beth Ann asked Andy for the smaller white photo album. It contained a few photographs Andrew had mailed from Vietnam and some handwritten notes about his service. One showed Andrew smiling in front of a helicopter. It was marked Chu Lai Air Base in spidery handwriting. A hand-drawn map showed the Bien Hoa Air Base some twenty miles north of Saigon. "One of Andrew's friends from home, George, was over there too," she explained. "He gave me those—after.

"He came to see me and talked about it a little. Andrew wouldn't never say much. He liked the helicopters. Went where they went. I don't know what happened. It don't matter much. Doesn't change anything. The helicopter was shot down, and he—" Her voice broke. "My boy died."

Beth Ann looked at Andy. "Me and Randy Keith made this book. I can't remember all the names without looking at it, but it seemed important not to forget. Andrew was full of life. So in love." She gripped his hand. "Why, him dyin' just didn't seem right, didn't seem possible.

"It was hard on your mama too. Law, she was changed when she came back after that summer. Drained somehow." Beth Ann wiped away a tear. "I wish I'd a known," she said again. "Ellie came to eat with us once or twice a month after Andrew passed. Tried to help each other. She was wrung out and had a lot of bad headaches. Grieving bad. We all was.

"I asked her to stay with us over Christmas that year, but she went with her brother. He was real nice. Had his wife and baby in the car when they came to get her."

"Her brother Ben?" Andy asked. "That's who raised me."

"Oh my." A tear rolled down Beth Ann's cheek. "I had no idea that little baby was Ellie and Andrew's. I could've helped her. Would have," she said as the tears fell.

"I guess it weren't up to me though. That school wouldn't have allowed it anyway. Them not being married." Beth Ann spoke with an acceptance grounded in a deep faith. "I saw you twice then. You was sleeping both times. That day at Christmas and then Ellie's funeral." Beth Ann blew her nose. "I'm sorry I didn't know, but I guess things happened the way they was supposed to."

Andy took her hand. "I think so. Can you tell me anything about my mother's death?"

Beth Ann patted Andy's hand. "Taking care of Ellie helped me get through missing Andrew so bad. Everbody needs some kind of work. Poor thing was sick a lot after she come back from Belford. She couldn't have taken care of a baby, but I'm sure she'd a wanted to." Beth Ann stared across the room for a minute. "Randy Keith and I ran her to the doctor more than once.

"Come summer, Ellie thought she was better, but she wasn't. Her legs was weak, but she were determined to keep going. We helped her set up her classroom that next fall. She fainted at the school once, but she rallied a little bit and was excited about knowing her students." Beth Ann reached for Andy's hand again.

"The principal called me when she didn't show up that Monday. Randy Keith found her. Everybody reckoned it was the polio come back. The doctor said maybe a brain bleed."

As Beth Ann finished her sad story, Jillian rose to give them some time alone. "I'm going to step outside." She saw Andy and Beth Ann hugging, comforting each other.

"Mind if I join you?" Jillian asked as she opened the screen door.

Randy Keith motioned to a chair. "Always nice to have company. I set out here a good bit."

They talked about the weather and circumstances of the visit. "Beth Ann said Mr. Rafferty bought you a drum set for Christmas one year. Do you still play?"

"Nah." Randy Keith laughed. "I never did much. Just banged around, acting like drummers on the TV. Andrew had more patience than me. He got purty good on that guitar. I made a lot of noise."

"And Mr. Rafferty didn't like noise?"

"That's for dang sure. Ol' Gene was okay but couldn't abide all the noise. He made a bit of noise about the noise."

Randy Keith snorted, then shook his head. "He was good to Ma. That's what matters."

"Sounds like he had a bit of a temper. What did Gene think about Andrew and Ellie?"

"Aw, his bark was worse 'en his bite," Randy Keith said. "Tell the truth, he wasn't crazy about Ellie. Ol' Gene didn't get to know her too good. He disappeared ever time she was here. Then he'd gripe about 'that college girl giving Andrew ideas above his raising.'"

Jillian wasn't surprised by Gene's attitude toward college, having heard the same sentiment growing up. Many people felt that what was good enough for them should be good enough for their children. Still, she wondered if Gene's objection had been about Ellie or education in general. "What did he mean by that, Randy Keith?"

"Oh now, Ellie thought Andrew orta go off to college. Said he could maybe be an engineer or somewhat. Gene didn't like that much. Said if Andrew was a man, he'd join up. Leastways keep working at the garage and earn his keep."

Jillian started to say how sorry she was, but Randy Keith continued. "We was gonna join up together, but I didn't make it. The Army wouldn't take me because of the epilepsy. I'd outgrown them seizures, but just Andrew got in."

Randy Keith shrugged. "Lotta water under that bridge."

They talked about his wife and his work, then Randy Keith said, "Reckon we orta go inside?"

Although invited to stay for supper, Andy and Jillian declined since they had to work the next day. Andy hugged his grandmother and uncle and promised he'd keep in touch. He handed Beth Ann a photograph from his wallet. "These are my boys, your great-grandsons. Now that I've found you, I'll send a larger photograph and arrange a visit this summer."

"Oh, Law, I'd love that," Beth Ann said. "I never expected a grandson, much less great-grandsons." She tucked the small photograph in the corner of a framed photograph of Andrew on the mantle. She hugged Andy and Jillian again and waved them out the door.

Andy was quiet as they began their journey home. "We know almost everything now. When mom gets home, I'll ask her about their role. I'd like to know why they kept quiet all these years. It wasn't fair to deprive me of a grandparent."

Jillian took Andy's hand. "I guess they had their reasons, misguided as they may have been."

"Did you know Randy Keith's wife died from diabetes?" she asked a few minutes later. "Kelly was a few weeks pregnant and passed out. He didn't find her until it was too late. She was twenty-six."

"Damn, that's rough. EMTs couldn't save her?" Andy asked.

"No such thing back then, Andy. Sometimes we forget how rapidly things change and how different things are in different parts of the country. Newton didn't get 911 service until the mid-80s, so Gentry and Belford probably didn't have it until a decade or so later. Even if they had, some rural areas don't have hospitals, so an emergency room could've been hours away.

"Randy Keith's father-in-law owned the garage where he and Andrew worked. Randy and Kelly lived in a little apartment over it. Randy Keith kept living there until he and Beth Ann moved to Kentucky about eight years ago, after Gene Rafferty died and Randy Keith retired. He says he keeps his hand in, whatever that means."

Andy looked at Jillian. "People really open up and talk to you. I know I did. Did you happen to find out what happened to their biological father?"

"No, I didn't think to ask."

Andy sighed. "I'll ask Beth Ann another time. We need to finalize things about the house, run the numbers, and see if our plans are fiscally feasible in this market. That'll be the final determinant, I suppose, but right now I'm leaning toward moving forward regardless. Everything started there, and I feel bound to the house, like we're the ones chosen to fix it up." Andy rubbed his neck. "Chosen by the house, not just Dad. Is that crazy?"

"No. As everyone keeps telling us in one way or another, things happen for a reason." Jillian turned toward Andy. "I don't want to market it as a private home, do you?"

"No. The Hixons believed in giving back. I'd like to do that too."

The ride back to Newton was quiet, with both lost in thought. Occasionally, one would comment about the passing scenery or share an idle thought, but mostly they rode in companionable silence.

Andy walked Jillian to her door but didn't come in. They stood holding each other close, without the fervor of the morning. Andy's need to be held and comforted soothed Jillian as well, so neither broke the embrace until a sharp yip reminded them that Willie wanted to be fed.

"Go take care of Willie." Andy kissed her softly. "I'm glad we were together today."

Chapter Twenty-Five

On Saturday morning, Andy stopped by with lattes. He and Jillian were eager to finally give their friends and Jillian's daughters a tour of Blackwater Manor. "Oh, Andy, thanks for the coffee, but there's been a change of plans. Larry has a migraine, and Stan's trying to finish a special sculpture."

"Would you rather have a girls-only day?"

"No, Elizabeth and Sarah are looking forward to meeting their mom's boyfriend in addition to seeing the house. The girls will join us for lunch." Jillian took his hand. "But you'll have to wait to meet James and Meg."

Andy grinned. "I'm looking forward to it, but let's eat at the Mexican restaurant. Last week's rain probably left the grounds too muddy for a picnic."

Jillian nodded. "True, and it may rain again today. Amy wants to browse in the junk stores this morning, so if you'd rather drive separately, I completely understand. Elaine will be here soon."

"Hmm. Have fun shopping this morning. I'll see you at lunch," Andy said with a kiss.

Jillian loved browsing in antique and junk stores. She never bought anything big or expensive but was drawn to small decorative pieces, old books, and items she could repurpose. Her favorite find had been a doll trunk that now held Willie's toys. Today, Elaine and Jillian were looking at old jewelry, while Amy roamed the store searching for furniture to refinish.

"Will this fit in your car?" Amy asked.

Elaine looked at the small shelving unit. "Yeah, but it's a plain Jane, isn't it?"

"It is now," Amy said, "but with a little paint and decoupage, it'll be lovely."

Amy added a corner table and a small mirror to her purchases, but neither Elaine nor Jillian found anything they had to have. *Wonder what style Andy likes. Hope it's comfortably cluttered.*

When Elaine parked her SUV at the Mexican restaurant a bit later, Andy was leaning casually against the back of his truck, hands in pockets.

Jillian hurried to greet him with a kiss. "I see the girls' car. Are you ready to meet them?"

"Already have," Andy said. "They're waiting inside. Two peas in a pod, like you said." He gave Jillian another kiss. "I thought I'd wait out here in case they were uncomfortable with just me."

"That was thoughtful," Jillian said as she took his hand and walked inside.

Jillian's daughters rushed to hug her and her friends as they entered the restaurant. "Doing any dancing?" Amy asked as she hugged the girls.

"Only the occasional victory dance when I win an argument," Sarah joked.

"Well, you both look great, so you're obviously getting exercise somewhere," Elaine said.

"Sarah runs, I do yoga," Elizabeth replied as they took their seats.

"We were a little early, so we grabbed this big table," Sarah said as a waiter took their orders and delivered chips and salsa.

"Mom mentioned you have three sons, Andy. I hope we'll get a chance to meet them."

"Oh, I'm sure we can arrange that, Elizabeth," Andy said, putting his arm around Jillian. "My boys will be in town this summer. We'll set something up then."

"I'm eager to see this house," Sarah said. "It's so bizarre to think about inheriting half a house. I mean, who does that?"

"We do," Andy and Jillian said together, then laughed.

"Did your mom mention she thought it was haunted?" Andy teased, then shared the story of Barb's search for the paranormal.

The waiter appeared. "Cheese enchiladas?" Sarah, Elizabeth, and Jillian raised their hands.

Elizabeth added salsa to her enchilada. "So, this house sounds amazing. Mom, I'm so glad you're finally getting to do a historic restoration."

Elaine added half of the sizzling fajita vegetables to her plate and passed the tray to Amy.

"I've never been one for touring old houses, myself," Amy said. "The history's interesting, but something about seeing how rich people lived bores me to tears. I hope you all come up with something more interesting."

"It's an exciting venture." Andy cut into his chili relleno and shared some of their ideas. "We're still not sure what we'll do, but we'll get there."

Their meal continued and discussion turned to their trip to Gentry and discovery of Andy's relatives. "Discovering a grandmother and uncle was pretty crazy," Andy said. "Who does that?"

"You do." Sarah laughed.

∞

WHEN ALL THREE CARS ARRIVED at the house, Sarah was the first to jump out of the car and stand in amazement. "Oh my gosh, you guys! This place is insane."

Elizabeth followed, standing quietly and taking it all in. "The pictures don't do this place justice. It needs work but has amazing potential."

"Are you kidding? It's gorgeous. And huge," Sarah rambled. "One family lived here? That's insane. Wait, ten kids? Now that's insane. I can't wait to explore."

Andy cautioned everyone about the steps and explained their plans for the outside, then opened the door. Elaine and Amy wandered off, admiring the woodwork. Sarah was more of a big-picture girl, so Andy walked her through the rooms quickly while Elizabeth and Jillian made notes and discussed furnishings.

"You'll need window coverings to prevent sun damage on all this wood," Elizabeth said. "I'll send you some information. I've found a source for the black-and-white marble floor tiles for the entry hall. That architectural salvage company I called in Chattanooga told me about them last week when I called about the door with the fan light. The entry is going to be spectacular.

"I'm thinking a two-tier Chippendale chandelier above the stairs, and I found a Virginia creeper pattern wallpaper. It's period appropriate and will tie together some of your colors. We'll look for a demilune console and a large mirror for the foyer. I'm waiting until you guys firm up your plans to do much more."

"I know, nothing we've discussed seems quite right, but I like your ideas for the foyer."

"Well, I like the wedding venue idea. I'll send you some pics of things Mary Kate saw in Savannah last month."

"If you guys go to Savannah, I'm coming too," Sarah said, entering the room. "This place is neat, Mom. Andy told me all about the history. We're going to the pond now."

"Don't let her run you ragged, Andy. Sarah's a ball of energy," Jillian said.

"It's good for me to run off all those tortilla chips I ate." Andy touched her arm. "We'll see you in a bit."

Elizabeth watched Andy and her sister leave the house. "I like him, Mom, but Liam said unresolved childhood trauma might result in abandonment issues. So please, be careful."

"Oh, Elizabeth, I appreciate your concern, but Liam's never met Andy. Despite Liam's psychiatric knowledge, I think it's unlikely in Andy's case. He was very young when his parents died."

"You're probably right, Mom. We're really happy for you and

glad Andy's so good to you. I'm not being negative about Dad, but you guys had issues. This seems better."

"Let's look at the dining room," Jillian said, patting Elizabeth's shoulder.

"Okay, then," Elizabeth said, following Jillian.

Jillian and Elizabeth discussed paint colors, then studied the hand-plastered border in the dining room. It had a botanical motif with swirls and roses. "The rinceau is quite well done, so you'll need someone highly trained to repair that damage in the corner near the window. If you go with the deep rose walls, I'd paint the rinceau either white or gold."

Amy and Elaine met them in the dining room. "We're going to need to leave soon," Elaine said. "I shouldn't have had that second glass of tea."

"Another storm's a-brewing," Andy said as he and Sarah came inside.

Everyone agreed it was time to go, so they parted ways, thinking of the work to come.

Chapter Twenty-Six

The following Friday, Andy brought Jillian some coffee and took a seat in her office. "Morning, beautiful. Sleep well?"

"Oh, Andy. I've hardly seen you this week. What's on your calendar today?

"I'm picking up Mom and Aunt Lois from the airport. Want to tag along? We can grab an early supper somewhere and hear all about their trip."

"Won't they be exhausted?"

"Nah. I'm sure they're ready to be home, but they'll be hungry, and I know Lois won't pass up a free meal."

"Are you going to insist Carol spill the beans?"

"No, I told her I knew I was adopted. I didn't get into it but said I'd have some questions when she was ready to explain. I kept my cool. I'm kind of proud of myself."

"You should be, Andy. Did she say anything?" Jillian asked.

"She started crying, then said we'd talk later. I want to talk to her, but I'm learning to not force things. Pick you up at three?" Andy leaned over the desk and kissed her cheek. "See you later, Miss Jillian."

Jillian watched Andy leave. He had changed so much in five months. He was no longer fighting the world. It was a good change.

As Andy parked at the airport, Jillian asked how much Carol knew about their relationship. "I haven't said anything yet. We had other things to talk about." Andy turned to her. "I'm taking the plunge, taking charge of Harrison's Realty. I want to be with you, and I think the time is right."

"You're leaving your job? Wow." *He's serious.*

"Come here, woman." Andy gave her a big hug, then took her face in his hands. "I love you, Jillian Peters, and I intend to say that every day for the rest of my life." With that, he kissed her so soundly that his words barely registered.

Andy and Jillian walked to the baggage claim to wait on his mother and aunt. *Does Andy realize what he said? Did he mean, really mean, forever? I love him, but . . . Wait. Andy isn't Paul, and I've changed. Marriage with Andy would be different.*

Jillian hugged Carol and greeted Lois as Andy gathered their luggage. They stopped at a buffet across the highway. Once their plates were filled and they'd found a table, Jillian asked if they'd had a good trip.

"Oh, honey, the best. We had a beautiful room and saw wonderful things. My favorite was the glaciers." Lois pulled out her phone. "See these natural ice carvings, so blue and beautiful." Then she scrolled through pictures of a logging demonstration, animals, their stateroom, and on and on, talking all the while.

Andy exchanged a grin with his mother. "It seems like you enjoyed the trip, Lois."

"Oh, I did."

Before Lois could get revved back up, Andy asked Carol what her favorite part had been.

Lois quirked an eyebrow. "I was monopolizing the conversation again. I'm sorry."

Carol smiled. "I'm always grateful for your company, Lois. My favorite part was just soaking in the scenery. Alaska is so beautiful. The sky was wonderfully blue much of the time, and we saw lots of animals. Eagles everywhere. Whales right from our stateroom balcony! Dall sheep and mountain goats on the cliffs. Oh, and puffins! All the migratory birds were returning. It was a wonderful trip."

Carol turned to Andy and Jillian. "Lois and I are thinking of moving in together, finding a smaller one-level place better suited to our needs. After I catch my breath, I'll stay at Lois's for several weeks, just to make sure we won't fight over whose turn it is to do the dishes."

Andy nodded. "Hmm. That could be a good arrangement. It's smart to make a trial run."

After taking Lois home, Andy turned to Jillian. "Where to, pretty lady?"

Carol answered for her. "Come home with us, Jillian. We have things to discuss. Honestly, I was never quite comfortable with Ben's strange bequest, so I'm relieved to see you two are still speaking."

After settling in the living room with some decaf, Carol said, "I imagine you've been a bit angry, Andy, both about what you've learned and with me for leaving you alone on this quest."

Andy set his cup down. "Yeah, truthfully, I was fairly furious at you and Dad both for leaving me in the dark. I want to believe there was some reason for that, but I can't imagine what it is."

"We were trying to protect you."

"Protect me from what?" Jillian put her hand on Andy's arm as his voice rose. "Did you imagine it would be easier to discover I was adopted at forty-nine than at five or ten? You should have told me!"

"Oh, Andy, we love you so much. We intended to be open, but Ellie died, and being orphaned, that was something Dad knew." Carol's eyes flooded with tears. "I told Ben we should tell you. It was playing with fire not to, but he didn't want you to feel orphaned. You see, Dad grew up feeling alone. He'd long given up on Ellie, thinking her adopted out, not knowing her new name or anything. Dad was grateful for a home with his uncle, but he always felt that little nugget of pain buried deep inside.

"As time went on, well, there just never seemed like a good time to talk about it. You were our son, always. We didn't want you to feel the pain of being alone. When Dad got sick, I said we should come clean, but he believed some journeys must be faced in their own time. I think Dad knew you'd need time to accept everything and someone to keep you calm and guide you."

Andy rubbed his face and smiled ruefully at Jillian. "Jillian's done that, or tried to, walking beside me the whole time." Andy looked at

Carol. "Do you think the master manipulator planned for us to fall in love along the way?"

"Your dad was a big believer in love, but he didn't manipulate you, Andy. He orchestrated the first step—bequeathing you both the home. Everything else resulted from your choices. You could've walked away. No one forced either of you to do anything." Carol sat back and sipped her coffee.

It's true. One or both of us could've walked away at any time.

Such was the genius of Ben's will. He'd left the decision up to them, but the opportunity had come from Ben. Their choices—to stay with the familiar and comfortable, sitting on the sideline, or get in the game. Choosing to take a chance, a step into the unknown, had made all the difference.

Andy blew out a breath. "I guess I can accept that, Mom. It's been a surreal experience, but somehow, I know I'm meant to move forward with the Belford house, even if we don't know exactly how." Andy and Jillian filled Carol in on all the possibilities for the house.

"My goodness." Carol paused. "All your ideas are fabulous. Ben would be pleased with any of them. I hope you'll forgive our secretiveness."

Andy ignored that. "We know what happened, but I'd still like to hear how you and Dad found Ellie."

"Well, we happened to see an announcement in the paper, an invitation to a party at Blackwater Manor. Dad had fond memories of his stay there, so we went. He showed me all his favorite spots in both the house and grounds. We were upstairs and overheard someone laugh and say, 'Baby Girl! It's so good to have you home!'

Your dad said he wanted me to meet someone special, meaning Francine, the owner's daughter. When we got downstairs though, this young woman with long blonde hair and emerald green eyes was standing there with a tray of drinks.

"When he saw her, Ben grabbed his chest and started sobbing. The woman set the tray down and put her arm around him. She didn't know him. She was so kind, led him to a chair and knelt beside him. Ben said she looked just like their mother and realized she had to be his baby sister, and sure enough, it was Ellen.

"Francine Hixon saw them and started praising God and hugging both of them. I don't think there was a dry eye in the house."

Carol sipped her coffee. "We kept in touch. Ellie was nineteen and had finished her first year at Tennessee Tech. Ben wanted her to come home with us, but Ellie had her own mind. She lived in the dorm over in Cookeville, worked at a daycare, and attended classes. We started eating together once or twice a month. She'd visit on major holidays but balked a little at your dad's big brother protectiveness. While glad to have family, she'd been independent a long time and wasn't going to be bossed."

"Gee, that sounds familiar." Andy laughed as Jillian elbowed him.

Carol smiled. "Nothing wrong with a little independence. Anyway, after Ellie graduated, Ben wanted to help her move to Gentry, but Ellie said she'd manage the same way she'd managed her move to Cookeville. She kept the relationship with Andrew secret for quite a while. She probably didn't want to admit that Ben had been right about her car being untrustworthy. She may have also worried about your dad interfering with her new boyfriend. She stayed with us a few days at Christmas that first year and got a phone call each night. Long distance," Carol emphasized. "That was a big deal back then."

"We met Andrew only once. Ellie eventually introduced us that summer. I warned Ben not say anything negative, but I needn't have worried. They were clearly in love, and Andrew was a sweet young man. We both liked him. He enlisted a few months later. I think you know the rest," Carol finished, wiping away a tear.

Andy nodded. "Mostly, but I'm still a little unclear how I came to live with you and Dad."

Carol sighed. "Ellie, Ben, and I cried a lot of tears and discussed many options." Carol looked at her son with concern. "Please understand that times were different, Andy. Ellie would've lost her teaching position if anyone had known she was pregnant and unmarried. We didn't know. I'm not sure anyone did." Carol took another tissue.

"She and Andrew intended to get married when he came home and start over in a different city, but they never had that chance. On the day you were born, Francine Hixon called and said Ellie was in labor. Sam was visiting that day, so he and Dad drove over to Belford while I ran around town gathering supplies. You were such a tiny thing, and Ellie was in bad shape. Dr. Humphrey had quit making house calls by that time, of course, but made an exception and tended you both.

"Ellie's concussion caused a lot of headaches and confusion. Her emotional recovery was a lot slower than her physical one. She begged us to take care of you. She needed and wanted to get back to work. Without a husband, it was her best option. We agreed to a sort of open adoption. We'd raise you as our own, but Ellie could see you whenever she wanted."

Carol hesitated, putting her hand to her mouth. "We didn't see a lot of her. Leaving you caused her great pain each time she visited, and of course, her health was deteriorating more than we knew. Dad and I agreed we'd tell you about her when you were older, but the time never seemed right. When she died, your dad felt orphaned all over again. I am so sorry for burdening you with all this now."

"Mom, it's okay." Andy moved to Carol's side, placing an arm around her. "I've struggled my whole life with that 'things happen for a reason' platitude. Lately though, I've come to appreciate the truth in it, or I've let go of trying to be the reason things happen. I don't know." Andy broke off.

"You've quit fighting, Andy," Jillian said softly. "You've accepted that this is the way things are. None of us can go back, so we have to find ways to move forward."

"Yes. We're moving forward. I had a great childhood, Mom. You and Dad were great parents. There's no point in wondering what life with Ellie and Andrew would've been like because it didn't happen that way. As Dad said, 'Life is all about trade-offs. Get a little of this, trade for a little of that. You don't get to have it all.'"

Andy hugged his mother as Jillian carried the coffee things to the kitchen. "I'm going to drive Jillian home, Mom. Don't wait up. I love you and will see you in the morning."

"It's a beautiful evening, Miss Jillian. Care to join me for a stroll by the river?" Andy asked as they headed back to her house.

"That sounds lovely. It's been a pretty intense evening."

Andy parked, grabbed a jacket from behind his seat, and tucked it under his arm before taking Jillian's hand. They walked without talking until they were past the playground. As the voices of children playing faded behind them, Andy turned toward Jillian. "I was serious, you know."

"Serious? About what?

Andy grinned slowly.

"Oh, at the airport. When you got me all flustered," Jillian guessed.

"Yes. I love you Jillian Peters, and I do intend to say it every day for the rest of my life if you'll let me." Andy put the jacket around Jillian's shoulders and drew her toward him. He kissed her softly before continuing. "I can tell you're a little worried about that. Probably wondering if it's too soon to get married, if I know what I'm doing, if you're ready for all this, so I'm not asking anything right now. I'm just telling you. I love you."

Jillian kissed him. "And I love you."

Andy tucked Jillian's hand under his arm and resumed walking, now whistling a song she did not recognize.

"That was beautiful, Andy. What's it called?"

"'Patience' from Guns N' Roses. I've got patience, Jillian,

because I know we're worth it."

Jillian was glad Andy was patient. She loved Andy. Of that, she had no doubt. She was just thinking about the trade-offs.

Chapter Twenty-Seven

Jillian and Andy returned to Belford on Friday to visit the Boyds and Martha Small, the librarian who had directed them to Miss Nola, before exploring the house at Blackwater Pond.

"You're sure about avoiding restoration to a private home, right?" Andy asked as they entered the town.

"I'm sure. My research indicates that none of these period homes would sell at a price that recouped renovation costs. Most buyers want newer energy efficient homes anyway."

"Do you feel cheated out of a commission?"

"No. Maybe it's naive, but we began this journey to honor your father's wishes. This whole experience has underscored trusting God and his timing. It's been quite the trip—intriguing, heart-wrenching, and fulfilling, somehow. It's more your journey than mine, but I'm grateful I've been along for the ride. I'm eager to see it through."

Andy parked the car, leaned over, and kissed Jillian. "You've been more than along for the ride. You've guided me through some dark places."

They walked to the Boyds' door hand in hand. As before, Faith met them, this time greeting them with hugs. "Aunt Nola's in the front room. I'll grab the coffee and join you."

Nola was waiting. Upon seeing Andy, she leaned forward and looked closely at him before sitting back with a satisfied sigh. "You're at peace. I reckon you got some answers."

"Yes, ma'am. We found my birth father's family, my mother filled in the missing pieces, and we've decided to move forward with the renovation of Blackwater Manor."

"Oh, that's good news," Faith interjected. She poured cups of coffee and passed them around. "Will you live there?"

"No, that's why we're here, actually," Andy said. "We want to make some sort of philanthropic gesture, but we don't know exactly what."

Jillian added, "Originally, we thought to create an inn, school, artist retreat, or wedding venue. But none seemed quite right. During our last visit, Miss Nola, you said something about wanting the children of this valley to know their history. Is that right?"

Nola put down her coffee cup. "Yes, I want them to know where they came from, about the sacrifices their ancestors made, and the things they accomplished."

"A museum." Andy looked at Nola and Jillian. "We'll create a museum . . ." Andy's words hung in the air, then everyone began speaking at once.

"With a library—a research area about genealogy," Jillian added.

"And exhibits about the founding families."

"You could have exhibits about the coal mines and railroads."

"And polio and servicemen."

"People could still have weddings there."

"Maybe host visiting artists or writers."

"Don't forget farmers."

Jillian jotted notes furiously as the ideas flowed and the coffee cooled.

"That's what we'll do," Andy said finally. "We'll develop a museum for all of Belford to enjoy. We'll honor the legacy of those who came before. I believe my father would be pleased."

"He'd be proud as punch, and you've made this old lady very happy." Miss Nola smiled. "I'd encourage you to get our neighbors involved, and I have one more request. As a founding member and seven-term president of the Richardson County Historical and Genealogical Society, I'd like our archives to have a permanent home. They're currently housed in the library, but much—"

"Oh, Miss Nola," Jillian interrupted. "We'll find room for the Historical Society, maybe with displays and a research area. Would that work?"

"Indeed it would," Miss Nola said, patting Jillian's hand. "I'm so excited to have a little project. Faith, I will count on you to help gather materials on the original families. Rex can bring down those boxes in the attic."

"Awesome!" Andy exclaimed. "We'll stop at the library on our way to the pond and ask about the Historical Society's needs."

Andy and Jillian said their goodbyes and quickly walked to the small library. Tall bookcases stood behind tables near the front window. Behind the circulation desk, a short, plump woman assisted a library patron. She waved at Jillian, then handed the man his books.

Jillian introduced Martha and Andy, then outlined their ideas for the property.

"How exciting!" Martha exclaimed. "The Society will have to vote on relocation, of course, but I'm sure the motion will pass!" She pointed toward the stacks. "Our space is limited, so only part of the collection is displayed. Many donated items are in storage, everything from hay forks to family bibles. I've actually hired a young woman through a grant to sort through it all. It'll be so nice to have everything in one location."

"I may know the young woman," Jillian said, thinking of Sarah's friend, but her words were lost as a group of children erupted through a back doorway.

"Story time's over." Martha laughed. "I'd better get back to work." She waved, then said, "Wait a second. Would you consider hosting a forum? People are going to be curious," Martha explained. "They'll have questions and concerns. You're likely to get more support if the community gets information firsthand."

Andy nodded. "That makes perfect sense. We're still tossing around ideas, but we want to hire local as much as possible."

"Community forums are the second Thursday of each month." Martha opened her datebook. "There's an opening June 13. Shall I pencil you in?"

Andy and Jillian looked at each other. "That's not much time," Jillian said.

"It's a good opportunity," Andy said.

"Let's do it. Put us on the calendar, Martha. We'll figure it out." Jillian hugged her. "Thanks for suggesting the meeting. It's an excellent idea."

"Martha's a real community asset," Andy said as they walked

outside. "It's helpful to have a liaison with the local community. She seemed excited to get some shelf space back too." Andy put his arm around Jillian. "I feel good about this. It's special."

Jillian returned his hug. "Yes, it is. Let's go see the house. I'm ready to set this dream in motion."

Chapter Twenty-Eight

Andy drove down Blockhouse Road. "Maybe we can get the road widened. Make a note, will you?" Slowing, he said, "There it is. Museum, sweet museum."

Andy listed needed improvements as he walked. "Repair stairs, plant grass, pave parking area, sidewalk to entrance. Remove porch and replace modern door with something more authentic." He reached in his pocket for the keys but came up empty handed. Cursing quietly, he said, "I don't suppose you have your keys?"

"Are you kidding?" Jillian shook her head in disbelief. "I gave my set to the inspector. They've been sitting in my desk drawer since he returned them. How could you forget the keys?"

"Well, I don't know, Jillian," Andy said grumpily. "I laid them out last night so that I wouldn't forget. Maybe they fell out."

Jillian could hear Andy grumbling as he checked the car. *Well, at least he's not blaming me.*

"No luck." Andy returned to the porch. "Any ideas?"

"We could just . . ." Jillian tried the door knob. "Well, that was always a long shot. Let's check the other doors. Maybe we'll get lucky." They walked down the steps toward the addition.

"Maybe we should leave a set with someone in town," Andy said, following her up the weedy path to the side door. "I can't believe I forgot the keys!"

"I wonder if Bobby Hixon hid a spare key somewhere."

"Who?"

"Bobby Hixon, the old caretaker. He lived here. Maybe he hid a key."

Andy sighed. "There's twenty acres. Where should we look?"

"Check the obvious places, under the doormat, under any pots. I'll look in his flowerbed and along the foundation."

Andy started feeling along the edges of the doorframe before looking under remnants of a long-faded welcome mat.

As Jillian used a stick to move aside leggy stalks of cosmos and cone flower and weeds, she could see Andy examining the grooves of the board and batten siding. Jillian fanned away the bugs that flew toward her face with her every step. Before long, she shouted, "Found something!"

Andy walked over as Jillian said, "Oh, never mind. It's a spoon. It's a nice one though," she said, handing it to Andy.

"Weird," Andy said, sliding it into his pocket. "What's the deal with all these turtles?"

"Ooh, one might be a key holder." Jillian picked up one of the half-dozen fake turtles of varying sizes hidden among the weeds. "Nothing." She picked up another of the little figures and lifted its concrete lid, but the interior was empty.

Andy reached for a one but drew back his hand. "Is that poison ivy?"

Jillian looked closely. "No, Virginia Creeper. Watch out for the vines with heart-shaped leaves though. They have briers."

"Add a gardener to the never-ending list of employees." Andy held a turtle up and shook it. They both heard a rattle. Andy opened the compartment and pulled out a key. "Aha! Let's see if it fits."

They walked up the front stairs again. "Okay, let's do this," Andy said as the key turned and the door opened. "Wow, it's bright."

"Yeah, Elizabeth recommended automated blinds to protect the wood," Jillian said.

"Good idea. This is an impressive room. We'll use the built-in bookcases to display photographs and artifacts. It'll make a great first impression."

"I'd like to include period furnishings with versatile uses. I think most museum displays will be in other areas," Jillian said as Andy jumped and pulled off a loose strip of wallpaper.

"Let's check out the basement."

They hadn't needed their flashlights upstairs, but the basement stairs were dark, the lone bulb long burnt out. Four painted windows along the front and two on each side barely illuminated the lower level. Some cardboard boxes were stacked along one wall, and two trunks sat in a corner near remnants of an oil-burning furnace and a few broken chairs.

Andy peered in dark corners while Jillian envisioned the future home of the Richardson County Historical and Genealogical Society. She sketched an arrangement of bookshelves and tables with computer stations along the wall.

Andy looked over her shoulder. "Leave room for more chairs and a projector for presentations. I'd save a good half of the basement for storage and utilities. Maybe a big closet for extra folding chairs and tables."

"Good idea. Did you find anything?"

"Some boxes and trunks for another day." Andy pointed. "We can place the water heater down here, a couple bathrooms, that sort of thing. What about a kitchen?"

Jillian gazed longingly at the trunks, which seemed much more interesting than storage and plumbing. *Later. We can look later.* "If we do the wedding venue, we'll need a large kitchen."

"Yeah," Andy replied absentmindedly. "Having a small kitchen down here makes sense."

Jillian was still staring at the trunks. "Andy, lets not wait. Just a quick peek."

"It's probably just the caretaker's things," Andy warned as Jillian started toward the trunks.

"Ooh, it's lovely." Jillian lifted out a blue satin dress and held it up to herself. "Look at that tiny waist and the off-shoulder collar. Imagine dancing the night away in this."

Andy watched with a bemused expression as Jillian danced holding the dress as if it were a partner. Finally, he approached and tapped her shoulder. "May I cut in?"

Jillian smiled as Andy took the dress and tossed it over his shoulder. He pulled her close, quietly singing, "Can't Take My Eyes Off of You," as they danced around the room. When he came to chorus, Andy stopped dancing and kissed Jillian softly, sensually.

"Holy moly," Jillian said, backing away. "Maybe we need to go dancing more often."

"I'll dance with you anytime, sweetheart." Andy replaced the dress in the trunk. "Should we go upstairs now?"

"Yeah, I think so." Jillian looked back at the trunk but followed him upstairs.

Handing Andy her notebook, she said, "Your turn. Okay, we'll pay homage to the original twelve founding families. Find photographs or paintings of each, maybe request artifacts and heirlooms to display alongside them. Hmm. If we host receptions or reunions, then we'll need seating."

Andy and Jillian went through each room, discussing possible uses. When they reached the subdivided rooms, Jillian said, "Let's leave some partitions to help people visualize the home's multi-use history."

"So we agreed to include displays about the babies born here, the orphans, and polio, which would be enhanced by photographs and personal stories, but is it ethical to display them?" Jillian asked.

"We'll probably need permission. I want to include Dad and Ellie's pictures somewhere. They weren't born here, but they were orphans who found a home here. We also need a section honoring the Hixons and everyone they helped."

"Absolutely. Downstairs somewhere. Okay, we'll ask Nola about the Hixons, and I'll check with UT. There may be a professor . . ." Jillian trailed off. "Sarah's friend, the one who interned at the Smithsonian. She'd be a great resource."

"Good idea. I'm all for calling in the experts. I don't have a clue how to set up a museum."

"I don't either, but my favorite museums share stories of real people, not famous ones. That's who we're remembering here, the regular people. I'm grateful for people like the Hixons, who worked to better things in their own little corner of the world. Walter and Malinda walked the walk."

Jillian and Andy continued planning exhibits honoring many aspects of the county and property's history. "What about upstairs, the servants' quarters?" Jillian asked.

"Hmm. I hadn't considered that. Storage or future expansion, I guess."

"Andy," Jillian breathed. "No one ever does consider the servants. But they were a huge part of the American economy. Indentured servants and free servants came from Ireland, Scotland, and England and worked in homes all over the country. We can dedicate the upstairs to their stories."

"I love that. Some of their descendants may be in the area."

As they walked down the stairs, Jillian realized they needed to consider accessibility. "We'll talk to the contractor about an elevator. We'll replace that nasty addition with public restrooms, a bookstore, and giftshop, maybe with local crafts."

"Good idea. We need to check with the County about zoning anyway. We'll ask about licensing for a commercial enterprise. Make a note, and we'll explore the possibilities."

The ideas continued to flow as they walked the property. Andy mentioned school fieldtrips, local artists, and authors or craftspeople, even hosting a music festival. When he suggested setting up log cabins to represent the earliest settlers, Jillian objected.

"Whoa, Andy! We're spiraling out of control."

Andy scratched his head. "Yeah, well, I'm just throwing out ideas." He reached for her. "Look, the reality is always different from the dream. But if we consider carefully, consult and hire the right people, budget accordingly, and phase in the different elements, there's no reason we can't do everything we've envisioned. Every great adventure starts with an idea."

Jillian took a deep breath. "True, but all I'm seeing is work, time, and money." Jillian looked toward the manor house and then back at Andy. "I want to be a part of this, but we live in the real world. We have bills and obligations. How can we do our actual jobs and create a museum?"

"Okay. We've been running on a high since we left Nola's. There's a lot to consider, including a budget. Let's walk." Andy held Jillian's hand as they made their way toward the river. "Don't fire me, but it would be a shame not to harness the potential of this pecan grove and river view."

"I'm just as bad." Jillian laughed. "I'm picturing a World War II victory garden."

"Nothing wrong with dreaming. Tomorrow we'll discuss how to get started, make some calls, do some research. I'll look into the legalities and practicalities. We'll set up a foundation to oversee the project, including payments. We won't draw a salary per se, but a stipend or reimbursement of time spent is entirely appropriate.

"Depending on the time required, you may need to lessen your load at the agency. Do you want to do that, or do you want to hire someone to oversee things?" Andy asked as he opened her car door.

Jillian's forehead furrowed. Just as it would've been easier to walk away, it would now be easier to hire someone than to participate actively in the renovation efforts.

She felt drawn to the familiar comfort of routine, yet . . .

A hawk's shrill cry sounded overhead. A clarion call? A siren's song? A call to adventure? When Andy settled in the seat beside her, Jillian leaned over and kissed his cheek. "I'm stepping out in faith. I'm all in."

◦∞◦

THEY RODE IN COMFORTABLE SILENCE through Belford, sipping their water. Jillian's thoughts centered on their dance with the blue satin dress. And that kiss!

As they started up Bay's Mountain, Andy spoke. "There's one more thing I'd like to include: a place for Beth Ann and Randy Keith. I'd like them to live closer, and I think Randy Keith would enjoy watching the comings and goings of the museum."

Jillian's eyes widened. *Is he joking?* It was a generous idea, but they'd just said things were out of control. "Andy, I'm sure you have the best of intentions, but please reconsider."

He looked at her quickly. "Why? What's wrong with building them a house? Are you objecting to the expense? Because—"

"No. Well, partly. It's more that you literally just met them."

"They're my relatives, Jillian. My only ties to my biological father."

"I understand that, Andy. I do, but it seems a bit patronizing to suggest that they need to live somewhere other than where they've chosen. They've managed without your assistance for years."

"My assistance? Is that how you see it?" Andy was quiet. "I'm not sure they chose to live in the middle of nowhere," he added grumpily. "Maybe they needed something cheaper. Why else move from friends and familiar places after decades?"

"Maybe so, Andy, but they've been there eight years, and it seems to work for them. I imagine they've made new friends and so forth. Why interfere?"

Andy huffed. "It's not that the duplex was terrible, but it's isolated. Belford at least has an ambulance service."

Jillian nodded but didn't say anything.

Andy took her hand. "Do you really think I'm interfering?"

"Interfering, meddling, butting in? It may be a matter of semantics, but I'm afraid they'll see it as manipulative."

Andy released her hand and glared out the windshield. "That's a little harsh."

Jillian spoke bluntly. "Is it? What would you call building a house for two people you barely know and moving them out of their home? How would you feel if someone you'd just met told you to move somewhere you've never visited, and oh, by the way, here's a house to live in. Wouldn't you be offended?"

"I think I'd be grateful. Glad that someone is looking out for me. Glad I don't have to worry about a mortgage."

"Glad that said person doesn't think you can handle your own business? Pay your own way? Maybe thinks you're too old to make your own decisions or know what's best for you?" Jillian retorted. "Would you not be the least bit suspicious of the person's motives?"

"They're my family!" Andy said firmly. "I want to help them."

"I know that. But Andy, how would Sam react if you suggested such a thing to him? Better yet, how would you feel if your mother bought you a house?"

Andy considered Jillian's words. "I'd resent it," Andy admitted. "I'd be angry. I said as much about Dad, who did, in effect, give me a house. I felt manipulated." Andy glanced at Jillian. "You've got a point. I thought I was being nice."

Wow. So this is what normal feels like. We can disagree and not be hateful.

"Oh, Andy, your heart's in the right place, but please don't overstep. Beth Ann and Randy Keith aren't looking for a handout. Get to know them better, learn about their situation. Some people are proud and easily offended. They want to be self-sufficient." After her impassioned plea, Jillian fanned herself and opened the vent.

"Listen, Andy, I know it'd be easier to visit them in Belford than Kentucky, and having better access to medical care makes sense, given their age. Maybe you don't have to give up on the idea. Just don't make their decisions for them."

◈

AFTER CHURCH A COUPLE DAYS LATER, Jillian changed from her spring dress to shorts and a T-shirt, both speckled with paint. She didn't have any definite plans. She might repot some plants, clean out a closet, or dabble with some watercolors. She hummed softly, heating leftovers. When the doorbell rang, Jillian was surprised to see Andy with his arms full of papers. She gave him a quick kiss. "What's all this?"

Andy dropped them on the kitchen counter. "I've been looking at house plans. I'm getting overwhelmed and could use a second opinion."

Jillian narrowed her eyes. "House plans for whom?"

"Uh, for the Belford property. We'll need some sort of caretaker, true?"

"So you just unilaterally decided this, partner?"

Andy frowned. "Yes, but . . ."

"Well?" Jillian prompted.

"Do you disagree that we'll need a caretaker on site?"

"No, but your motivation in building a caretaker home is a bit transparent, Andy. It seems you're still planning to coerce Beth Ann and Randy Keith to move."

"I'm not a fan of your word choice, Jillian. I'm not forcing anything. Yes, I hope they'll decide to move, but I promise not to manipulate them." Andy opened the refrigerator, retrieving a water bottle. "I'm not pushing but will eventually offer them an opportunity to move somewhere nicer, with better access to medical care, a better variety of stores, and so on. I have their best interests at heart. Truly."

Jillian sighed. "I know, but you may feel hurt if they decline your offer."

"I bet Randy Keith would jump at the chance to be useful, to get back to work."

"He's seventy years old, Andy. Maybe he enjoys retirement."

"And if he does, that's fine, but I think he'd enjoy being a caretaker. And, honestly, I started thinking about my own situation. I'm practically fifty, getting ready for a major career shift. Will I just sit on the porch in twenty years? My dad was eighty-six and still coming into the office, right? My mom—"

"Your mom was ready for retirement a long time ago, Andy. She stayed because your dad wanted to and because they kept hoping you'd take over."

"Yeah, I know. My point is, most people want to be useful and feel needed, not fade away in some little backwater, watching television. Look at half the people in DC. Look at Mick Jagger. Hell, look at Miss Nola, ninety or thereabouts, teaching for forty years, then writing history books. Everyone needs a reason to get up in the morning. Beth Ann still cooks, but what does Randy Keith have to do?"

Hmm. He's got a point. Elaine's nearly seventy and plans to keep working. Amy's not dancing anymore but refinishes furniture. Stan has his art. I don't know what I'll do in retirement, but I won't be sitting on a porch, watching the cars go by.

She smiled. "I guess it can't hurt to ask. Have you eaten?"

They sat together and talked as they ate. Andy said, "I know the house needs to be one story, but how big, how many bedrooms, what sort of kitchen—all those decisions confuse me."

"There's a lot to consider. Not just today's needs but long term." Jillian laid her hand on Andy's arm. "It's hard to think about, but realistically, if—and it's still a big if—if Beth Ann and Randy Keith move to the property, they may only use the house ten or fifteen years.

"Since it'll be on Blackwater Manor land, you should think in terms of an unknown future caretaker, possibly with a family, so probably four bedrooms, using one for an office. Add safety features in the bathrooms, regardless of who lives there," Jillian said.

"The extra rooms could come in handy when my boys visit too. We all had a conference call last week. Beth Ann invited them for a visit, and Randy Keith promised to take them fishing."

Jillian held up her hand. "Andy, they haven't agreed to anything yet."

"I know, I know, but I think they will."

"How are we paying for this house?"

Andy stood and started clearing the table. "If Beth Ann and Randy Keith agree to move, I'll pay for it." Andy looked toward the window. "Leila bought out my interest in our family home. Prices in Philly are much higher than here. There should be enough to build a modest house."

"But, what about . . ." *Why wouldn't he reinvest in a house for himself, for us?*

"The money feels tainted, which I know is stupid, but I'd feel better not using it for us."

Tainted? Jillian didn't have the luxury to forego a share of a home sale, but she had thrown away perfectly good clothes after witnessing Andy and Leila's fight. *I guess I understand that.*

After examining the plans, they opted for an 1800-square-foot ranch with four bedrooms, three bathrooms, and an eat-in kitchen. "It's kind of a plain box, but the floorplan seems to make a lot of sense," Andy said.

"It does," Jillian agreed. "You can always add a front porch to give it some character."

"True, and we know what a porch-sitter Randy Keith is."

Jillian ignored that. "How about a screened porch in back?"

"I think the boys would enjoy that. Okay, that's settled." Andy pushed back his chair, stood up, and looked at Jillian. "You've got paint on your shirt. Did I interrupt something?"

"Just noticing, huh?" Jillian laughed. "I'm being lazily productive today."

"I like that idea. Want to be lazy together?" Andy put his arms around her waist. "Watch a movie? Go for a walk? Or, I know, let's take a last ride in the Jag. I'm trading it for a work truck with two bench seats. I've got a pretty good deal lined up with a dealership in Knoxville. How do you feel about being squired around town in a truck?"

Jillian laughed. "The tattoos fit. Get a ball cap and you'll be all set."

"That's part of the deal, honey. Buy a truck, get a cap," Andy joked. "I needed something larger with room for you and my boys. I'm flying them in next week. We'll go meet their new relatives, see Gentry and Blackwater Manor, meet Miss Nola." He paused. "And meet you."

Jillian's heart thumped. She was excited to meet the boys but also nervous. How would they feel about a potential stepmother, especially one nothing like their mother?

Andy was still talking. "I want them to meet all the important people in my life. They know we've been seeing each other but not how much you mean to me. They should know that. It's time you met my sons." Andy squeezed her hand. "I'll explain the depth of our relationship while we're traipsing around the countryside. The boys are pretty excited about meeting their great-grandmother. A little weirded out, but they've handled it well."

He kissed her. "Get changed. We'll drive around the mountains, see what we can see, maybe find another short hike."

Chapter Twenty-Nine

Jillian didn't see much of Andy during the next week. He'd picked up his new truck and squired his boys, not her, around the state. Eager to hear about their trip, she was glad to see a new pickup in the realty office lot on Thursday.

"Morning, Barbara. Any messages?"

"Only two, Jillian, but Mr. Harrison wants to see you. He's in Mr. Harrison's old office."

Ben's office had been vacant since his illness. Tom, as acting manager, had moved into Carol's larger office, but no one had replaced Ben. Jillian put away her purse and walked down the hall. Through the open door, she saw Andy reclining in his chair, feet on desk, eyes closed, headphones on. Jillian crept inside and quietly closed the door. She tiptoed around the desk, planning to surprise Andy with a kiss. As she leaned over him, Andy pulled her into his lap, muffling her squeals with a kiss.

"God, I've missed you, woman!" Andy growled.

"You scared me! I thought you were sleeping."

"I was just resting my eyes."

"When my dad says that, he's sleeping," Jillian protested, kissing Andy again. "Let me up. I shouldn't be sitting in the new boss's lap."

Jillian stood and straightened her skirt.

"Speaking of your dad, when can I meet your parents?"

Jillian sighed. "I offered, Andy. My parents are, well, difficult. Dad said he's happy for us, and Mom said she hopes this relationship lasts, but neither cared enough to choose a time to meet you."

"I'm sorry, Jillian."

"It's okay, I'm used to it. A different dynamic would be nice, but this is what I have. You'll meet them eventually." Jillian changed the subject. "Do you remember me mentioning Sarah's friend Skylar when we were exploring Blackwater? She's an archivist working with the Historical Society. I spoke with her while you were out of town and asked if she'd be interested in working for us."

Andy's brow furrowed. "How many hours?"

"Ten to fifteen hours a week for now. She's grant-funded at the library part-time."

"Okay, I guess we can swing that. Nola mentioned some family photographs she's been given. We'll need to catalog those."

Jillian smiled. "How was your visit with Miss Nola?"

"Great. She quizzed the boys. I'd warned them she might. They were impressed. Faith insisted on feeding us all, of course. I'm not sure she realized how much teenage boys eat. There weren't many leftovers." Andy laughed.

"Did they like Blackwater Manor?"

"Oh yeah. How could they not? Well, you know, impressed by its size and age, but it's a house. BJ's more interested in our family ties. Seth liked the pecan grove. We had an impromptu tag football game to run off some of our lunch."

"So . . ." Jillian prompted. "Did you tell them about us?"

"Of course. We stayed at a resort near Fall Creek Falls. Nice rooms, good prices, good all-you-can-eat buffet."

"Andy. What did you say? How did they react?"

"Well, we got to the resort about two," Andy began, drawing out his story. He tossed a coin in the air and caught it. "Went horseback riding. When we reached the meadow, I had the boys dismount." Andy tossed the coin again and again after each sentence. "We watched the horses while I tried to figure out how to start. Will said, 'It's okay, Dad. We know. You're in lurve.'" When Andy mimicked his son's mispronunciation, he tossed the coin higher and dropped it.

Andy picked up the coin. "I confirmed his intel and explained how we'd met and how you'd helped me through all this and how I feel about you. I told them we will marry one day."

Although Andy had made his intentions clear and Jillian was quite sure she loved him, she was still uncertain about marriage. Marriage with Paul had confined her, limited her, somehow. Trying to fit in a mold he'd shaped had sapped her creative forces. She knew Andy wouldn't intentionally seek to control her, but she worried about her own response to marriage. *Would I change as I did with Paul?*

Slapping the coin on the desk, Andy finished, "Seth said that was fine, as long as you didn't mother him because he's already got one mother, and she's enough trouble as it is. He asked what to call you. I said Miss Jillian for now. Would you prefer something different?"

Jillian, who hadn't thought that far, shook her head. "No, that's fine."

"Will said he wouldn't interfere in my love life if I stayed out of his." Andy grinned. "He has a new girlfriend. Beej said that if you make me happy, then he's happy, so I told them we'd get together for dinner before they head back to school. End of story."

"I'm glad they're okay with it, Andy. I don't know what we would've done if they weren't."

"We'd have worked it out. Hell, by the time talk of marriage ceases scaring you, they may be old men," Andy teased. "Want to hear about Gentry?"

Jillian colored a little, realizing Andy had seen her jump. "Yes! Tell me everything."

"Well, there's not all that much to tell. After gorging ourselves on the breakfast buffet, we loaded up the truck and drove to Gentry. I showed the boys where Ellie worked, where we'd eaten lunch, and then drove on to Kentucky.

"Randy Keith was sitting on the porch, same as before. He shook each boy's hand, called him by name, saying how proud he was to meet them. Beth Ann oohed and aahed over them and cried a bit. Said Seth was the spitting image of her Andrew at that age, made a fuss over Will and his green eyes, then told BJ how handsome he was. We looked at photographs, and they encouraged the boys to ask questions.

"Will asked why they had double names, and Seth asked what to call them. We decided on Grandma.

"Beth Ann gave each boy a box with copies of a few photographs, a letter from Andrew in each, and one of his yearbooks. He'd been on the annual staff and played baseball, just as I had. I liked hearing that." Andy grinned. "She went to a lot of trouble. She even made necklaces of Andrew's guitar picks strung on a leather cord."

"That's so sweet."

"Yeah, she also gave each boy two books from the Narnia collection, saying Andrew loved them all. She gave me *The Last Battle* so we'd have the full set. Oh, and a bag of homemade cookies. She's got this grandma gig figured out."

"She sure does. I'm sure she's thrilled finding a grandson and three great-grandsons. What did the boys think? What happened next?"

"Oh, they were pretty amazed. Seth gave her a big hug. BJ and Will were less effusive, took their time looking at pictures and admiring the books. Will put on the necklace. I don't think he's taken it off." Andy grinned.

"Randy Keith suggested they go for a walk, so I got a chance to ask Beth Ann some personal questions. I asked about their father. I knew she'd married Gene Rafferty when the boys were teenagers, but no one had ever said what happened to Mr. Keith.

"I was worried about offending her, but she'd expected questions. They never married. She took his name because she was pregnant. Beth Ann grew up in Hopewell, which is bigger and 'up the road a piece' from Maple Branch. She was in high school, working at a diner, when she met Raymond Keith, a traveling salesman. He took a shine to her but neglected to mention he had a wife. She fell in love, realized she was pregnant, and told him they needed to marry.

"He explained about a family back in Lexington but promised to take care of her and the baby. He sent her a check every month for five years. She's not sure what happened to him, just cashed the checks and went on with life." Andy shook his head. "Crazy, right? When the boys were ready to start school, Beth Ann and her sister moved to Gentry and rented some rooms together. Beth Ann just went by Mrs. Keith.

"She was a little embarrassed, said she'd never told anyone. The boys thought their father was dead and didn't ask any questions. Can you believe that?"

"She had a hard road. I'm glad she had her sister to help."

"Yeah. I told her she was really brave, but she said she just did what she had to to get by."

"I guess it's like Sam said, 'Times were different.'"

Chapter Thirty

Jillian was anxious to meet Andy's boys, who had one more week in Tennessee before returning to Pennsylvania. Andy suggested going to Bruno's, which offered casual dining right beside the river.

Half an hour before they were due to arrive, Jillian stood in the middle of her bedroom, surveying clothes strewn across a chair. Nothing she'd tried on seemed right. She didn't want to appear to be trying too hard or not trying at all. Jillian knew Leila always dressed like a fashion model but hoped the boys wouldn't expect that from her.

"Oh, forget it," Jillian muttered. "I'm wearing shorts." Jillian returned the clothes to the closet and pulled on a pair of green shorts and a simple navy blouse. She brushed her hair, added some lip gloss, and grabbed her purse.

Willie's barking alerted her to their arrival. *Oh good, Andy's wearing shorts too.* He gave her a quick kiss. "Nervous?"

"A little," she admitted.

"I've warned them to be on their best behavior. You know how that goes." Opening the truck door, Andy indicated the boys in the backseat. "BJ, Will, and Seth. This is Miss Jillian."

Jillian noticed that although BJ's hair was dark brown, almost black, he looked a lot like Andy. His hair was shorter but curly like his father's. In the middle of the bench was Seth, the youngest and only blond. Will had Andy's green eyes, but his hair was dark like BJ's. He also had Andy's grin. Jillian felt sure he was a fun-loving soul.

They exchanged pleasantries and drove down the hill. Jillian asked their ages and how they liked school. Seth was eleven, Will fifteen. They liked school okay. Jillian didn't want to interrogate them, so she gave Andy a chance to break the somewhat awkward silence, but BJ spoke first. "This is a nice neighborhood, Miss Jillian. Have you lived in Newton long?"

Jillian smiled as the other two boys snickered at their brother's attempt at polite conversation. She turned toward him. "I have, BJ. I've lived in Newton for most of my adult life. I understand you're at Furman. Do you like it?"

The conversation continued, friendly, if somewhat stilted, until they arrived at Bruno's. The boys were impressed with the river and pleased to sit outside. They ordered burgers and fries, with chicken fingers for Seth and Jillian, who suggested they take turns asking questions while waiting on their food.

"Seth, what's your favorite subject at school?" Jillian started.

"Math. Um, how old are you?"

"Out of line, bud," Andy said.

"But Mom told me to ask," Seth objected.

Jillian's smile froze as she felt Andy momentarily stiffen. She didn't mind anyone knowing her age, but she worried about Andy's response.

"It's a rude question to ask an adult, son. Try again."

Seth looked confused but asked, "What's your favorite color?"

"Green. Will, if you could have a pet, what would it be?"

"An iguana. Or a tarantula. Yeah, a tarantula. That'd be cool. Uh, when were you born?"

"Will!" Andy warned.

Will grinned impishly. "Just kidding. Just kidding. What's your favorite song?"

Jillian laughed. *Will's cheeky. I'm glad he was comfortable enough to joke around, but Andy should have let me answer Seth.* "I don't know, Will. It's hard for me to pick favorites."

She listed a few titles but was interrupted by the arrival of their food.

Seth half raised his hand. "Can I ask another question?"

"You just did, doofus." Will punched his brother in the arm.

"Of course, Seth. What is it?" Jillian said.

"If you guys get married, will your kids be our brother and sisters?"

Jillian gulped. She could explain step siblings, but the bigger question was the 'if.' She was still thinking when Andy put his arm around her and reached out a hand to his son.

"When we get married, you'll have a new brother and two new sisters, but they're already grown-ups, so they won't live with us. And your new brother will be getting married soon, so you'll also have a new sister-in-law."

"Oh, okay, that's cool. Lots of kids at school have stepbrothers and sisters. As long as I don't have to share a room with any of them, I'm good."

Marriage was a big step. Marrying someone with children still at home was even bigger. Teenage boys could be messy. And stinky. Jillian needed to think more about that, but Seth was a sweetheart. "I promise you won't have to share a room with any of my children." Jillian laughed. "Now, Willie might decide to sleep with you, but that's a whole different ballgame."

Jillian explained about her little dog and his fondness for visitors. After their supper, they took a walk along the river. The boys raced on ahead while Jillian and Andy strolled hand in hand.

"I think that went pretty well, don't you?" Andy asked quietly.

"Yes. They're good kids, Andy."

"And not at all nosy." Andy pointed to BJ, a few feet in front of them.

BJ turned and smiled at his father. "I figured you'd talk about us as soon we got out of earshot."

"A man could ask for a little privacy, son, but of course we're going to talk about you. I imagine you'll do the same before the evening is out."

BJ bowed and tipped an imaginary hat at his dad before jogging ahead and half-tackling Will.

"Hey, Dad. Look!" Seth yelled, pointing at the water. "Can we do that?"

"I don't think so, buddy. That's probably his canoe."

"Actually, Bruno's rents canoes and paddle boards," Jillian said. "If you're interested."

"Do you want to?" Andy asked, surprised.

"It might be a good bonding experience."

"Hey, guys? Miss Jillian says they rent canoes at Bruno's. Anybody up for that?"

A chorus of yeses and excited cheers rang out as the boys returned to Andy and Jillian. They walked back to the rental booth on the lower level of the restaurant. Jillian offered to wait and watch, but the boys protested, saying they could all fit, so BJ took the rear, Will the front, and Seth the middle.

"It's been years since I was in a canoe," Andy said, climbing in the back of their canoe.

"Me too. Hope I don't fall in," Jillian joked, taking her seat in the front.

The boys promised to stay in sight. They would head toward the bridge and let that be their turnaround point. It wasn't long before the boys outpaced them.

Andy grunted. "I guess all that tuition money is going to good use. They've obviously been canoeing recently." He paddled a few more strokes. "This was a good idea. They're having fun."

"Looks like they're waiting on us to catch up. I bet they challenge us to a race."

"Oh, I'm sure of it. Now that we've remembered how to paddle, I think we can take them. Are you game?"

BJ did indeed challenge them to a race. Andy agreed on the condition that the winners buy ice cream. They boys were so excited they didn't realize what he'd said. Although Jillian and Andy put up a good fight, the boys were the clear winners in the race to the bridge.

The delight on Andy's face warmed Jillian's heart; his love for them was obvious.

To keep the boys close on the return trip, hopefully at a slower pace, Jillian started singing "Row, Row, Row Your Boat," and the boys joined in. That and "Michael, Row Your Boat Ashore" got them close to the restaurant. "Anybody know another rowing song?" Jillian asked.

Will grinned and started singing "Splish, Splash, I Was Taking a Bath." Pretty soon, he splashed water toward Andy. Things escalated quickly as the boys laughed and splashed water toward their dad, who splashed back while Jillian shielded herself pointlessly. As quickly as it began, the fight ended. Jillian's joy at seeing Andy's carefree interactions with his boys almost outweighed her concerns about living with teenagers again.

Laughter rang out as the canoes drifted toward the dock. Jillian didn't mind being wet. She smiled, realizing that BJ and Andy, each positioned at the rear of the canoes, were sizing each other up, silently challenging the other to a final race to the dock. As each simultaneously began paddling again, Jillian heard a splash and felt her canoe wobble. She saw Andy jump into the water moments before the canoe tilted and she fell in.

The water wasn't deep, but it was cold. Jillian stood up and looked around to see both canoes upside down and all four Harrison men standing sheepishly looking at each other. She burst out laughing.

Andy took charge. "Seth, Will, go to the dock and be ready to grab these canoes. Jillian, you okay? BJ, let's flip the boats over and push them to the dock."

Jillian swam to the dock and hoisted herself up. It wasn't graceful, but she managed. *Good thing I wore shorts.* She stood with Will and Seth, watching Andy and BJ attempt to flip the canoes without filling them with water.

Andy and BJ managed to flip the canoes and push them to the dock. After Andy checked on the boys and Jillian, he disappeared into the river outfitters shop, where he purchased five towels.

The boys were rather subdued, shivering and dripping on the dock.

Are they worried about Andy's reaction or just cold?

"Ready, gang?" Andy asked after passing out towels. He held out his hand to Jillian and pulled her close, then started walking toward the car. The boys followed silently.

By the time they reached her favorite bench, Jillian had realized it wasn't Andy's reaction the boys were afraid of, but hers. She pulled Andy to the bench, sat down, and said, "Well? Doesn't anyone have anything to say?"

All the boys started talking at once, each taking responsibility for singing the song that started the splashing, for joining in, for having to get one more good splash in, and for falling in the river. Even Andy said he'd overreacted by jumping in after Seth, who'd fallen in trying to splash Andy one final time. They all apologized for getting Jillian wet and ruining her hair and clothes.

"Please don't be mad at my dad," Seth said.

Jillian hugged him and looked over his head at Andy. She felt bad for Seth and worried about him being worried about her getting mad. The poor child had obviously been around too much fighting. "I'm not mad, Seth. This has been an evening we'll never forget! My clothes aren't ruined, and I'm no wetter than anyone else in this family. I'm grateful for these new towels, but I'd rather have dry clothes than the ice cream you boys owe us though."

"Yeah, I think we'll take a raincheck on that," Andy agreed.

Will stood and leaned over his father, shaking his head from side to side. "Here's your raincheck, Dad," he said as water flew everywhere.

Everyone laughed and jumped away as Andy playfully wrestled his middle son and gave him his own raincheck. As they walked to the car, Jillian held Seth's hand, already loving Andy's boys.

AFTER BEING BAPTIZED IN THE RIVER, Jillian felt more at ease with the idea of marriage. Andy had taken charge, but he'd not been angry. He'd been concerned with everyone's safety rather than embarrassed by the unexpected events. Watching Andy navigate troubled waters without raising his voice or losing his cool helped allay any lingering fears about his mood swings and temper.

Over the next few days, Jillian, Andy, and the boys shared meals at home and at Dimitri's, hiked in the mountains, and attended a Smokie's baseball game. Andy seemed eager for everyone to enjoy themselves, but he didn't try to force or control the boy's interactions with Jillian.

As their visit neared an end, Andy stopped by her house to bring some papers to Jillian. "These are the permits and licenses for Blackwater Manor. Copy them for our files, then stick them in sheet protectors for display."

"Need anything else, boss?"

"No, ma'am." Andy grinned. "I know that look. I could do this myself, but I'm hoping you'll notice what you're copying and let me know if I've overlooked anything. I think I've got everything, but I'm not as well organized as you are."

"I'm teasing. I'm happy to make your copies, Andy." Jillian hugged Andy. "I'm feeling a little blue. I'm going to miss you and the boys."

"Well, I just happen to have something for you to remember me by," Andy said, pulling a rectangular box from his pocket. "Because you hold the key to my heart," Andy said, grinning and handing her the box. "And, yes, I'm fully aware of how hokey that sounds."

Inside the box was a bracelet made of two silver spoon ends connected by a crystal heart and key charm.

"Oh, Andy, is this the spoon I found at Blackwater?"

"Yeah, I found it in my pocket when we got home. I threw it on the dresser and forgot about it until we went to Gatlinburg. I didn't know spoon bracelets were a thing but saw some there." Andy grinned again. "Stan made it, with a little help from some guy he knows."

"Oh, Andy, I love it." Jillian fastened the bracelet around her wrist.

Andy would be gone for several days as he delivered the boys to their mother's, then returned by way of Kentucky, where he'd pick up Randy Keith and Beth Ann. Andy had booked some rooms in Belford's only inn. They'd attend the community forum on Thursday, visit Miss Nola, tour the house, and spend some time exploring the countryside before heading home. Andy would return to Belford on Monday for the groundbreaking.

"Guess I'll see you at the library on Thursday," Jillian said.

"Or we could grab some supper, and you can tell me again how much you're going to miss me. The boys are staying with Mom and Lois tonight."

"Oh? I'd prefer dancing with you," Jillian said, moving close to Andy.

"Mmm, even better. Will you wear that blue satin dress?" Andy asked with a lingering kiss.

Chapter Thirty-One

The Belford library held community forums the second Thursday of each month. Topics ran the gamut from political debates to organic gardening, home décor, parenting, health, or literal chicken feed. Andy and Jillian had prepared a short presentation about the house at Blackwater Pond, with photographs and plans for the museum.

Jillian thought it was sweet that the Raffertys wanted to attend the forum. The parking lot was nearly full when she arrived, so Jillian hurried inside to find Andy. "Where are Beth Ann and Randy Keith?"

"Still at Nola's. Faith and Rex will see they get here in time to see our spiel." Andy double-checked the connections and quickly ran through the presentation slides. "We've reserved some seats for them up front. Are you ready?"

"I'm a little nervous," Jillian admitted.

Andy rubbed her shoulder. "It's going to be a good meeting. I can feel it."

Before long, the rows of folding chairs were filled and people were standing alongside the room's perimeter. Library staff found more chairs, and promptly at seven, Martha bustled in, welcomed everyone, and introduced Jillian and Andy.

After polite applause, Andy took center stage. "Thanks for coming out tonight. Last December, a week before Christmas, I came to Belford for what I believed to be my first visit. Snow covered the ground, but despite being in town to bury my father, Belford was charming. Some two months later, Jillian and I returned to tour the big house out at the pond."

Andy showed slides of the home's exterior. Most people seemed to be familiar with the exterior views, but a few whispered to their neighbors. "We didn't know what to expect, and to be honest, we didn't get to see a whole lot that first visit."

The audience was quiet, politely listening to Andy's story, but Jillian noticed some frowns and bodies shifting. *Were they bored? Confused?* She attempted to inject a little levity. "The windows were boarded up, so we explored by flashlight. I was worried about mice but also afraid of what might be lurking in dark corners, like bats or ghosts." There were a few smiles but no laughs. "Perhaps you'd like to see what we found after the boards were removed."

Andy showed the interior photos as Jillian pointed out architectural features. The final interior slide, showing the beautiful spiral staircase dominating the front hall, elicited admiring comments. "We're here to discuss our plans for the home," Andy said, "but if anyone has any questions, this seems a good time to ask."

A tall older man stood. "All I want to know is how these plans you're going on about are going to affect us. This is our town. Where are you from anyway?"

Andy looked surprised but nodded his head. "It's a fair question, Mr. . . ." He paused, giving the man a chance to identify himself.

"Clive Rogers. I've lived here all my life. There's been talk of renovating that house more than once over the last forty years, but nobody's done nothing. What's your plan? Why are you here?"

A teenager with bright pink hair pulled at the man's arm, trying to get him to sit down, but a few nodded in agreement, murmuring encouragement to Clive.

A woman in flowered scrubs said, "Sit down, Clive. Give the man a chance."

Several people laughed, and someone called out, "You tell him, Janelle."

"Thank you, ma'am. Mr. Rogers, I appreciate your candor." Andy moved a step closer and looked around. "I get it. Change is hard, especially when it comes from strangers. But I hope you'll listen long enough to understand that my father was not an outsider." Andy paused, looking at Clive Rogers. The older man nodded.

"My dad, Ben Harrison, chose to be buried in the Belford City Cemetery. Why? Because he lived here, right out there at Blackwater Pond after World War II as one of many orphans supported, loved, and cared for by Malinda and Walter Hixon and their daughter Francine."

Andy smiled. "Through some unusual circumstances, I've recently discovered that my birth mother too grew up at Blackwater Pond and that I was born there."

Now the audience was surprised. They probably hoped to hear more about those unusual circumstances, but Andy skillfully turned the conversation back to their plans.

"Jillian and I inherited the house after my father's death, but we don't intend to live there."

As Andy laid out the plans for the museum, Jillian observed expressions of wonder and delight as people imagined their families being honored, their histories being shared, or their children being educated.

"We hope our plans will impact your community in a positive way. We will hire local as much as possible. We've set up a website so folks can apply online, but some paper applications are in back if you'd rather do that." Andy pointed toward the door. "To bring our ideas to fruition, we need you. We need construction workers, contractors, gardeners, and designers. Later, we'll need people to staff the museum, help curate the collections, and maintain the facility."

Jillian spoke, "This is a multi-faceted, multi-year, multi-use project. As a part of that, we're considering hosting different events on the property—festivals, meetings, reunions, and perhaps weddings." Andy glanced at her in surprise. "So we'll need event staff, caterers, wedding directors."

"I ain't sure anybody around here needs all that. I dang sure don't, and I don't want it," Clive Rogers said.

"Now there's a surprise," a wry voice sounded.

"Clive, you don't have to want it. You don't have to need it. Far I can recall, what a man does with his own property is his business," a man in the front row called out.

"Or a woman!" someone added.

Jillian was afraid that the meeting would descend into chaos when several people stood at once, wanting to speak. Martha, who had joined them at the front, took charge.

"Susan, you first, then we'll hear from Brad, and then Penny."

"Thanks, Martha. Well, for those that don't know me, I'm Susan Crabtree, owner of the Crabtree Inn. I just wanted to say that a venture like this will have a positive impact on my own and other locally run establishments. Right now, I'm the only game in town, so to speak, but, um, I'm not afraid of a little competition. I welcome it. Sometimes I have to turn folks away. We could use another B&B. Oh, and some locally owned restaurants would be good too." She looked around the room. "What I'm saying is that economic growth is good for all of us." The audience clapped as Susan took her seat.

"Right, well, I agree with Susan. I'm Brad McTeer, a descendant of one of the original families." Unlike Susan, Brad seemed to be speaking primarily to Andy and Jillian. "I'm proud for you to honor our history. Susan's right. If a town doesn't move forward, it moves back. Too many little towns around here have pretty much dried up and died. Now, if you were wanting to build a big, fancy subdivision or golf course, I'd have a different attitude, but this sounds like a win for all of us."

When the applause died down, a teenager rose to speak. "Uh, my name is Penny Cook. I just wanted to say that I'm glad you're doing something with that old house. My great-grandmother was one of the orphans too. She would've liked knowing somebody's taking care of that house." She paused and looked around at the audience before speaking more forcefully. "More than that, she'd like the town growing. Too many of us graduate, leave, and don't look back. Which is sad, 'cause Belford's a nice place. We need jobs. So thanks."

Martha indicated they needed to wrap up the meeting, so Andy thanked everyone again while Jillian passed out cards with the website address.

Some people lingered to express their excitement or concerns and pick up or fill out applications, but most scattered pretty quickly. As Andy and Jillian packed up their materials, library staff returned the room to its usual setup.

"Wedding venue?" Andy asked. "Where did that come from?"

Jillian looked at Andy in surprise. "It's been mentioned every time we've talked about the house. Do you truly not remember?"

Andy frowned. "I remember hearing it mentioned but not seriously discussing it. I don't think we should pursue it until the museum is up and running. I wish you hadn't mentioned it tonight."

"Well, I didn't mean to surprise you, Andy, but a wedding venue is a viable use of the property, one that could be quite profitable."

"But profit isn't our motive. We agreed on a philanthropic use," Andy insisted.

Their whispered discussion was interrupted as Martha congratulated them on a successful meeting. "Don't mind Clive. He's one of those people who always has to disagree to begin with. By the time the museum is finished, he'll be telling everyone it was his idea."

Jillian laughed. "I know the type."

Andy eyebrows shot up as he looked at her.

Oh, good grief. I didn't mean him! Jillian shook her head slightly, then turned to greet the Boyds and Raffertys. "I see you've all gotten acquainted," Jillian said after hugs all around. "What did you think of the meeting?"

"Why, it was nice," Beth Ann said. "Such an interesting crowd. I can't wait to see the inside of that big house tomorrow."

Randy Keith stood beside her, smiling and looking around. His gaze rested on a tall woman with iron gray hair, placing a completed application in the box.

Andy joined the group. "Everything's loaded. Ready to head back to the B&B?" Andy put his arm around Jillian's waist. "Do you want to join us for Belford's version of a nightcap? I think Susan has hot chocolate or lemonade, plus cookies."

"No," Jillian said as they stepped outside. "I better get over the mountain before dark."

"I'll walk you to your car." Andy handed the truck keys to Randy Keith. "Be with you in a few minutes."

"So, pretty good meeting tonight," Andy said.

"It was. A bigger turnout than I'd anticipated. We collected a lot of applications," Jillian added, holding up the box. "It's getting real."

Andy kissed her. "Do you want me to look at those? Or you could come back to the B&B with us and we could look at them together." He kissed her again. "Or not."

"As nice as that sounds, no. I'm not the one on vacation."

"I could wake you up early," Andy suggested, wagging his eyebrows. "Make sure you get to work on time."

Jillian laughed. "You've got a thing or two to learn about small towns, Andy. People talk. Let them focus on the plans, not our sleeping arrangements." She moved from the embrace. "Beth Ann and Randy Keith are waiting."

Andy glanced toward the truck, then kissed her once more. "I love you. Call me when you get home. Can't wait to see you in a hard hat next week."

"I will, Andy. I love you. Have fun."

As Jillian drove home, she wondered about Andy's objections to using the home as a wedding venue. *I'll review the applications tonight and research wedding venues tomorrow. Extra income can't hurt.*

―――∽∾∽―――

AS SOON AS JILLIAN ARRIVED HOME, she put Willie outside, then called Andy to let him know she'd arrived home safely. She made some tea and opened the back door. "C'mon, Willie. I want to review those applications."

Jillian sorted the applications by the type of work people had selected: construction, museum, other events, and maintenance. She wasn't surprised the largest stack was for construction workers. Andy could choose those workers. Only two had applied for the museum. One was Skylar Wilson, the archivist she'd spoken to about helping them part-time. The other was, surprisingly, a teenager. Setting aside the younger applicant, Jillian reviewed Skylar's application and the resume she'd stapled to it. *She came prepared! Wow, good experience, good references.*

There were a number of applicants for waitstaff and set-up crews for 'other events,' including several experienced wedding directors. *Awesome. I'll follow up with them later.*

Glancing through the applications for maintenance workers,

Jillian saw a familiar name. Randy Keith Rafferty, age 70.

Oh my goodness. How sweet. Jillian remembered Andy's conviction that Randy Keith wanted to work. She looked at his experience. In addition to being an auto mechanic, he'd been the volunteer maintenance man for his church for the past forty years, handling HVAC and AV equipment, electrical and plumbing problems. *I guess that's what he meant by keeping his hand in.*

Jillian took a picture of the application and sent it to Andy. "I think we've found our caretaker."

Chapter Thirty-Two

Jillian and Carol left early Monday morning for the groundbreaking. Carol handed her a steaming cup of coffee as they crossed the river on the way out of Newton. "It's been years since I've been out to Blackwater Pond." She sipped her own coffee. "I am so pleased with the plans for the property, Jillian. Ben's intuition was spot-on. You and Andy are doing good things for the community."

"It's creating a buzz in town," Jillian admitted. "So many people have asked us about it and offered items for display. Miss Nola suggested early on that we involve people in town. James created a website Faith Boyd has been updating. It already has about one hundred followers, most from Belford and the surrounding area, but some from out of state."

"That's amazing. Are you taking pictures today?"

"A few," Jillian said. "I'd asked the archivist to take more, but she declined since the local paper will get some. James will need photographs for the website."

"I didn't know you'd hired an archivist."

"Yes, Skylar went to school with the girls, and Sarah reconnected with her recently. She works part-time at the library on a grant and now part-time for us. She has experience from an internship at the Smithsonian! It's too perfect to be coincidental."

"She'll be a good asset. Ben always said to trust in God's timing. How big a role do you think you and Andy will play in the running of the museum?"

"Truthfully, not much," Jillian admitted. "Neither of us has the education or experience for day-to-day operations, nor do we want to be on-site all the time. So, once the museum is up and running, we'll likely offer Skylar a full-time job. She's highly qualified, and Martha can't say enough good things about her."

"I imagine it will take a while to get everything situated."

"Oh, yes. We hope to open the museum sometime next year, but we'll be working in phases, so it'll be years before everything is finished. We have a plan and lots of long-term goals, but we'll take things one day at a time."

When they arrived on site, Andy hugged them both and led Carol to a row of chairs. Henry Pickett, the construction foreman, handed Jillian a hard hat and asked Andy if they were ready to get started.

"Just about. We're waiting on a few folks. Jillian, is Miss Nola coming?"

"No, Faith said they'll wait to see the finished product." Hearing a car approaching, Jillian said, "I think that's Skylar and Martha Small."

"We'll wait five minutes for the reporter, Henry," Andy said. "If no one from the paper shows, we'll take pictures with our phones."

"Time is money," Henry replied. "Your money, but another car's coming."

Two men rushed from the car, one with cellphone in hand, the other with several cameras around his neck. Henry barked orders to his crew and sent the spectators back behind a line spray painted on the grass. The photographer started shooting pictures right away, while the reporter waited to speak with Andy and Jillian.

They wore matching hard hats, watching as the excavator ripped away the roof and walls. In no time at all, the sagging addition was gone. The excavator cleared away rubble from the front steps, and Henry's crew marked off the location of the planned addition.

"That was fast! You want a turn with that thing, don't you, Andy?" Jillian laughed.

"Oh yeah," Andy said, grinning. "It seems fast now, but it'll go a lot slower inside. Henry's crew will dig the foundation today and put footers in, which have to sit awhile. Henry coordinated use of the excavator with the contractor for the caretaker's house, so they'll dig that foundation today too."

Andy and Jillian walked over to the spectator chairs and discussed the history of the manor and their plans with the reporter.

"Thanks for the interview. I'll be submitting the article to the Newton paper as well. I'm happy to do follow-up articles as needed. We in the valley are proud to see this house being restored. I know our readers are interested in your plans."

"Please encourage your readers to visit our website. We're trying to build a list of people with connections to the manor. You might say we're actively soliciting contributions of people's stories," Jillian said.

After the reporter and photographer had left, Andy turned to

Jillian and frowned. "Care to keep me in the loop with things like that? Since when are we actively soliciting stories?"

"I'm sorry, Andy. It just occurred to me that if people share their stories and photographs, we'll have names to contact for permission to use their stories in the museum. Maybe some of them will have worked here. I want to share the servants' stories too."

"I get that, but I don't like being caught unaware. First the wedding venue and now this."

"Andy, I've mentioned the wedding venue repeatedly. If I'd thought about soliciting stories before today, I would have mentioned it, but it really did just occur to me when he was here."

Andy rubbed Jillian's shoulder. "Okay, we've both got a lot going on. This is pretty exciting, huh?" They watched as the first window was removed and breathed a sigh of relief as it was loaded safely on the big truck. The windows would be refurbished by a company in Atlanta.

"Ready to head to the library, Carol?" Jillian asked. "I think most of the exciting stuff is over, and it's too nerve wracking to watch all the windows being loaded."

<hr>

"INTERESTING READING?" Jillian asked Skylar about fifteen minutes later.

"Definitely. This ledger lists the household and farm employees, beginning in 1872, when construction started. Many seem to have been local men, but the brick masons were mostly Scottish immigrants, and an Italian man was the plasterer. Enrico V. Fabbri. He's probably responsible for that fancy border in the dining room."

"Not everyone would find those ledgers interesting. I'm glad you're working with us, Skylar."

"I find them fascinating. I don't know if the Bunches were being philanthropic or opportunistic, but two of the house servants were only six. They probably cleaned, chopped vegetables, polished wood. One was orphaned, but the other was the daughter of 'a dissipated and improper woman, father dead,'" Skylar read.

"That's harsh. I wonder how she wound up with the Bunches."

"Probably a court ruling," Skylar said.

They continued discussing the ledger and listings of men employed as blacksmiths, saddlers, and farmers. "It's amazing how many people were required to maintain the manor," Carol said.

"It is, and how many tools were needed. You really need a barn to store and showcase all the donations," Skylar suggested.

"Good idea, but I don't know how we'd fund it." After looking at Skylar's pictures of wagons, plows, yokes, and corncribs, Jillian knew it needed to be a priority.

Jillian and Carol walked across the street to the Boyds' house. After looking at photographs and artifacts Nola had been given, Jillian mentioned that many of the servants had been orphans.

"Malinda and Walter did not see servitude the same way we might today. Walter accepted his position as a town leader and wealthy man and believed it was his God-given duty to employ servants and help them help themselves. He believed people needed employment, so although his actions were charitable, he never gave anyone anything for free."

"Many of Belford's residents share in the history of the home and the valley, so they should have a part in preserving that heritage. Have you considered asking for financial donations?" Nola asked.

Jillian was surprised. "No, ma'am, we haven't. Right now, at least, the funds from Ben Harrison's estate are adequate for our needs," Jillian answered carefully.

"It is not your needs that concern me at this moment, dear," Miss Nola said. "Remember what I said about dignity and paying one's way? The people of this valley will feel more invested in the museum and be more likely to participate in activities you have there if they are partners with you."

"What should we do?"

"Allow people to help. Organize some volunteers to sort donations or set up exhibits. Perhaps remove wallpaper or prime walls."

"Volunteers could prepare garden paths or plant flowers," Carol suggested.

"Some groups could carry food out to the construction workers," Faith chimed in.

"Don't be afraid to ask for financial contributions. Dollars and cents add up," Nola insisted.

Jillian smiled at Nola. "You are so insightful. Faith, can you set up a way to accept contributions online?" Jillian laughed. "This gives barn raising a whole new definition."

Chapter Thirty-Three

One Saturday morning in late August, Jillian sat on her patio, waiting on Andy and imagining a future with him by her side.

"You're cute when you're daydreaming. Thinking of me?"

"I was thinking of your boys and living arrangements. Will they stay in boarding school or live with us?"

Andy sat down, holding her hand. "I'm shocked, sweetheart. Pleased as all get out, but shocked you're ready to think about that. I thought you were still running scared."

Jillian shrugged. "I'm feeling more comfortable with the idea. So, what do you think?"

"They'll stay in boarding school but spend holidays and summers divided between us and Leila. School is a good, steady environment for them. Seth, especially, has been a little shaken. I don't want to rock their boat, metaphorically speaking." Andy laughed. "We've been drenched enough."

"True." Jillian smiled at the memory. "Where should we live?"

"It doesn't matter to me, babe. Mom's offered her house. We can live there, here, or find a new place. Whatever you like." Andy's phone buzzed. He checked it but didn't answer. "Sorry, I was hoping that was Henry. He's supposed to call with some numbers."

"Hmm. I don't think there's enough closet space for two here, but I love this house and this neighborhood, especially the proximity to Amy and Stan."

"We can add on, Miss J. I know you've invested a lot of yourself here."

"True, but I don't want to be selfish. Paul accused me of being a control freak more than once."

They moved to the swing, and Andy put his arm around her. "I don't see that. You seem to let things happen as they will. I admire that."

"I did try to control things though, Andy. I've fussed about Paul and blamed him for our marriage falling apart, but I'm to blame too. My fear of things going wrong caused me to try to micromanage the universe. Since I've relaxed, things go a lot smoother and fewer bad things happen. Or maybe I'm just more able to handle them."

Andy nodded. "Micromanagement is something I'm still working on. I guess it comes with the territory, being a parent, being a boss, being single. Relaxing is hard." Andy grinned. "Did you take up jogging like I did? I see you as more of the yoga type."

"Ha. I walk, I don't run, and I've never been to a yoga class in my life." Jillian threw a toy for Willie, who was begging to join them. "I stopped trying to control everything when I realized Paul wasn't going to change. I had tried to avoid divorce, but it was the only way out, so I had to figure out a way to be okay. Once I did that, I saw that there are many ways to live.

"My attempts to manipulate and control God and everyone else were unsuccessful, so I had to accept that I wasn't in control of the universe. And you know what?" Jillian reached for Andy's hand. "It was a relief! I'm a much nicer person now."

Andy had been listening intently. "How did you try to control God?"

"By bargaining." Jillian gestured. "'Look, God, I'm doing this, so this is what should happen next.' I was laying out all these big plans but still going in circles. 'Wandering in the wilderness' because I couldn't see the bigger picture. Actions have consequences, seen and unseen. Since I can't control anything beyond myself, I had no business attempting to control what I couldn't see."

"Bargaining is one of the stages of grief, you know: anger, depression, bargaining, acceptance."

"You forgot denial," Jillian said. "I was in denial for a long time. I grieved the loss of my marriage, Andy. That's one of the reasons I kept you in the friend zone for so long. I needed to be sure you'd moved beyond those stages of grief."

"I may have been the King of Denial about the state of my marriage and about my role in its demise, but I knew it was over when I filed the papers," Andy said. "I'm still working through some of those other stages, more in regard to Dad than the divorce though." Andy stood and stretched. "So what do you do now? Now that you've accepted that you're not in control?"

"I go with the flow," Jillian said. "I trust that God or fate or the universe has the master plan in hand, and I trust that things will happen as they're meant to."

"I've never known you to give up."

"Going with the flow is not giving up or being passive. It means actively choosing a path, an action, but surrendering control of the outcome, trusting things will turn out okay." Jillian stood and took Andy's hands in hers. "It's hard to explain. It's like, well . . ." Jillian paused. "When the canoes flipped. They weren't supposed to do that." They both smiled again.

"Giving up equates to passively staying in the water. Fighting for control might mean blaming each other, wasting time and energy emptying water from the canoe, and pretending it never happened. Instead, we surrendered to the situation. We actively chose to swim to the dock, climb out, and put the canoe to rights. We accepted what happened and moved forward in an appropriate manner. Does that make sense?"

Andy kissed Jillian softly. "It does. I like the way you think."

He tossed the toy for Willie. "You know, I was at fault too. Leila cheated repeatedly, but I probably gave her reason to. I had ideas of supporting my family and spent too much time at work."

"I don't think you can blame yourself for her cheating, Andy. That was her fault, her choice," Jillian protested as she returned to the swing.

"Yes, but lavishing gifts isn't the same as being emotionally available. I shut down my emotions so much that she accused me of being an automaton. Even during the first affair, I didn't lose my temper or show her how hurt I was. I thought I had to be strong, to be man enough to take it.

"I was wrong. I ignored her feelings, and then I didn't tell her how angry and hurt I had been, so I didn't give her a chance to understand mine." Andy paused. "I get it now. Loving someone means trusting them with your emotions. You've seen me hateful, furious. Hell, you've seen me cry, and yet, here you sit."

"Here I sit, loving you, Andy." Jillian reaching for his hand. "Yes, I've seen you furious, but I've also seen you laugh and encourage, comfort and love. I've become more trusting of your emotions. I like that you share them with me. That frees me to share mine. Not something I did in the past."

Jillian and Andy hugged for a long time before Andy said, "I'm grateful to have you in my life, lady. You know, I don't think we need to force the issue of where to live. When the time is right, we'll know it, and the right place or right idea will come along."

Jillian leaned back and smiled at him. "Way to go with the flow, mister!"

"Speaking of time, we've been working double duty lately, Andy. I'd like us to take next weekend off and view some old houses turned into wedding venues in North Georgia and Knoxville. It would be nice for us to have some time together to catch our breath. I'd also enjoy seeing how the homes are furnished. See if my ideas make sense."

"I can't, Jillian. Whatever you want to do as a wedding venue is fine. That's in the future. Let's focus on the museum first. All this will calm down soon, and we'll go where ever you want."

"But Andy, weddings could be a profitable use of the manor."

"I don't have time, Jillian. Besides, your job is aesthetics, mine finances, remember?"

Their conversation was interrupted by Andy's phone. "It's Henry,

I'd better take it," he said, frowning.

Lately, all of Henry's phone calls had been bad news. They'd had trouble sourcing the basement flooring. Since the room would house a bank of computers, they needed to raise the floor and install vinyl tiles to cut down on static electricity.

Jillian worried about Andy's stress level. He was attempting to learn the ropes at Harrison's Realty while coordinating all the aspects of the renovation. The whole house had been rewired, walls painted, and floors refinished. The basement reno was holding up construction of the kitchen and bathroom.

"Henry, what's up?"

Jillian couldn't hear Henry's answer, but Andy wasn't pleased. "It's how much?! Geez. A cubic yard? I don't know, man. I'll get back to you."

"What's wrong, Andy?"

"The price of concrete has gone up again. With labor, it's over a hundred bucks a cubic yard. Do you know how big that barn is?"

"But the fundraiser will pay for the barn, right?"

"Not for its foundation." Andy rubbed his neck. "Don't worry about it. I'll figure it out."

"Maybe we can—"

"Jillian, I've got it. My job is finances." Andy leaned over and kissed her. "I'm headed to the office. I'll see you later."

Well, he's super stressed. I know the wedding venue's a good idea. Maybe Amy and Elaine will ride with me. I'll talk to Andy about it later, when things calm down.

THE NEXT TWO MONTHS FLEW BY as construction and renovation continued at a fever pitch. Money trickled in, helped along by a challenge to descendants of Belford's founding families from Miss Nola. Jillian knew Elaine and Amy had contributed, and when a substantial donation was made anonymously, she suspected Carol was the donor. They'd use the barn for displays of farming equipment and potentially as a wedding or dance venue.

Once the exterior work was completed, groups of volunteers worked on the landscaping. A local Boy Scout constructed a gazebo as his Eagle Scout project. The Boyds traded off weekends with Martha Small and her husband to oversee volunteer efforts. Miss Nola had been right to suggest allowing other people to be a part of the restoration.

Jillian had worked some with Skylar on museum exhibits but focused her efforts on the lower floor. She planned a versatile space with both period elements and serviceable reproductions.

Chapter Thirty-Four

The days passed quickly as Jillian and Andy coordinated the myriad aspects of their Belford adventure and continued their work at the realty office. Andy grew more confident in his abilities, but Tom agreed to stay on as general manager through September. Jillian accepted a stipend from the newly established Blackwater Manor Foundation to compensate for any income lost by shifting clients to other agents.

One Thursday, Jillian arrived at work early and opened her email. The Owens, some former clients, were moving again and wanted a quick sale. Jillian made a face. The market had stalled. Houses weren't moving quickly, and unfortunately, the Owens' home was unique. Nicknamed 'Noah's Ark' by local agents, the home featured a prow-shaped deck with brass railings and a mountain view. The interior had oddly shaped rooms and sunken floors in the living room and den. Jillian knew it would bring a nice commission but wouldn't sell quickly. *I don't have the time to fool with it.*

Jillian made her way to Elaine's office. "Hey, early bird, heard any flood warnings lately?"

"What?" Elaine asked from behind a pile of papers she was frantically sorting.

"Sorry, a client wants to sell Noah's Ark. Interested?"

"No, oh no. Can't you see I'm already drowning?" Elaine barked, then snickered. "That house is pun-worthy." She shook her head. "I can't, Jillian. I already have three of your listings, plus I'm working with Andy on those rental houses, and he's not listening to me. His prices are too high for the market, and—"

"It's okay, Elaine. I'll talk to Andy about the rental houses." Jillian backed out of the office.

Maybe Betsy will help with Noah's Ark.

Jillian knocked on Andy's office door. He'd been sequestered in his office pretty much all week. Jillian opened the door and saw him, head down, brow furrowed as he studied stacks of papers.

"Andy? You've hidden yourself away back here for so long I've lost count of the hours. What's going on?"

"It's just business. Nothing to worry about." Andy looked up and closed a file.

"Nothing to worry my pretty little head about." Jillian bristled, walking in and closing the door. "Is that what you mean? We're partners. Don't shut me out. Talk to me."

"It's nothing I can't handle, Jillian. You have enough on your plate," Andy said patiently.

"Is it realty business or Blackwater Pond business?" Jillian persisted.

Andy sighed and leaned back in his chair. "You may as well sit down. I can tell you're not going to let this go."

Jillian sat, but her tone made her mood clear. "You say that as if my tenacity is a personality flaw rather than determination to be part of the conversation. If it's honestly none of my business, I'll let it go, but if it concerns the house, then it is my business." She glared at Andy, warning him. "I don't need to be told again that my concern is aesthetics and yours finance. We agreed we'd share details and be open about budgeting. What's bothering you?"

"Okay, all right." Although unsaid, Jillian could hear Andy's thoughts: "I give up. You win."

Kudos to him for not voicing them.

"It's complicated, but you're right. You should be involved. We have some difficult decisions to make. I'd hoped to find a solution myself." Andy huffed. "We're short of money, a lot of money. I keep going over the numbers, hoping to find a mistake, to find a miracle, but there isn't one." Andy rubbed his eyes. "The thing is, construction costs have skyrocketed, and with the market downturn, I haven't been able to move the rental houses as quickly or as profitably as we'd planned. Inventory is down, so investors should be interested, but—"

"But prices are higher than they want to pay," Jillian interjected. "Investors want a deal. That's natural. Can you offer some incentives?" *I feel sure Elaine has suggested all this.*

Andy frowned. "That sounds like desperation to me. I'd rather wait for the right buyer."

"But doesn't waiting threaten the museum project?"

Andy waggled his hand. "Delays more than threatens. We might do a soft opening with exhibits but without the furnishings. Or we might postpone the work in the basement. That's a pretty sizable investment with the kitchen and computer stations. I suppose we could delay construction of the barn and redistribute those funds."

"Andy, no. We can't do that without losing the townspeople's support. They contributed those funds. We have to follow through. Besides, we need the barn."

"Okay, okay. I was brainstorming." Andy ran a hand through his hair. "I guess we're back to the rental houses. What kind of incentives would you suggest?"

"Well, um, offer some seller financing at a reduced interest rate, or cut prices for investors who buy multiple houses. I know Clark is still interested in the three properties off Windsor Drive."

Andy stood and looked at Jillian sharply. "Clark?"

"Clark Grebe, from Sweeney's," Jillian started.

"Oh, I know exactly who you're referring to," Andy said heatedly. "But I wasn't aware that you were talking to him."

"Excuse me?" Jillian stood up. "What is that supposed to mean?"

"Seems to me you've been running around behind my back, talking to an old boyfriend, to someone you know I don't like. He's pushy and rude."

Jillian laughed sharply, involuntarily. "Clark Grebe? He's not an old boyfriend."

"Are you saying you never dated him? Because I remember differently."

"No, I'm not saying that we never went out. We did, maybe three times. I'm saying that your overreaction is unwarranted and unwelcome."

Andy fell silent.

"Where is this coming from, Andy? What's going on?"

He sat down and stared moodily out the window.

"Andy?"

"I don't want you talking to Clark Grebe," Andy said quietly. "I don't trust him."

"But do you trust me?" Jillian asked. "Because that's the more important issue here. Clark Grebe means nothing to me. He's in the business, so I see him around town, but we are not dating. Clark Grebe is not an issue, and if you can't see that, we've got bigger problems than rental houses." She turned to leave.

"Jillian, wait, please. I'm letting old fears haunt me." Andy breathed in and out slowly. "Leila cheated on me repeatedly, as did Marie Whitworth back in high school. As did Paige. Clark makes me uneasy. Maybe I'm overcautious, a little scared of history repeating itself."

Oh my God. He's jealous of Clark.

Jillian spoke firmly, "I'm not a cheater, Andy, and I've done nothing to warrant your suspicions. I have no intention of defending my actions or integrity in that regard, now or ever. You either trust me or you don't. It's as simple as that."

"Maybe I don't trust myself. What's wrong with me? Why did they all cheat on me?"

Why did they all cheat? Jillian backed out of the door. "I, I don't know. I've got to think. I can't have this conversation right now."

Jillian hurried from Andy's office, stopping in her office only to grab her purse. "I've got an appointment," she called to Barb as she hurried out the door.

Jillian parked at the river and started walking. *I can't believe this.*

Where did that jealously come from? Clark, of all people. And the money, why hasn't he talked to me about this before?

We can't cut back on furnishings. We need to do this thing right if we're doing it at all.

Jillian's steps slowed. She realized she had walked past her favorite bench and was almost at Bruno's. *Oh my God. We can't stop work at Blackwater Pond. We've come too far.*

Realizing she should have stayed with Andy to work things out, rather than scurried away, Jillian began running toward her car. *The wedding venue. I'll show Andy those figures.*

"Jillian!" Andy came running toward her. "Thank God, you're here." Andy hugged her. "I saw your car, but when you weren't at your bench . . ." Her hugged her again. "I was wrong to question you about Clark. I'm sorry. Insecurity in past relationships is one of the issues I've been working on with my counselor recently."

"I was wrong to leave, Andy. I needed to think, but I wasn't running away."

"My reaction to Clark was stuck in the past, Jillian. Counseling dredges up a lot of weird thoughts." Andy hugged her again. "Mark—that therapist I told you about—he and I've spent hours discussing all the cheating lately, so it's been on my mind. Trying to figure out why, you know. There's not a lot of info on partners of cheaters, actually."

"That's not very helpful."

"Yeah, well, there are some things that ring true, always helping others, not setting boundaries. Wanting to be the hero. Sounds familiar, right? I think that's why I've been so frustrated lately. I thought I should be the one to find the answer to our financing woes."

Jillian reached for his hand. "Andy, I have an idea."

"And I want to hear it, but I need to get some things off my chest first." Andy held her in his arms and brushed a curl from her face. "Jillian, our relationship has been different because you are different from those other women. You're capable, smart, hardworking, curious, and more organized than I'll ever be. All good things. You don't have a bottomless pit of need you expect me to fill the way my exes did."

"But I do have needs, Andy. I need you to see me as a partner, not a, a clinging vine, unable to stand on my own."

"A clinging vine—that's a good description of those past women." Andy took her hand as they walked. "I repeatedly chose women who needed a man to prop up their egos. I'm glad you're different, but to be honest, I find your independence both attractive and scary."

"What? Why?"

Andy stopped and looked at her. "Sometimes, I feel you don't need me at all."

"But I do, Andy. I need your time, your trust, your honesty." Jillian rubbed his back. "Andy, I too reverted to old patterns when I left the office. But I don't need to hide or run away anymore. I need you to see me as capable and independent, because I am. But I also want you to know, to trust, that I choose to be with you. Not out of economic need or fear of being alone, but because I love you."

Andy picked up Jillian's hand and kissed it, looking out over the water. "I want a partner, Jillian. I want to share my life with you, to be open and honest about everything."

"I want the same. You've said you weren't always emotionally available with Leila. I need you to let me in. I need to know what you're thinking and feeling. I promise not to run away. Can you promise not to shut me out?"

They started walking again. Andy said, "I can. I promise not to shut you out. I'll continue with therapy, continue working to be the man you deserve. Right from the start, I've admired your honesty, Jillian. It was refreshing compared to all the lies and demands from my ex. I don't know why I put up with that so long."

"It's hard to see the forest when you're focused on the trail."

"Um, isn't that 'hard to see the forest for the trees'?" Andy asked.

"Oh, it totally is, but I see life as a journey. I had to find a trail before I left my forest."

Andy laughed and hugged Jillian. "I love you. I love all your metaphors and philosophy. I need to tell you one more thing. Before I realized you'd left the office, I called Clark Grebe. I told him to put together an offer on the three houses on Windsor. I hinted that I was in the mood to make a deal. If it's at all reasonable, even if we have to take a loss based on today's value, we'll sell so we can move forward with our commitments."

"I think that's wise, Andy. Ben recouped what he paid for those houses years ago. When we get back to the office, I'll explain how using Blackwater Manor as a wedding venue is a good way to finance our other plans."

Chapter Thirty-Five

Early one morning in late September, Jillian drove to Belford to see the completed interior painting and wallpapering before continuing on to Chattanooga, where she'd collect the girls for their shopping adventure in Savannah. Seeing Andy, who'd been staying in Belford a night or two each week to keep an eye on things, was a bright spot in what promised to be a long day.

The driveway, about to be paved, was blocked, but Jillian enjoyed looking around and seeing how much work had been accomplished outside. *The landscaping looks great. Oh, there's one of Stan's turtles in the flowerbed.*

She soon spotted Andy walking up from the barn site and hurried to meet him.

"Hey, stranger. It's so good to see you."

"It's good to have you right where you belong, here in my arms." They walked to the house, hand in hand. "Can you believe we've actually done this, Jillian? A year ago, I didn't even know you. Things change in a hurry when they decide to change, don't they?"

"They do. I never imagined any of this when I was getting ready for Ben's funeral. I almost didn't go because of the weather. What if I'd chickened out? We might never have met."

"I don't know about that. We're meant to be together. I've never felt such a strong connection with anyone. Let's go see the product of your labors."

"Oh, wow." Jillian sighed. "It's so beautiful. The marble floor makes this entryway."

They continued touring the house, commenting on all the completed renovations and those as yet unfinished. They'd focused their efforts on the first floor so that they could begin offering the house as a wedding venue as early as January. At the base of the stairs, Jillian embraced Andy. "Can you imagine the wedding pictures? Brides are going to love this staircase." She walked into the living room. "It's hard to believe this part of our journey is ending."

"Speaking of brides," Andy said, taking her hand. "Jillian, the ghosts are at peace, and now is our time. Our journey is beginning."

Jillian's heart swelled. No fear. Not just contentment, but love.

Andy held a small white box. "Beth Ann gave this to me when the boys and I visited. She'd found it in Andrew's dresser years ago. I found a jeweler to create a new ring from the old.

"We've been crazy busy lately, and along the way, I've realized that I want a slower pace. I want a different sort of richness now. I want to spend my days with you. You bring me peace and laughter. You challenge me and excite me, and I want you by my side.

"I reclaimed my roots on this journey, I found my heart, and now I've unburdened my soul, as Dad knew I needed to do. I'm a better man for having you in my life."

Andy knelt before Jillian and opened the ring box to display a princess cut stone surrounded by a halo of tiny emeralds. "Jillian

Renee Peters, will you marry me?"

Jillian's face was wet with tears. She was shaking but ready to open her heart and claim the love Andy offered.

"Yes, Andy. Yes, with all my heart, I will marry you." Jillian knelt and kissed Andy softly. "You were worth waiting for. I love you today, tomorrow, and the rest of my life." Jillian punctuated her answer with kisses.

"I had the center stone, Ellie's stone, reset. If you don't like it, or if you think it's weird—"

"Oh, Andy," Jillian interrupted. "I love it. Their story brought us together. It's beautiful and unique and perfect. Truly."

Chapter Thirty-Six

Jillian left Belford a little later than planned. As she drove over the mountain toward Chattanooga, she admired the ring on her left hand. She hadn't expected to become engaged this morning. *Maybe we'll shop for a wedding dress in Savannah.*

The historic Georgia city boasted a number of antique stores and markets for reproduction furniture. Elizabeth had arranged for them to view some specific pieces as well as browse, hopefully locating rugs and decorative accents for Blackwater Manor that were within the foundation's budget.

After picking up her daughters, they'd stop in Acworth so Meg, a Savannah native who was sure to know the best places to eat and shop, could join them.

JILLIAN KNOCKED ON THE GIRLS' DOOR a second time.

"Hey, Mom," Elizabeth said, "Come have some coffee. Sarah's not quite ready."

Sarah rushed into the kitchen and hugged Jillian, nearly spilling her mother's coffee with her enthusiastic embrace. "I'm so glad you're here, Mom."

Seeing her older daughter's swollen eyes, Jillian realized that what she'd assumed was enthusiasm may well have been desperation. "Have you been crying, Sarah?"

Sarah nodded as Elizabeth firmly said, "I've told you before, Sarah. He's not worth your tears."

"I'll tell you everything after I find my shoes," Sarah said.

Elizabeth held up a hand, refusing questions. "She came home early last night and wouldn't talk about it. Honestly, I'm tired of hearing about Brandon. He's not good for her. He never has been."

"She had to discover that by herself." Jillian cradled her coffee cup in both hands, unconsciously revealing the ring on her left hand.

"Mom!" Elizabeth squealed. "Sarah, get in here!"

Jillian was momentarily confused, then smiled. The girls were thrilled and peppered her with questions until Jillian reminded them they needed to get started on their journey.

After loading the car, Sarah sighed heavily. "I'm happy for you, Mom, but I'm feeling blue. I don't think I'll ever get married. I'm done with men."

"Sure you are, sis."

"I'm serious," Sarah insisted. Brandon had canceled plans with Sarah one too many times. She felt unimportant and taken for granted. "Get this, Mom. When I told him how I felt, he said I was being dramatic and needed to get over myself!"

"I hope you told him right then that it was over."

"That's the worst part, Mom. I didn't. I was all, 'You're right.

Sorry, I'm such a drag.' I don't know what's wrong with me. I don't want to be treated this way, yet I let guys walk all over me. Brandon is like Jerry, who was like Ethan, who was like Brad."

"Oh, honey." Jillian looked at her daughter in the rearview mirror. "Maybe you do need a break from men. What's the longest you've been between boyfriends?"

"About three months," Sara admitted. "After Blake and I broke up." Blake had been Sarah's college boyfriend, one she'd been sure she'd marry.

"I remember Blake," Jillian said. "To be honest, you seem more upset about Brandon."

"I'm not upset about Brandon," Sarah protested. "I'm mad at myself for wasting my time in dead-end relationships. I'm tired of playing. I want true love but don't know how to find it."

"Oh, honey, maybe you do need a time-out. I'm sorry your dad and I didn't model a healthier relationship."

"Mom, don't—"

"No, let me finish, please. It wasn't healthy. We established patterns, probably based on our own parents, that didn't allow either of us to grow. We married too young, and neither of us knew how to communicate or to trust. We grew apart instead of growing together."

"Mom, you're not to blame for my inability to find a good man."

"Maybe not, but here's what I've observed, Sarah. You like the flirtations, the chase and pursuit. Real love isn't a race or a game though. It takes work, time, and trust. You have to be open and honest."

"Falling in love is exciting, but being in love is better," Elizabeth added.

"Yes, it is," Jillian said quietly. "Sarah, real love means you're home, you're safe, you're accepted. It's real, and you can take what life throws at you because you're together and stronger because of it." Jillian looked at Sarah's reflection. "Why don't you take some time? Decide who you are and how you'll be treated. Then, if you decide you want a man in your life, the right one will come along. I'm sure of it."

"You know what Liam would say?"

"No, Elizabeth, what would your almost-a-psychiatrist boyfriend say?"

"He'd say the constant in all these relationships is you. If you want to change the pattern, you have to change. Not your personality but your expectations, behavior, and boundaries."

Jillian changed lanes, preparing to exit the interstate to Meg and James's condo in Acworth. The area had grown tremendously since she'd moved to Tennessee. She was glad she didn't have to contend with Atlanta traffic every day.

"I'm so excited to look at dresses for your wedding, Jillian," Meg said as they started their journey anew after touring the condo and visiting with James a bit. "I know the perfect place."

"I'll be your bridesmaid, Mom, since I'll never be a bride," Sarah joked sadly.

"That's not true," Meg said firmly. "Once you figure out what you want, just put out some positive energy and life will get better. You'll see."

Jillian smiled to herself and thought about furniture as the younger women continued to discuss how best to manifest their futures. They still had a five-hour drive in front of them.

THE NEXT MORNING, they rose early and enjoyed a leisurely breakfast at a charming cafe. Feeling quite full after feasting on Belgian waffles topped with whipped cream and strawberries, the women walked around downtown, popping in and out of stores, including some where Elizabeth had contacts. Jillian agreed the fainting couch they'd discussed was a good selection, and they found a demilune for the entry. Two stores later, they located rugs and urns and decorative pieces.

"Thanks, girls. Together we've accomplished so much more than I'd have been able to do alone," Jillian said, realizing how much fun she'd had shopping with all three of the girls. Meg already felt like one of the family.

"I love the dining room suite I picked out," Meg gushed. "And the paintings. You've got a great eye, Elizabeth."

"Happy to help. Are we ready to switch gears and try on some gowns?"

"Later," Jillian said. "I want wine and somewhere to rest my feet."

"Sheridan's it is then." Meg laughed. "I'm pretty sure their wine selection is why my mother insisted we get my gown there. We'll be your personal shoppers while you rest!"

Persuaded at last, Jillian lounged at the back of the store, fortified by a glass of wine and canapés, thinking of her upcoming wedding while the girls looked at gowns. *Nothing fancy, just friends and family. Maybe along the river somewhere.*

Jillian's thoughts were interrupted by Sarah and Elizabeth and Meg coming toward her. "Mom, we found the perfect gown," they said in unison, holding out an emerald green silk dress.

The dress was perfect. Jillian put down her wine glass and followed the girls into the dressing area. As they helped her into the gown, Jillian remembered trying on bridesmaid's dresses in her twenties. This time though, the gown perfectly suited her womanly figure.

It was lovely. A classic silhouette exactly the color of Andy's eyes. The sleeveless bodice had a rounded neckline that showed off her curves. Sarah handed her a deep rose poinsettia brooch to pin at the cinched waist, and Elizabeth held out a coordinating bolero jacket.

"You're beautiful, Mom. Don't you love it? Can't you see yourself standing on that staircase at the House at Blackwater Pond, surrounded by poinsettias?" Sarah asked.

She could and she did. Of course they would be married there. It was the perfect location. She knew Andy would agree. The house had brought them together, and together they'd found the joy they'd been missing and the love that was meant to be.

Author's Note

This book began, as most do, with a question: What if? What if two lonely people met at a funeral? What would draw them together and pull them apart? Then the title came to me. Blackwater suggested something mysterious, and so the book began.

The House at Blackwater Pond is the first of two books set in the fictional town of Belford, a town loosely based on a place my father called home. A place where time seems to move at a different pace.

I owe friends and family a huge debt for their love and support, reading early drafts, asking about my progress, offering encouragement and careful criticism. Your comments were invaluable. To Linda, who read multiple versions, Christine, who helped me wrangle the secondary plot into the background, and Taylor, who took my vision and turned it into a website, I offer my sincere thanks. I could not have done it without you.

To my readers. Thank you. I hope you've enjoyed reading the book as much as I enjoyed writing it. Book 2, *The Art of Love at Blackwater Pond,* is Sarah's story.

Let's keep in touch. Follow my progress, read the blog, sign up for my newsletter or drop me a line at terrigilbertauthor.com.

Printed in the USA
CPSIA information can be obtained
at www.ICGtesting.com
LVHW022041270924
792331LV00004B/270